PRAISE FOR A. R. TORRE

Every Last Secret

"Deliciously, sublimely nasty: *Mean Girls* for grown-ups."

—*Kirkus Reviews*

"Torre keeps the suspense high . . . Readers will be riveted from page one."

—*Publishers Weekly*

"A glamorous and seductive novel that will suck you in and knock you sideways. I love this story, these characters, and the raw emotion they generated in me. I devoured every word. Exceptional."

—Tarryn Fisher, *New York Times* bestselling author

"Raw and riveting. A clever ride that will make you question everyone and everything."

—Meredith Wild, #1 *New York Times* bestselling author

THE
GOOD
LIE

OTHER TITLES BY
A. R. TORRE

THE GOOD LIE

A. R. TORRE

THOMAS & MERCER

Published by Thomas & Mercer, Seattle

www.apub.com

Amazon, the Amazon logo, and Thomas & Mercer are trademarks of Amazon.com, Inc., or its affiliates.

ISBN-13: 9781542020169
ISBN-10: 1542020166

Cover design by Shasti O'Leary Soudant

Printed in the United States of America

Dedicated to Eva. I love you.

CHAPTER 1

The prestigious street still held secrets of the horror. The missing-person flyers were tacked into the Canary Island palms, their colors faded from the elements, the edges of them curled from rain and wind. The white-brick mansion at the end of the street no longer had police cars parked in its circular drive. The press vans and cameras had slowly moved on to other stories. The iron gates, which had been necessary to keep the well-intentioned public at bay, were deserted. The weight of silence hung in the sunny Los Angeles air.

Scott Harden stumbled down the palm tree–lined sidewalk and toward the large gates. As he moved, the white house swayed before him, the view blurred by sweat burning the corners of his eyes. His monogrammed polo shirt, stained from weeks of wear, stuck to his back. Bruises and cuts from the stiff rope circled both wrists, and he quickened his steps, moving into a jog as he grew closer to the home. As blood oozed from the incision on his chest, he staggered to a stop at the gates' security panel.

He pressed the code into the keypad, leaving bloody fingerprints behind. The gates chimed and hummed as they slid open.

~

Nita Harden stood before the bathroom mirror and tried to find the energy and motivation to pick up her toothbrush. Her counter, once clustered with perfumes and expensive cosmetics, was empty. Her blonde locks, which had always been kept up with biweekly visits to the salon, now had a half inch of dark-gray roots. Wearing a black yoga suit that hung from her frame, she looked nothing like the put-together socialite who had clawed her way to the top echelon of Beverly Hills society. Did bad breath matter when your son was missing? Did *anything* when each day was just a horrible waiting game for someone to discover his body?

The Bloody Heart Killer was reliable. He kidnapped handsome and popular teenage boys, like her Scott.

He held each boy prisoner for a month or two, strangled them and mutilated their bodies, then discarded them like bags of trash. There had been six boys before Scott. Six naked bodies found, a heart carved into their chests. It had been almost seven weeks since Scott had disappeared. Any day, his body would show up, and she would be called to the morgue to identify her son.

The tones of their security system chimed, and she looked up from her toothbrush, listening as it played one of the custom sounds of the front gates. When they built the home, each of them had picked a unique gate code and notification sound. Every time she pulled her Jaguar up to the gates and used her remote or personal code, the gentle tinkling of bells would sound. Her husband's was the UCLA fight song. Scott's was a simple trill . . . Her toothbrush clattered into the sink as Scott's personal chime sounded through the large bathroom.

A fresh pang of raw emotion ripped through her heart, and she let out a painful cry at the familiar ring, one she had taken for granted for years, one that instantly brought to mind Scott's big grin. He always came bounding in with his backpack slung over one shoulder, beelining for something to eat. She moved to the large window at the end of the bathroom and peered down at the front yard, expecting to see one of his friends' cars, or the van of their cleaning crew or landscapers, any of whom Scott might have given his code to. No vehicle appeared through the foliage, and she cupped her hand to the glass and tried to see down to the entrance gates.

A figure moved stiffly down the center of their crushed-shell drive, one leg dragging a bit and drawing a long line behind him. Her breath caught painfully in her throat at the familiar gray polo, identical to the dozens that still hung in Scott's closet. His face wasn't visible, his attention forward, but she knew that build instantly. Whirling, she tripped over a copper clawed foot of the tub and fell to her knee. Hiccuping out a sob of emotion and pain, she bolted to her feet and through the arched opening that led to their bedroom. Barreling into the hall, she knocked past a maid as she rounded the staircase and sprinted down the stairs, her hand tight on the banister, her vision blurring with tears.

"George!" she screamed, her head whipping in the direction of her husband's study, where he often worked from home. "George!" Without pausing to see if he was home or had heard, she yanked at the heavy bronze handle of the front door and swung it open far enough to squeeze out.

Her bare feet churned against the crushed shells, the pain ignored as she tore down the middle of the drive, screaming out her son's name.

Scott's head lifted, and he staggered to a stop, his features exhausted as his mouth wobbled into a smile. He slowly lifted his arms, and she crashed into them.

Her son, against all odds, was home.

CHAPTER 2

I listened to John Abbott's voice mail and wondered if this was the day he would kill his wife.

"Dr. Moore," he rasped, his voice uneven and emotional, "call me back. She's gonna leave me for him. I know it. This is it."

John—who always arrived five minutes early for our appointments, in pressed clothes and meticulous shape, who wrote my checks in painfully neat block writing—sounded as if he was falling apart. I listened to the end of his voice mail, then pressed the screen and played it again.

Sighing, I returned his call. I had determined, over a year of one-on-one psychiatry sessions, that John suffered from pathological jealousy. We had spent the first two months focused on his wife and her supposed infatuation with the landscaper. John was resistant to behavioral therapy and staunchly opposed to the thought of taking phenothiazines. After weeks of urging, he took my advice and fired the landscaper, which resolved the situation. He had now found a new source of worry—their neighbor. His suspicions seemed to be unfounded, which wouldn't be too alarming if he didn't also suffer from a growing compulsion to kill said wife.

As I waited for him to answer, I opened up the fridge and pulled out a gallon of milk. Whether John Abbott had the capacity to kill was up for debate. Still, the fact that he had consistently considered it for almost a year was validation enough.

He didn't answer, and I ended the call and set my phone on the counter. I poured a tall glass, then moved aside the stiff lace curtains and peered through the window above the sink. Through a fine layer of pollen, I saw my cat knead her claws along the polished red finish of my convertible's front hood. Knocking at the glass, I tried to get her attention. "Hey!"

Clementine ignored me. I downed the milk in one long gulp and tapped the window harder. No reaction.

Rinsing out the glass, I stacked it in the top shelf of my dishwasher and eyed my cell phone. This was the first time John Abbott had called my cell. Unlike Rick Beekon, who couldn't book a tee time without getting my approval, John was the sort of client who viewed a call for help as being weak and incapable. For him to leave a voice mail on a Tuesday morning was significant. Had he caught Brooke? Or had his paranoia and jealousy hit a breaking point?

She's gonna leave me for him. I know it. This is it.

Loss, for a man like John, could be a world-breaking concept, especially since he had a singular focus on and distorted view of his wife. That focus had grown into an obsession, one with a violent thread that hovered toward maniacal.

I called him again, my concern mounting as the phone rang and rang with no response. The possibilities appeared, unwelcome in my mind. The pharmacist with the perfect handwriting and two missed appointments this month standing over his wife, a bloody knife in hand.

No, I corrected myself. Not a knife. Not with Brooke. It would be something else. Something less hands-on. Poison. That had been his recent fantasy of choice.

I checked the clock on the microwave. Over two hours since he had called me. Anything could have happened in two hours. That's what I got for sleeping in. The Ambien, which had seemed like a great idea at 3:00 a.m., had cost me this missed call.

One more call, I told myself. I'd wait a little bit, then try him once more and then move on with my day. Obsession, as I frequently told my clients, never affected outside situations. They only made your internal struggles—and resulting personal actions and decisions—worse.

I fixed a piece of toast and ate it, chewing slowly and deliberately as I sat at my dining room table and watched an episode of *Seinfeld* on my cell phone. After I'd wiped down the counters, rebagged the bread, and washed my hands at the sink, I tried him again.

And just like the first two times, he ignored my call.

~

At nine forty-five, as I headed to the office for my first appointment, John Abbott failed to show up for his shift at Breyer's Pharmacy.

There was immediate concern. The man was a tyrant about punctuality, so much so that two junior pharmacists had quit in tears after being subjected to his long and almost violent rants on time accountability. After his tardiness stretched to ten thirty, then eleven o'clock, and repeated calls to his cell phone went unanswered, the three staff members convened at the back of the medical racks over what to do. The line of customers, which had never extended past the adult-diapers section of the aisle, now stretched all the way into herbal remedies. At the front, a man with a bushy white mustache and cowboy hat cleared his throat.

A decision was made to find John's wife on Facebook and send her a message. With that task complete, they waited another fifteen minutes, then dispatched the most junior and expendable member of the team to drive to his home.

Joel Blanker was twenty-one years old and a pharmacy intern from Little Rock, Arkansas. He liked Dungeons and Dragons, Latin women, and chicken tenders with extra ketchup. As I listened to Phil Ankerly mull over a documentary he'd watched on Ted Bundy, Joel parked on the street and texted the assistant pharmacist to let him know that John's car was there, parked in the drive behind a white sedan. The instructions

Joel received were simple: Ring the doorbell. Ask John if he's coming to work. Duck and cover if he starts to yell.

Joel began at the one-story home's front door, his armpits damp from the Los Angeles heat as he listened to the chime echo through the house. After a second ring, and with no sounds from inside the home, he moved around to the carport. Knocking gently on the side door, he waited, then hesitantly cupped his hands to the glass and peered in.

At the sight of the blood and the body, he stumbled back, his dress shoe catching on the carport's curb. His cell phone skittered across the ground and came to a stop against a support pillar. He crawled across the cleanly swept surface and picked up the phone. Ignoring the fresh spiderweb of cracks across its display, he unlocked the device and jabbed the digits for 9-1-1.

~

After my second morning appointment, I swung by the Forty-Fifth Avenue gym. My concerns over John Abbott's voice mail faded as I changed into gym clothes and climbed onto a treadmill. I dialed up the speed and scanned the row of television screens, zeroing in on one that showed a newscaster's face, the words BH KILLER in bold font under her chin. Settling into a comfortable jog, I kept my eyes on the press conference's closed-captioning thread, trying to understand what the update was covering. The camera view switched to show a handsome teenager in a button-up shirt and khakis standing beside his mother, a bashful grin on his face as she gripped him around his waist.

"... grateful to have him home. Please give us privacy as we spend this time with our son ..."

I jabbed the "Stop Session" button on the treadmill and grabbed my phone. Despite the halt in pace, my heartbeat increased. Had the latest Bloody Heart victim escaped? Along with most Angelenos, I'd spent the last three years glued to the coverage, following each tragic case from disappearance to death. An escaped victim, especially one in healthy condition, seemed impossible. This was the time frame when a victim's dead body was typically found, his penis crudely removed, his nude corpse given the same amount of care as a discarded cigarette.

This killer was unique and precise, his expertise proven through six victims. I was stunned that he would be careless enough to allow for an escape. Could this be a copycat killer? A hoax? Or a weak moment in strategy and execution? I unlocked my phone and searched for the latest news article, then glanced back up at the muted television.

". . . escaped from the BH Killer and ran for miles until he found his way home . . ."

There it was. Confirmation in black and white. How had Scott Harden escaped? I stepped off the machine, hurried through the busy cardio area, and hit the stairs, jogging down the wide steps toward the gym's lower level. As I reached the bottom step, the phone's display changed and my ringtone sounded through the headphones. The call was from my office, and I put my second earbud in place and answered it. "Hello?"

"Dr. Moore?" Jacob spoke in a hushed tone. I pictured him at our reception desk, his wire-frame glasses slipping down his nose, a bead of sweat already halfway down one side of his acne-scarred forehead.

"Hi, Jacob." I pushed open the door to the ladies' locker room and grabbed a fluffy monogrammed towel off the top of the stack.

"There's a detective here to see you. Ted Saxe. He said it's urgent."

I squeezed past a cluster of neon-clad yoga enthusiasts and found my locker. "Did he say what it's about?"

"He won't tell me, and he's refusing to leave."

Shit. It had been almost six hours since my voice mail from John Abbott, and I'd heard nothing but silence. Had something happened? Or was this visit about one of my other clients? "I'll head back now." I balanced the cell phone against my shoulder as I worked my running shorts past my hips. "Oh, and Jacob?"

"Yes?"

"Don't let him go in my office. And don't give him any information. I don't care what he asks for."

Our part-time receptionist, who tuned pianos and ate shark-shaped gummy snacks for lunch, didn't miss a beat. "Done and done."

"Thanks." I ended the call and paused, my shorts around my ankles, my red-cotton thong in full display of anyone in the area. Scrolling down to John's voice mail, I quickly deleted the file, then went into my deleted voice mails and cleared out the backup record of it.

The act was instinctual. My psychiatry training would blame it on a childhood history of covering my tracks and hiding anything that would spur my alcoholic mother into rage. But here there wasn't a risk of a belligerent housewife slapping me across the face. The ramifications of John Abbott harming his wife—if that's what this was about—would be much worse. A potential investigation into my practice. A review by the medical board. Media attention on me and my clients—clients who demanded complete confidentiality.

After all, I didn't treat workaholics with insecurity issues. I specialized in killers. Depraved, volatile killers.

Setting my cell on the bench, I stepped out of the shorts and spun the combination dial of the locker, anxious to get to the office and get this over with.

~

Detective Ted Saxe was a tall officer in a cheap gray suit, his shield hanging from a lanyard around his neck. I unlocked my office and gestured to the duo of soft green chairs that faced my desk. "Please, take a seat."

Out of spite or stubbornness, he stayed on his feet. I made my way around and dropped my purse in the side drawer of my desk before sinking into my leather rolling chair. "How can I help you?"

Leaning forward, he dropped an evidence bag on the middle of the clean wooden surface. I picked up the clear bag and examined the item inside.

It was one of my business cards, the discreet style with just my name, doctor designation, and the office number. On the back was my cell phone number, written in my handwriting. I glanced back up at him. "Where'd you find this?"

"In John Abbott's wallet." He removed a set of aviator glasses off the top of his bald head and looped them through the neck of his button-up shirt. This guy was straight out of central casting. Thin and hard, with jet-black skin and a distrustful scowl. "Do you know Mr. Abbott?" he asked.

The lingering concern that John Abbott would act out morphed into alarm. What had he done? Placing the evidence bag down, I cleared my throat as my mind worked overtime through the possibilities. "Yes. He's a client of mine."

The American Psychological Association's Ethical Principles of Psychologists and Code of Conduct was firm on the confidentiality owed to clients. It was also clear that that confidentiality could be broken if I thought my client was a danger to himself or others.

John Abbott's prior sessions, in which he described his struggles with wanting to harm his wife, technically fell into reportable arenas. His voice mail this morning could easily classify as an alarming incident worthy of police intervention.

But it had only been a voice mail. An insecure man saying the same thing he had said to me in a year's worth of sessions. Just because he toyed with the idea of killing Brooke didn't mean he ever would, and if I called the police every time one of my clients thought about killing someone, I'd put a lot of innocent people in jail and deplete my client list.

The truth is, wanting to harm or kill someone is a common part of the human mental circus. While there are some moral saints out there who have never wished ill on anyone, twenty percent of human beings have weighed the pros and cons of killing someone at some point in their lives.

Five percent have the moral flexibility to act on the possibility.

A tenth of a percent obsess over it, and the best intentioned of those seek psychiatric help with their fixation. My clients were the best of the worst, and I felt a fierce sense of duty to protect them while treating their most honest confessions.

After all, their thoughts weren't actions. People didn't die from mental activities. It was only if those thoughts turned into actions . . . that was the dangerous risk in this game I played with clients on a daily basis.

Now, with a detective sitting across from me . . . the signs were clear. In John Abbott's game, I had lost and the risks had won.

Saxe cleared his throat. "John Abbott didn't show up to work this morning. His coworkers grew concerned, and one went by to see if he was okay. That's when the police were called."

I placed a hand on my chest, rubbing the soft silk of my dress shirt and willing my heartbeat to calm. I was about to ask if John was in custody when the detective continued.

"The bodies were both on the kitchen floor. The pharmacy employee saw Mr. Abbott's through the window."

All my thoughts skittered to a stop. *Bodies? Mr. Abbott's?*

"It looks like Brooke Abbott had a heart attack while they were eating breakfast. We found her husband next to her. An apparent suicide."

I frowned. "What? Are you sure?"

"The man was stabbed in the stomach. The angle and situation lead us to believe it was self-inflicted."

I tried not to picture Brooke Abbott, whom I had met just last month in a freak run-in at the grocery store. A pretty woman. Kind eyes. A friendly smile. She had greeted me warmly, with no idea of the dozens of conversations I'd had with her husband about why killing her was a bad idea.

A year of sessions, and Brooke Abbott had died of a heart attack within hours of him calling me? I didn't believe it.

"What were you treating John for?"

I clicked my tongue. "That's confidential, Detective."

"Oh, come on," he scoffed. "The patient's deceased."

"Get me a warrant," I said. "Look, I'm sorry, but I'm bound by a code of ethics."

"And I'm sure you stretch the boundaries of that code." He snorted. "We all know what your specialty is, Dr. Moore." He finally sat, which was unfortunate, because I was now ready for him to leave. "Doc of Death? Isn't that what they call you?"

I sighed at the moniker. "Violent tendencies and obsessions are my specialty, but they aren't the only type of disorders I treat. Many of my clients are perfectly normal and pleasant individuals." The lie rolled out smoothly. I hadn't had a normal client in a decade.

He smirked. "Killers," he said. "You treat killers. Current, future, and past. You'll have to forgive me, Doc. I call it like I see it."

"Well, like I said, I can't discuss Mr. Abbott."

"When's the last time you spoke with him?"

The tap dance was beginning. I chose my words carefully, mindful that they were probably already aware of his calls. "Our last appointment was two weeks ago. He canceled the one scheduled for this week. And he called me this morning. I missed his call and called him back several hours later, but he didn't respond."

Saxe didn't seem surprised by the information, which meant that they already had his call log. Thank God I hadn't left a voice mail. "What did he say when he called you?"

"Just asked me to give him a call."

"I'd like to hear that voice mail."

I sighed. "I deleted it. I'm sorry, I didn't think anything of it."

He nodded, as if he understood, but if he was looking at this as a heart attack and suicide, he didn't. "That number on your card, that's the one he called?"

"The number on the back, yes. That's my cell."

"You give your cell phone number to all your clients?" He frowned. "Even the dangerous ones?"

12

"It's a cell phone." I sat back in the chair. "It's not my home address or the code to my front door. If they abuse it, then I stop working with them. If I need to change the number, I'll change the number. It's not a big deal."

"Coming from someone who looks at dead bodies all day, I have to say, Doc—I don't think you take your safety seriously. You're an attractive woman. All it takes is one of these sickos becoming obsessed with you, and you're going to have a serious problem."

"I appreciate the advice." I forced a smile. "But they aren't sickos. They're normal people, Detective. Some people struggle with depression; others struggle with violent urges. If my clients didn't care about protecting others, they wouldn't be in my office."

"Is that why John Abbott was seeing you? He didn't want to hurt people?"

I kept my features pleasant. "Like I said, I treat clients for a variety of things. Some just need someone to talk to. You want to know more than that, I need a warrant."

"Hey, I had to try," he said, raising his hands in surrender. Glancing toward my window, he studied the park view for a long moment. "Any reason I should look at this as anything other than a suicide?"

He was questioning the wrong death. "Not that I'm aware of."

"Would you swear to that under oath?"

"Absolutely." *Just please don't ask about Brooke.*

He nodded slowly. "I'll be in touch if I have any more questions, Dr. Moore." He pushed on the arms of the chair and stood. "Thank you for your time."

I walked him to the lobby and gave a reassuring smile to Jacob, who watched us with interest. Returning to my office, I closed the door and let out a shuddered breath.

The chances were high, very high, that this was my fault. I'd had one job to do, and I had failed in an epic way with Brooke—but also John. Because of that, two people were dead.

CHAPTER 3

"This isn't your fault." Meredith squinted at me over a brussels sprout–laden tuna fish sandwich. "Tell me you know that."

"While I appreciate your emotional life raft, you're wrong." I stabbed my fork into a piece of melon and prosciutto. "He sought treatment with me because he wanted to kill his wife. He killed his wife. He killed himself. If I'd done my job properly, they'd both be alive."

"Okay, first, you have no proof he killed his wife." She spoke through a mouthful of food, one finger lifted in the air as she started to count off a list of bullshit. "She had a heart attack."

"Someone can trigger a heart attack." I set down my fork. "He was a pharmacist. Trust me."

"Then call the detective. Have him run a tox screen." She waited, her sandwich hovering before her mouth.

"You know I can't do that," I said grudgingly, lowering my voice as I glanced around the crowded downtown café.

"You *can* do that," she pointed out. "You just don't want to. Because then I might be right and you'll have to release this self-imposed guilt and move on with your life in a happy and productive manner."

This was why I shouldn't have befriended a fellow shrink. We couldn't have a simple lunch without analyzing each other.

I studied the stamped design along the rim of my plate. "I *shouldn't* do that," I amended, "for several reasons." I could waste our entire lunch going over why that was a horrible idea. If I was wrong, and Brooke's death was natural, I'd be a laughingstock who'd tried to tarnish my own client's name. If I was right and my client had killed his wife, I'd be under a microscope, would have to turn over his files, and for what? For justice on a man who had already imposed his own death sentence? It was a waste of government resources and time.

Meredith took a sip of herbal tea and shrugged. "Whatever. Dig your own mental grave. Did you call that guy whose number I gave you? The handyman?"

"I did *not* call the handyman." I tore off a piece of bread. "I appreciate the matchmaking, but I already have one new man in my life, and I don't need another."

"A pack of Mr. Clean sponges doesn't count." She frowned at me and picked a sprout off the front of her blouse.

"Yeah, well. He's the first man inside my house other than my brother in . . ." I squinted and did the depressing math. "Eighteen months? So, I'm counting it as a step in the right direction."

"Even more reason to call Mimmo. Have you had an Italian before?" She let out a low whistle. "Honey. It's a spiritual experience. Besides, he's a total sweetheart."

"So you said." I placed a forkful of cold melon in my mouth.

"Oh, did you hear?" She perked up, her handyman forgotten. "They caught the Bloody Heart Killer."

Amid the news of John Abbott's death, I'd forgotten. "I missed the full story. What happened?" I took a sip of ice water. "The kid escaped?"

"Right. That Beverly High senior—the one who's been gone seven weeks? He—" She took a sip of tea, paused, then coughed, her fist in front of her mouth as she hacked out whatever was bothering her. "Sorry about that."

"The BH victim," I prompted her.

"So he escapes from the guy and makes it back to his Beverly Hills mansion, where his parents freak out, prodigal son has returned, blah blah blah, and they call the police. Turns out the kid knows who the killer is." She pointed her finger at me. "Get this—the guy's a teacher at Beverly High."

"Wow." I leaned in closer. "What do we know about him?"

"Loner. Never married. Harmless-looking guy, looks like a mall Santa Claus. Won teacher of the year a decade ago."

"That's interesting." I mulled over the information. "I wonder why he just now targeted a Beverly High kid. Normally it's the first victim who's in easy and close proximity."

She shrugged. "Killers are your thing. I'm perfectly happy to stay on my side of the office with my orgasm-hungry lacrosse moms."

"Speaking of which . . ."—I glanced at my watch—"I've got an appointment in forty-five, so I need to wrap this up."

"Yeah, I've got to run over to the dry cleaner anyway." She half raised her hand, catching the attention of our waiter, who fished the bill portfolio out of his apron and placed it on the table.

I reached for it. "I got it. Thanks for the counseling session."

Placing a few bills down on the table, I stole one last sip of water and stood. I needed to hurry. A wannabe killer was probably already in my lobby, tapping her four-inch stilettos and waiting.

CHAPTER 4

"You know, most killers start with a close family member or friend."

This fact was delivered by Lela Grant, who wore a bright-yellow dress with a white cardigan and had a designer purse tucked between her turquoise-blue heels. In the first thirty minutes of our appointment, she had complained about her husband, chattered enthusiastically about the addition of a salad bar to her country club's lunch hour, and shown me photos of two chaise lounge options she was considering for her lanai. After we made the excruciating choice to go with the white-and-green-cushioned bamboo chaise, we finally circled around to why I was treating her: her violent fantasies toward her husband's sister.

"Yes, I'm aware of that statistic." I drew a small line of roses along the top of my notepad and made a mental reminder to order a funeral spray for John and Brooke's service.

"The problem is that she lives so close. He's going to want to go to her house for Christmas dinner, and what can I say? I have no good excuse. Sarah's house is bigger than ours, her kids haven't seen him in months, and she makes some lemon pie he won't shut up about. I mean, it's *lemon* pie. How spectacular could it be?"

I shrugged. "I don't like pie."

"Well, a pie is a pie. I told him that, and he got offended. Let me tell you, I've made a hundred pies for that man, and he's never raved about any of them. I should be the one who's offended. Honestly, Gwen—I don't think I can sit at her table and watch her waltz in with that dessert and not turn violent. Do you realize how many knives are going to be at that table?" Her cheeks sucked in with worry, an act that further ballooned her injected lips. Her forehead, defying all natural odds, remained perfectly smooth.

"You're not going to pick up a knife and stab her," I said patiently.

"I think I am. You don't know how often I've seen it in my head." An almost dreamy calm came over Lela's face as she worked through the bloodshed in her mind. Her lids snapped open. "Can't you give me a doctor's note? Something to get me out of this?"

"We have two months until Christmas," I pointed out. "Let's take things one at a time." I moved the conversation in a better direction. "I'd like you to tell me something nice about Sarah."

"What do you mean?"

"Share something that you like about her. A redeeming quality."

She looked at me as if I were insane. I waited patiently, my hands folded over each other on the pad. Lela wasn't a killer, though she certainly wanted to be. She was bored, had watched too many female-murderer documentaries on TV, and hated her sister-in-law. Who didn't hate someone? I had a list of at least three people I'd rather do without. Would I grab a turkey knife and go for their jugular? No. But neither would Lela. She just liked the idea of being interesting, and the thought that she had a secret and underlying homicidal inclination was a rainy-day fantasy she had embraced with maniacal vigor.

"I'm going to give you some homework." I picked up my pen. "Before next week's appointment, come up with three things that you like or admire about Sarah." I held up my hand to stop her objection. "Don't tell me you can't come up with three things. Figure it out, or postpone our next appointment until you do."

She twisted her watermelon-colored lips into a grimace.

I gave her a reassuring smile and stood. "I think we made good progress today."

She reached down and gripped the handles of her purse. "I hate this homework."

I stifled a laugh, then threw her an emotional crutch. "If we're going to keep your impulses in check, we have to retrain the way your brain looks at Sarah. Trust me, this is important to your treatment." *And your marriage,* I added silently.

"Fine." She huffed to her feet. "Thanks, Doc."

"Of course." I rose and swallowed the new and foreign swell of insecurity that was rising in my chest. I'd been wrong to believe that Brooke Abbott was safe from her husband.

Was I missing the mark on Lela Grant, too?

CHAPTER 5

I stood in a sea of black-suited strangers and listened to everyone talk about John as if he were a saint.

"It was Christmas Eve and he came into the pharmacy, just for me. Someone had stolen my bag at the gym, and I needed more heart medication . . ." The older woman put her hand over her large bosom, right next to a gold butterfly broach.

Oh, bless John and his heart medicine to the rescue. Honestly, it's the nicest people you have to worry the most about. Ed Gein, the killer who famously created suits of women's skin, was described as the nicest man in town. Dr. Harold Shipman, who murdered over two hundred patients, would make home visits and had a soothing and polite bedside manner. Part of the game, for many killers, is the con of the innocent, the hiding of the monster, the successful deception that proves to them that they are smarter and therefore superior.

"On the rainy days, John brought in my newspaper. Said he worried about me making it down my drive with my cane . . ." A younger man with braces on his legs spoke in a hushed tone, and I maneuvered around the group, beelining for the coffee station.

"You could just see the love they had. You know, it would have been their fifteen-year anniversary this year . . ." Another tight cluster of mourners, this discussion led by a woman with short-cropped hair that was a bright shade of magenta.

Sure, fifteen years of him hovering over her with a critical eye. Picking her apart for harmless conversations and friendships. In a year, I had barely scratched the surface of where John's insecurities and control issues came from, but they seemed to swell and ebb around Brooke's behavior.

They had been married fifteen years, but John's complicated mix of emotions for his wife had only ramped into violent inclinations in the last year. He had first sought my help when an argument between them had led him to wrap his hands around her neck and squeeze until she fainted. The act had given him a rush of sexual endorphins and caused her to emotionally withdraw . . . which was akin to a child running from a large dog. Ears went up, tail twitched, chase time on.

John may have brought newspapers in for neighbors with disabilities and opened the pharmacy on the weekend for heart-medicine distribution, but he had also calculated medicine combinations that would kill his wife and mused about locking her in his car trunk on a hot summer day to "teach her a lesson" about loyalty and trust.

With the exception of his first choking incident, the rest of his fantasies we had controlled through regular sessions and prescribed medications, the latter of which he often skipped or ignored altogether.

I stopped at the end of a long receiving line. Ahead of us was a trio of family members. I watched their faces as the line shuffled forward, curious if any of them had seen the monster behind the man.

"Strangling her would be best. For my enjoyment, I mean. I like the idea of looking in her eyes. Of her understanding what is happening. Otherwise, I'm worried she'll get distracted by the pain."

I'd spent the last four days thinking over our sessions. Each night, I'd listened to the recordings of our appointments, focusing on the excited lilt of his voice as he had described the different ways he would hurt her. In hindsight, there were far too many signs, a gradual ramp-up of intensity between his first visit and last. I'd heard it and made notes, yet I'd been foolish enough to believe that the power of my counsel was enough to keep him in line. My ego, that was what had killed Brooke.

I paused in front of John's sister, her mascara streaked down her cheeks. "I'm so sorry for your loss," I told her. I stepped to the side and repeated the routine with his brother. They were both thin and bookish—a marked contrast to John's large frame.

"Mrs. Caldwell." I nodded to Brooke's mother, who was sagging in place, her face etched in deep lines of sorrow, all color faded from her skin.

I did this. I'm the reason she no longer has a daughter.

I could have broken my physician's code of silence if I believed my patient was an imminent and violent threat to others.

I could have gone to the police. Shared everything John told me.

But then what? They would have questioned him. Questioned her. And then released him. You can't arrest someone for thinking about killing someone. They would have let him go, she might have left him over the event, and he might have killed her then.

Justification. The problem with the initials after my name was that I could smell my own bullshit.

~

I snuck out early and ended up at a bar two blocks down from the funeral home. I claimed a booth in the back, one tucked behind a pool table and beside a crooked dartboard. It was quiet, the bar half-empty, and I slid into the plastic seat and pulled a metal bucket of dusty peanuts toward me.

The waitress was heavily pregnant and lumbered over with a disinterested yawn. I saved her a few extra trips by ordering a bucket of beer.

"Getting anything to eat?" Her gaze drifted over my black pantsuit with the sort of curiosity that indicated ironed outfits rarely made their way through the doors.

"Just the beer." I forced a smile.

"You guys with some sort of convention?"

"Excuse me?"

She pointed toward the entrance. "You and him."

I followed her direction and saw a man in a three-piece suit on a stool at the bar. "No."

She shrugged. "Okay. If you need more peanuts, let me know."

The jukebox started up, some twangy song about Amarillo in the morning. I eased down in the booth until my head rested against the cushion. I hadn't been to a bar in a decade, which might be why I was still single. It was hard to find a boyfriend when you spent the bulk of your time surrounded by fellow shrinks and psychotic patients. The last time I'd stepped foot in a bar, the delicate sounds of a pianist played as hushed conversations were held beneath expensive light fixtures. I'd sipped a handcrafted drink garnished with spices and served in a smoked tumbler.

This place was the polar opposite, the sort of establishment where mistakes were made and sorrows were drowned, which was exactly why I'd paused by the entrance and pushed open the door. If I could drink away the last two hours, maybe I could go to sleep without the vision of Brooke Abbott's mother sobbing against the side of the casket.

"Here." The waitress was back, heaving a metal pail full of Bud Light bottles onto the table. "If we fill up, you'll have to move to the bar. The booths are for parties of two or more."

I nodded. If they filled up, I'd be out the door and flagging down a taxi. I took a beer from the ice and twisted off the cap, chugging it until my brain flexed in response to the chill.

~

Two beers later, I returned from the bathroom and reclaimed my seat, my remaining bottles cockeyed and waiting in the ice. I picked up a sticky menu tent and reviewed the short list of offerings.

"I'm sorry to interrupt, but I made a vow a long time ago to stop any woman who was about to make a huge mistake."

I looked up from the card and into a face that looked as tired as mine. He wore it better than I did, his handsomeness almost magnified by the deep lines in his brow. "What mistake is that?"

"You were thinking about the fish dip, right?" The corner of his mouth crooked up, revealing a hint of straight teeth. He was my age, late thirties, and I checked for a wedding band, my interest rising at the sight of his bare ring finger.

Not that a relationship was what I wanted. Right now, with guilt weighing down every thought, I just needed a mistake. One filthy, mind-numbing mistake. If it came wrapped in an expensive suit and bedroom eyes, even better.

"I was actually thinking about oysters."

He winced. "As a man who's spent the last hour sampling every item on that menu, I recommend the wings and nothing else."

"Sold." I set the tent card down and held out my hand. "I'm Gwen."

"Robert." He shook it firmly, but not to the point of dominance. "Bad day?"

"Bad week." I gestured to the other side of the booth, inviting him to sit. "You?"

"Same." He slid in, and his leg bumped against mine. "Want to talk about it?"

"Hell no." I pulled out a bottle and offered it to him. "Beer?"

He took it. "I have to say, I've never seen a beautiful woman drink alone for so long without being approached."

"I think I put off a pretty clear 'Stay away' vibe." I glanced around. "Plus, there's no one here."

"Which is shocking, given the ambience," he deadpanned.

I laughed. "Yeah. But I don't know, it fits my mood." I leaned forward and wrapped my hands around the bottle. "With this glass, rich and deep, we cradle all our sorrows to sleep." I gave a wistful smile. "My dad used to say that. Though he was a scotch man, not Bud Light."

He studied me. "What are you doing here? You seem like more of an uptown girl."

I had to smile at the polite dig. "A snob," I amended. "That's what you're saying?"

"I'm saying you carry hand sanitizer in your purse and played Taylor Swift on the jukebox," he pointed out. "To say you don't fit in here is putting it mildly."

I warmed at the knowledge that he had been watching me, then immediately reminded myself of why I was there. Punishment. Atonement. Two people were dead on my watch. "I was in the neighborhood." I caught the waitress's eyes. "You?"

He grimaced. "Attending a funeral."

I paused, surprised. "The Abbott funeral?"

He raised his brow. "Yeah. You?"

"Same." I frowned. "I didn't see you there." Not that I'd been studying the crowd.

"I left pretty early. I don't do well at funerals. Especially lately." A shadow passed over his face. "It's been a bad year for me with deaths."

I didn't need my psychiatry degree to know to avoid that minefield. The pain was radiating off him, and if it was from this funeral, my guilt was about to get worse. I gave a slight nod in response.

His eyebrows pinched together in thought. "Who were you a friend of? Brooke or John?"

A friend? I'd be lying either way. "Brooke," I said, and wished it were true.

He nodded. "John was my pharmacist."

"Wow." I took a sip of my beer. "Good for you. I don't even know mine's name, much less would attend her funeral."

"My son had diabetes," he said quietly. "We were frequent customers."

Ah. Had diabetes. A bad year for funerals. Unless someone recently found a cure for juvenile diabetes, I had an answer for the haunted look in his eyes.

"Well." I lifted my beer. "To John and Brooke."

"To John and Brooke." He clinked bottles with me, then downed the rest of his without flinching.

The waitress paused by our table and pulled the empty bucket of ice toward the edge. "Did you want to order something?"

"Yes. A dozen wings, please. Mild."

"And another bucket of beer." Robert threw an arm over the back of the booth, and his jacket gaped open, revealing the expensive lines of his vest. A custom suit. The glint of a Rolex peeking out of the sleeve of his jacket. A comfort level in this atmosphere where he obviously didn't fit, bred from pure confidence. A businessman or attorney. Probably the latter.

"I really shouldn't have any more." I turned my watch so I could see the dial. Seven thirty. It felt so much later.

"I'll drink them all." He reached in his pocket and pulled out two pills. Putting one in his mouth, he put the other on the bar napkin in front of me. "Take this. It'll help with your hangover tomorrow."

I looked at the round white tablet without touching it. "What is it?"

"B6. You're supposed to take it prior to, during, and after drinking, but any of it helps." He nodded to the pill. "Go ahead. It doesn't bite."

I slid the napkin toward him. "Not gonna happen. It's all you."

He chuckled. "You're either anti-remedy, drinking to punish yourself for something, or you don't trust me."

"The last two." I took a small sip of beer. "No offense."

"None taken." He picked up the pill and put it on his tongue, a flash of white teeth showing before it disappeared in his mouth. "What are you punishing yourself for?"

"I made a mistake at work." I moved my beer in a small circle on the table, watching as it left a path of condensation.

"Must have been a big one."

"It was."

"Let me guess." He tilted his head to one side and did an obvious up and down of my pantsuit. "Accountant."

I curled my upper lip in distaste. "No."

"Studio exec."

I laughed, because in this town, everyone wanted to be in the movies. "No. Psychiatrist."

"Ah. Definitely not anti-remedy, then." He studied me. "Expensive watch and bag, and the freedom to be entering bars in questionable areas of town just in time for happy hour. You must have a private practice. Let me guess, housewives with inferiority complexes?"

"Private practice, yes. Housewives, no." I narrowed my eyes at him. "If you're a cop, you aren't a great one."

"Definitely not a cop. I sit on the other side of that courtroom." He gave an unapologetic smirk. "Defense attorney."

I sat up straighter, my interest piqued at the specialty. "White-collar crimes?"

"Mostly criminal."

"Here in Los Angeles County?"

"And Orange."

"Personal or property crime?"

He regarded me over the top of his beer. "You're suddenly full of questions."

"I'm called in for expert testimony a lot. I'm surprised our paths haven't crossed."

"There are thousands of cases a year," he said slowly. "I'd be surprised if they did. What's your specialty?"

I was too drunk for this interview. I cleared my throat and attempted a mask of composure. "Personality disorders and violent compulsions."

"You get more interesting with each moment, Dr. Gwen."

"Wings?" A man in a cowboy hat stopped by our table, a basket in hand; they were really pushing the western-bar concept too far.

I raised my hand. "Those are mine."

~

My house was closest, and I was laughing when I stumbled out of the taxi, my fingers latched through his as we made it across the dark stepping-stones and up the stacked-stone steps of my house. From the swing at the end of the porch, Clementine mewed. Robert stared into the darkness. "Nice kitty."

I ignored him and got the door open. He followed me closely, his hands roaming as he peeled off my jacket and kissed the back of my neck. I dropped my head back, enjoying the soft press of his lips against the neglected spot, one that sent a tremor of need down my spine. My last sexual encounter had been the result of a blind date and had involved a half-hearted erection and lots of stifled yawns on my end as I'd eyed the clock and yearned for bed.

The foyer lamp was on, the light picking up the turquoise colors in the oil painting of Alcatraz Island. Robert pushed me against the navy wall, palming my breast through my shirt as his mouth settled on mine. He was a talented kisser, confident yet gentle, and I sank against the molding and let him take control. I kicked off one heel, then the other, dropping in height as he undid the top button of my blouse.

"Come on." I pulled to one side, tugging on his hand as I led the way up the dark wooden stairs to my bedroom. Pushing open the door, I felt a wave of calm and reassurance at the perfectly made bed and orderly room. While I had chosen dramatic and dark colors for the living room and foyer, my bedroom was all crisp white, from the walls to the bedding to the soft, plush rug that stretched over the walnut floor. The only color came from the neat stack of novels and the fresh lilies on my bedside table and the large fireplace, which shimmered with inlaid mirror shards, set into brick. I'd paid a fortune for that fireplace, and it'd been worth every penny.

If he was impressed by the room, he said nothing, staying silent as I crawled onto the taut expanse of the white monogrammed duvet and turned to face him.

He pulled off his jacket slowly, then unbuttoned his shirt, giving me time to think, to analyze, to back out. Maybe it was the alcohol, maybe it was the fact that I hadn't been with a man in over a year, but there was no hesitation in me. I unbuttoned my pants and shimmied out of them.

The bed sank as he joined me on it, and I reached for him, greedy for the warmth of his skin and the reconnection of our kiss. The heat of our bodies joined, and it was exactly what I needed—a living connection in a day filled with death.

CHAPTER 6

I woke up to the smell of toast and coffee. It was comforting and familiar, reminiscent of my childhood, and I closed my eyes for an extra
moment before jerking fully awake.

My bedroom was in perfect order, as it always was. Dresser clean
and uncluttered. Curtains pulled closed. Clock at a forty-five-degree
angle to the vase of lilies, which were beginning to wilt. My watch on
the bedside table, next to the novels.

The smell of food was out of place. So were the footsteps coming
from downstairs. The lawyer. I pinched my eyes closed and tried to place
his name. Robert. Robert without a last name. We'd debated the death
penalty during the cab ride here. Oh my God, my car. It was still in the
parking garage three blocks down from the funeral home.

I slowly sat up, appreciating the sore ache of my muscles. Robert
had been . . . A grin pulled at my lips. Fantastic. Was that what sex
was supposed to be like? God, to think of all the years I had wasted
on mediocre lovemaking. I pulled back the covers and swung my legs
over the side of the high bed, surprised that I was naked except for an
oversize Star Wars T-shirt that I'd purchased online. Robert had liked
the shirt, chuckling as he had returned from my closet with it in hand. I
looked around for my underwear but didn't see it. Pushing to my feet, I
winced at the pain in my head. I should have taken that B12 . . . or B6,

or whatever it had been. Just the fact he was up and cooking breakfast was proof it worked.

I brushed my teeth and pulled on a fresh pair of underwear and a pair of faded jeans. Buttoning up the fly, I quietly made my way down the stairs and toward the kitchen.

The grin that stretched across my cheeks fell as soon as I passed the open double doors to my office and saw Robert standing at my desk, looking down at an open client file. John Abbott's file. I'd left it out, my review abandoned yesterday afternoon when I'd stopped to dress for the funeral. As I watched, he lifted up the edge of a page.

"What are you doing?"

He looked up, unperturbed by my tone. "I thought you said you were Brooke's friend."

I entered the office, my anger growing at his lack of apology. "These are confidential patient files."

"Confidential patient files for John Abbott." He tapped the page. "John was a patient of yours?"

"You need to leave," I snapped, my warm and fuzzy feelings fleeing at the thought of what he had seen. What was the liability here? I'd left patient files out in the open, but in the privacy of my own home. Had he broken any laws? Had I?

He dropped the file and stepped away from the desk.

"What are you doing in here?" I closed the file and wrapped a rubber band around it. "Is this what you do? You sleep with someone and then go through all their things?"

"I had to check my work messages. My cell's battery is dead." He nodded to the phone on my desk. "I didn't have a charger, and you don't have a phone in the kitchen. This was the first room where I found one. I'm sorry. His name caught my eye."

I opened my drawer and pushed the folder into it. "You should go. I can order a car for you if your phone is dead."

He didn't move, and my frustration grew.

"You know what confidentiality I'm bound to. You have a very similar one with your clients," I said.

"You should have told me that you were John's shrink."

"Why?" I gave a strangled laugh. "You were a stranger in a bar. I didn't owe you confidential information about a client."

"A dead client," he pointed out.

"It doesn't matter. My legal obligations don't change." I crossed my arms over my chest and glared at him.

"Okay," he said finally, his jaw tight. "Fine. No need to call me a car. Thank you for the hospitality."

He picked up his jacket from where he'd folded it over a chair and walked into the hall. I stayed in place and listened as his dress shoes sounded down the hall and out the front door. There was a quiet click as it latched back into place. From the kitchen, something wafted smoke in the air.

I picked up the phone's receiver and listened to the dial tone. I studied the bank of buttons, then reached forward and pressed the redial button. An unknown number with a 310 area code displayed. Holding my breath, I listened as the phone rang once and then went to a voice mail for Cluster & Kavin Law Firm.

I hung up. So, he had called his office. Cluster & Kavin . . . I paused halfway through to the hall and inhaled sharply, suddenly aware of who Robert was.

Robert Kavin. The father of Gabe.

CHAPTER 7

Robert Kavin stopped at the end of Gwen's driveway and looked to either side, surveying the quiet neighborhood. It was well established, the yards neatly tended to, the cars all tucked behind garage doors. He'd liked her house, liked the perfect order and care it held. It was a home with character, her style elegant with an edge. The skull paperweight tucked into her bookcase. The framed blood-spatter prints hanging in her powder room. The rich navy walls. Books everywhere. Art that seemed to have a story behind every piece. He wanted to know those stories, wanted to unlock the brilliant and sexy woman who had crawled on top of him in the back seat of the cab with an infectious laugh that had contrasted with her professional exterior.

His warm feelings toward her had dissolved the moment he saw that file on her desk. He'd only had a chance to read a few pages before she had interrupted him, but it had been enough to know that her sessions with John Abbott had been highly personal in nature. Personal and full of violence.

He glanced back at the two-story Tudor and headed left down the street, cursing himself for his phone's dead battery. He hadn't paid attention to his bearings when the taxi took them home last night, but he headed north, hoping the road would lead to a neighborhood exit, preferably one with a gas station or strip mall nearby. He fisted his jacket in his left hand and moved to the shaded side of the street. Even in October, the California heat was a bitch.

If his son were here, he'd laugh at him. Gabe would make some crack about Robert getting literally screwed. He'd ask why he'd stormed off instead of talking things out with Gwen. And if Robert would say that he tried to, and she had clammed up and spouted about confidentiality, Gabe would point out that he'd have done the same thing.

Which was true. Twenty years of dealing with clients—some really terrible clients—and he'd never broken their confidence. Granted, a one-night stand had never gone through his case files, either. He grimaced at the thought of what his reaction would be if one did. Calm reactions weren't his strong suit.

A Volvo with Stanford decals passed, and he watched it go, reluctant to flag down a stranger. Ahead, a cart path sign said CLUBHOUSE with a small arrow. That couldn't be too far.

The neighborhood felt familiar, like the one Gabe's first girlfriend had lived in. Her parents had thrown a Fourth of July party and all but forced him to attend. It had been in the middle of the Zentenberg trial, and he'd barely had the energy to stand, but he'd gone. Talk about a painful three hours. The same conversation over and over again about the Chargers, then the forest fires, then the election. A nonstop circle of dull conversation.

If Natasha had been alive, she would have gone to that party with him. She liked that stuff. She could stand there, a drink in hand, and laugh at stupid comments as if they were the wittiest thing she'd ever heard. And it didn't come across as fake, which was commendable, considering that she always ripped apart the person as soon as they were out of earshot. It was one thing he hadn't missed about her. The backbiting and judgment that never seemed to stop.

Around the curve, the golf clubhouse appeared. He stepped over a curb and turned down the wide drive, his pace quickening at the prospect of a phone and air-conditioning. He glanced at his watch, wondering if the bar would be open, despite the early hour.

Right now, what he really needed was a drink.

~

The bar was open and empty, his scotch order taken with a grunt. Leaning back on the stool, he stretched his back, sighing as something popped into place. He was too old for marathon sex, and last night had been the first time in a while that he had been so . . . active.

Gwen had been a surprise in bed. Passionate and needy, but also confident. She hadn't covered herself up when he looked at her, or apologized for the cellulite along her thighs. Maybe that confidence came from sitting across from killers all day.

His mood darkened, and he pulled the drink closer.

". . . a tearful reunion."

He glanced at the television and caught the tail end of a video with a family embracing. His mood soured further.

"Crazy stuff, right?" The bartender leaned against the bar, his palms tucked underneath his armpits.

"Yep." Robert stared into the glass. Scott Harden and his miraculous escape was the last thing he wanted to hear about.

"You heard about this, right? That missing kid—you know, the one they thought was taken by that serial killer? He escaped from the guy."

The missing kid. Not Gabe, who hadn't been able to escape. Scott Harden. Lucky Scott Harden.

Robert's emotions rose as the television announcers recapped the escape and reunion. The camera cut to a summary of the BH history, and he downed the rest of the watered-down drink. Gabe's name was mentioned, and he slammed down the tumbler. Pulling out his wallet, he retrieved a twenty-dollar bill and placed it on the bar. "Thanks."

"Sure."

His anxiety rose as he heard Gabe's name again. Were they showing the photos? His bare foot hanging out from under the tarp? A bloody letter jacket?

He made it out of the lobby and through the front doors and saw the taxi moving down the drive toward him. Raising his hand to catch its attention, he closed his eyes but couldn't block out the image, the one they always showed. His son, smiling into the camera with his football jersey on—the one taken just eight weeks before he was killed.

CHAPTER 8

Nita Harden had expected her son to be skinny. Somehow, against all odds, her son had grown thicker. Now, as Scott sat in a wingback chair in the study, his white button-up shirt was snug against a chest dotted with small cigarette burns that were starting to scab over. Seated before him, Detective Erica Petts adjusted a dial on a voice recorder, then set it on her knees. She'd been the first to the house when Scott had disappeared and had listened to countless questions, tears, and complaints from George and Nita during the duration of his absence.

"If you get tired or need a break, just let me know. And take your time if you need to think over a question." The detective leaned forward in her chair, her full attention on Scott.

"Yes, ma'am." He was such a polite boy. That was one thing that George had done a great job of. Back in first grade, Scott was using *please* and *thank you* before he knew how to write. Nita's pride swelled as she watched him rub the side of his handsome face.

"Okay, we're recording this, just so we don't miss anything." The other cop settled into the third chair in the cluster. Detective Ed Harvey was a big, burly man with glasses. He'd always put off a clear "Get out of our way and let us do our job" vibe that had infuriated her. Now that Scott was home, Ed's attitude had switched to one of suspicion, though she couldn't figure out of whom.

Nita leaned against the wall, knotting her hands as she watched Ed offer Scott a soda. It was a brand he didn't like, and she left the room and hurried to the kitchen. In the large double fridge, she found a can of root beer. Returning to the study, she crept forward and set it down next to him on the desk.

"Thanks, Mom." He smiled at her.

Erica cleared her throat. "How are you, Scott?"

He gave a shy smile. "I'm good. Glad to be home."

She gave a short laugh. "I bet you are. Got any big plans?"

"Well, my mom is fixing lasagna tonight. I'm pretty excited about that. Then we're going to watch *Die Hard*."

Nita had suggested a less violent movie, but Scott had rolled his eyes and cajoled George into siding with him. Not that it had taken much work. She couldn't refuse him anything. Right now, her heart felt like it would burst every time she looked at him.

She couldn't sleep at night out of the sheer relief and joy of having him back under their roof. She had broached the idea of bringing a cot into his room, but her husband had stopped that idea with a firm shake of his head.

"Great movie," Ed interjected. "Love Bruce Willis."

"Yeah." Scott cracked the top of his root beer.

There was a pause, and Nita shifted her weight to her other foot.

"You were gone for forty-four days, Scott." Erica clicked her pen into action. "How much do you remember about the day you were taken?"

"Everything. I mean . . . well, I remember everything leading up to when I blacked out. Then I remember being at the house."

"Okay, so let's go to the last thing you remember, before you blacked out."

"Well, we had that football game, against Harvard-Westlake." He scratched the back of his head. "And I, uh, showered after the game. A lot of the guys were talking about going to get food, so I grabbed my gear and headed to my truck."

Scott's truck had been his seventeenth-birthday present. A huge silver four-door with off-road tires and an engine that was too loud, but he loved it. When he was missing, she had climbed up into it and sat for hours, desperately inhaling the air, needing his scent.

"But you never made it to the truck?" Ed asked.

"No, I did. Next to my truck, someone was parked there. It was, um, the science teacher from school. Mr. Thompson."

"This man?" Erica pulled a photo out from a folder on her lap. Nita eased around to get a better look at the image. It was a man in his late fifties, with a neat white beard, a receding hairline, and a kind smile. It was a staff photo in which he wore a lanyard and had a name tag clipped to a slightly crumpled white button-up. She stared at it. This was the monster who had taken her son. The man who had tortured and killed six others. The man whom she must have passed a dozen times at Beverly High and never noticed. Where had her motherly intuition been? How had it not screamed at her, with a giant glowing spotlight on his face?

"Yeah, that's him."

The problem was, she had grown lax. Assumed that because Scott was 170 pounds and practically an adult, he was safe. A stupid assumption, one she would never make again.

"So, what happened?" Ed asked.

"He needed help getting something out of his trunk. I bent over to help him, and he stuck something in my neck. Whatever it was, it knocked me out like that." Scott snapped his fingers.

"Where were you when you woke up?" Erica asked.

He hesitated. Lifted his soda to his mouth and took a sip. Glanced at his mother. "Uh—in a room. On a bed. I was tied to it."

Nita held eye contact with him until the moment he looked away. Her stomach cramped. During the weeks of Scott's absence, as they grew certain the BH Killer was involved, the police had shared information with them about the other victims. The details about what the autopsies had shown . . . Nita let out an involuntary shudder.

Scott had always been a fairly innocent boy. No serious girlfriends, though he'd had plenty of crushes over the years. Before his disappearance, she would have put her hand on a Bible and sworn he was a virgin. Now, her gaze dropped to his bandaged wrists. They had been the first thing she took care of, after she fixed him a plate of food and helped him into a hot shower. She had called Erica while Scott had been in the bathroom, and the detective practically screamed at her to get him out in order to preserve evidence.

But Scott had been filthy. And he'd already known who took him, so why did evidence matter? It didn't. What mattered was healing. The police needed to wrap up their questions and leave him alone so that he could return to being a normal teenager with his family.

"Do you know where this house was? Was it this one?" Ed produced a photo, which Scott glanced at.

"Maybe. When I left, I just ran. I didn't look at the house."

Nita watched him carefully, saw the moment he rubbed the side of his face with his forefinger. It was one of his tells, and she frowned, wondering what he was lying about.

"Were you in a bedroom? His bedroom?" Erica asked.

"No, I don't think he lived there. I was drugged most of the time, so I'm not sure."

The two detectives glanced at each other.

"You need to arrest him." Nita spoke up. "Before he disappears, or before he comes here."

"We have officers with Randall Thompson now." Erica met her eyes. "We're waiting on a warrant to search his home. Don't worry. He won't be out of our sight."

"What if he says he didn't do it?" Scott asked. "If it's my word against his?"

"The evidence has a vote," Ed said. "It'll be fine."

Scott nodded, but he looked unconvinced. Nita moved forward. "You've asked enough questions for tonight. He's exhausted, and we should have our attorney present if you have any more."

Her husband watched from his place by the door and nodded his approval. He had wanted to call their attorney first, but Nita had argued with him, insisting that the most urgent thing was to get the teacher locked away. She walked the officers to the front door and hugged Erica goodbye, whispering a thank-you in the woman's ear. Pausing at the door, she glanced back at her son, who was still seated. He glanced back at her, then quickly looked away.

Her unease grew. Her son was keeping something from the police. What could it possibly be? And why?

CHAPTER 9

Cluster & Kavin Law Firm was housed in the same building as the Creative Artists Agency, which meant that once a week, Robert Kavin bumped elevator elbows with a celebrity. It was a factoid that had once earned him enormous street cred with his son, back when he was young enough to be impressed. That magic had left around puberty, replaced by a bored expression that only seemed to react when money, his car, or girls were involved.

One day soon, Robert would set all his files on fire and move to a shack on the beach. He'd wear board shorts and a baseball cap and not shave for a year. He'd handle cases about beach access and rental deposits and represent sandy daiquiri bars that paid in alcohol and coconut shrimp. This sleek building, pressed and starched suits . . . all that would be left behind.

"You're daydreaming again." His receptionist spoke from her spot next to him in the elevator, a knowing smile stretched across the older woman's face. "Let me guess. Aruba?"

"I'm thinking Uruguay now." The elevator doors slid open, and he held his hand against the opening, gesturing her forward. "Lower tax rate. Want to join me?"

The stately grandmother of three chuckled as she stepped off the elevator. "I can't convince Fred to take the forty-five-minute drive to

Costco. There's no chance of getting him on an airplane anytime in this century."

They rounded the corner and passed through the tall glass doors and into the law-firm lobby.

"Is Martin here?" He pulled his keys out and flipped through the set, finding the one for his office door and pushing it into the lock. Out of the three firm partners, he was the only one with the additional layer of security, but he didn't care. That was the difference between him and someone like Gwen, who left her files out for anyone to see. Carelessness like that was how cases were lost, secrets were spread, and careers were destroyed.

"He's been here since seven."

"Imagine that." He flipped on the lights and tossed his keys on the desk, then headed to his partner's office.

Martin was on the phone and met Robert's eyes as he came in. Nodding toward the conference table at the end of his office, he held up his finger in a "Just one minute" gesture. Robert took one of the leather rolling chairs and plucked a sticky doughnut off a discarded plate on the edge of the massive desk.

"There's coconut in that," Martin warned as he ended the call. "I swear, Joy's teaming up with my wife to get me to lose weight."

"I like coconut," Robert said through a mouthful.

"Right." Martin picked up the end of his tie and examined it, scratching at a spot with his fingernail. Glancing back at Robert, he paused. "I'm assuming you heard about Scott Harden returning home."

"I did." Robert wiped at his mouth. "One of the detectives called."

"Do they have any leads?"

"Actually, the kid said it was one of his teachers. They brought the guy in for questioning, and Judge Glenn gave them a warrant this morning."

"They find any evidence?" Martin tented his hands atop his stomach, his full attention on Robert. Between the two of them, they had freed hundreds of accused criminals from a life behind bars, and most of the time, a missing piece of evidence had been the weak link that had dictated the verdict.

"They found a shoebox in his house." He met the man's eyes. "It had souvenirs from each of the boys, including Gabe."

Martin winced. "I'm sorry, Rob."

"It's fine." He took a final bite of the doughnut and forced himself to chew, his mind refusing to let go of the detective's words. *They found some of Gabe's hair in the box. It matches his DNA. There's a few other things here. A key chain. We'll need you to come down and identify it.* Robert coughed, then swallowed, willing his voice to remain calm. "They're charging the teacher for all six murders and putting him in Central."

"Well." Martin's bushy white eyebrows raised in the middle of his dark forehead. "That's great. That's got to give you some peace."

Robert stayed silent.

"What?" His partner hunched forward. "What are you thinking?"

"Something's wrong." Robert shook his head. "It's too easy. Scott Harden escapes, makes it all the way back home without this guy catching him. And he knows the killer? BH's other victims didn't attend Beverly High. So why break routine? Why take a kid who can ID him? It's too risky."

"You're looking for reason and forgetting that the BH Killer is a human. An unstable human. Don't look at it through a prosecutor's lens."

"I have to. I'm pointing out the same things they will."

"Robert . . . ," Martin warned him.

"There's not enough to go on. It's the word of a teenage kid and a box that could have been planted—"

"Come on." Martin's voice was calm and comforting, and there was a reason he was one of the most successful attorneys in California. He could manipulate a jury's entire mood with just the lilt of his voice.

"You've got a victim's eyewitness and evidence. He's it. We'll make sure he pays for what he did."

"I'm worried it's not him." Robert leaned back and crossed his arms, steeling himself for his partner's response to his next words. He had been up all night thinking over Randall Thompson's arrest and the evidence against him. The man would need an attorney, and the public defenders would be playing hot potato to avoid the representation. Martin had always given him a fair amount of leniency in things that involved Gabe, but what he was about to say wouldn't go over well. "I want to represent him."

Martin stared at him for a long moment, then laughed. "Is that a joke?"

"As I said, I don't think it's him."

"No, you said you're worried it's not him."

"Fine." He sighed and amended his statement. "I don't think it's him."

His partner in the firm moved closer to the desk and rested his elbows on the surface, pinning him with laser eye contact. "This is Gabe's killer we're talking about. Your son was like my own. I'd be more in support of you saying you want to deliver justice via a prison shank. *You don't think* isn't good enough, Rob. You want this to go to trial without cutting off this asshole's balls, then fine. But sitting on his side of the defense table?" He studied him. "If you were anyone else, I'd think you were trying to sabotage his case, but you're too ethical for that."

"I don't have an ulterior motive here. I don't think he's the guy, which means the police have stopped looking for the real guy." Robert shrugged and hoped it came off as believable. "I've thought it through, Martin. I'm reaching out to the courts this afternoon to set up a meeting."

Martin let out a sigh. "You're a grown man, Rob. You know the case better than anyone. But this feels rotten. I don't know what to tell you."

"You don't have to tell me anything. I'm not asking permission." Robert balled up the napkin and tossed it into a round wastebasket beside Martin's desk. He needed to end this meeting, before the questions began. Martin would nail him with brilliant, precise, and unavoidable inquiries that Robert wouldn't have answers for because it made no logical sense for him to come within a thousand feet of the Randall Thompson case, not unless he was standing opposite him in the courtroom.

"Okay, but one last thing that has to be said. This is a huge conflict of interest." Martin stood and walked around the desk, his arms crossing over his wide chest and pinning the front of his blood-red tie into place. "You lose this case, and he'll sue us. Say that you intentionally botched it. He'll say you destroyed evidence and led witnesses and didn't properly represent him."

"I'm not going to lose."

Martin let out a frustrated laugh. "What am I missing here? You think he's innocent? Fine. Let the police and public defender handle that. There's nothing good that will come from your involvement."

"I need to meet with him. See what he says. Being his potential attorney gives me face time that I wouldn't otherwise have." He squeezed the man's thick shoulder. "If I don't believe what he says, I'll walk. You know I'll walk."

Martin shook his head. "He's not going to want you as his attorney. I can't imagine he wants to discuss his activities with the father of one of the boys he killed."

Robert said nothing. He'd spent the evening digging for everything he could find on Randall Thompson. The man worked as a high school science teacher, drove a five-year-old Honda Accord, and lived in a two-bedroom teardown. He couldn't afford to pass up free legal representation from the top criminal defense attorney in Los Angeles, no matter who that attorney's son was—had been. Robert released Martin's shoulder and headed for the door, pausing when his partner spoke.

"The press is going to crucify you for this. I know you think he might be innocent, but what if he's not? What if he killed Gabe and all those other boys?"

Robert glanced back over his shoulder and pulled the door open, wishing he could tell the man everything. "Just trust me."

The big man winced. "That's the problem. I don't."

CHAPTER 10

I stood at the dining room table and studied a puzzle piece and the box, trying to find a match between the two. Clementine wove between my legs, her tail tickling the backs of my bare knees. I twitched away. "Clem, stop."

She leaped onto the closest chair and mewed for attention. Setting the box on the table, I petted her head and stared down at the board.

Today was not a good day. My two o'clock appointment had gone completely silent on me, which might have been a pleasant change of pace if I wasn't already paranoid about my skills as a shrink.

I never used to worry about this. I'd always been a little overly cocky, convinced that I could wave my pen, open my mouth, and spew out a brilliant dialogue that would twist my clients' brains into performing however I wanted them to. But ever since John and Brooke had died, I had sunk further and further into the belief that my emotional radar was temporarily—or maybe even permanently—on the fritz.

Take my last meeting with John. He'd been furious at Brooke. I remember sitting across from him and feeling the spittle hit my cheek as he had ranted about the man he thought she was seeing.

I hadn't believed it, but my job wasn't to judge his wife's innocence—only to filter and analyze his thinking. The majority of trust issues were rooted in real-life experience, originating as far back as childhood. John had continually balked at discussions of his adolescence, which only gave further credence to his trust issues as a natural defense mechanism. If my psychological tuning fork had been in proper pitch, I would have ignored efforts to diagnose the root of his insecurities and instead focused on the more glaring possibility—that his anger would cycle out of control and into physical violence.

From my television in the living room, a game show came on. I glanced over and watched the host bound toward the stage, high-fiving the audience as he went.

I've always held an ugly hypothesis about marriage—that at some point, one spouse secretly wishes the other would die.

It's not a popular theory. When I broach it at psychology events and forums, it always sparks an argument, some doctors jumping into denial with gasps and sputters and an insistence that they've been married forty years and NEVER ONCE wished death on their spouse. But deep inside, in the dark place that they squash down and pretend doesn't exist . . . I know there's always been a true and weak moment where the thought—the hope—flickers. For most people, it's fleeting. For some—like John—it was a splinter. A deep splinter that broke off under the skin, the sort that was almost impossible to remove unless you peeled back the entire area, and no one would do that, so it festered. It grew infected. It killed and ate away at surrounding healthy tissue and throbbed and ached and dominated every thought and action until it controlled an entire life.

I had listened to so much deliberation and thoughts about hurting Brooke that it had become background noise. I'd become desensitized to it. I had accepted the fact that John fantasized over killing Brooke and had stopped being aghast at the idea because I didn't believe it would ever happen. They'd been married fifteen years. If he was really going to kill the woman, he would have done it already. So what *if* he thought Brooke was having an affair? He'd been almost as irate a year earlier, when she'd parked on a hill and hadn't fully engaged the emergency brake and the sedan had rolled into a parked car.

This wasn't my fault. I pushed a five-sided piece into place and mentally chanted the words, trying to find truth in them.

This wasn't my fault. I'd argued with him in Brooke's defense. Stood up for the woman. Pointed out all their history and his false insecurities.

This wasn't my fault. Maybe she really did have a heart attack.

I lifted my wineglass and took a deep sip, holding the smooth merlot on my tongue for a moment, then let it seep down my throat.

The doorbell rang, a sharp ding-dong of intrusion, and I turned at the sound as Clementine sprinted past me and hid under the couch.

~

Robert Kavin stood on my front stoop, a bouquet of flowers in hand. I paused in the foyer and hesitated.

It was late, almost nine. Too late for a pop-in, though I had a staunch policy against them at any hour. I could just ease back around the corner and into the dark hall. Stay away from the windows in the hope he would lose interest and head home.

"Gwen." He placed his hand on the door. "I can see you through the glass."

Of course he could. I had hoped the dim interior light would hide me, but luck hadn't been kind to me lately. Swallowing a curse, I flipped open the dead bolt.

"Hi, Robert," I said crisply, as coldly as I could considering the fact that he held out a bouquet of pink tulips, his face contrite and apologetic. It had been years since I'd gotten flowers. I took them from him and struggled not to bury my face in them and inhale their scent.

"I know it's late, but I needed to apologize."

With the flowers in hand, I had limited ability to bar the door, so I settled for my stoniest tone. "Go ahead."

"I shouldn't have looked at the file. Shouldn't have gone in your office. Honestly, I shouldn't have even fixed breakfast without you. I'm sorry."

I digested the apology and found that it tasted sincere. A stronger woman would have argued some key points, dressed him up and down for his actions, then ripped the heads off his flowers and thrown them back into his face, but it was chilly outside, my sleep shorts weren't warm enough to combat the open door, and it was hard to be cruel to anyone who had suffered the loss of a child. "Okay," I said agreeably. "Thanks for the flowers."

He looked surprised at the easy acceptance, then slowly nodded, stepping back from the door. "Sure. I really am sorry."

"Yeah." I studied him in the porch light. He was in a suit, this one without the third piece, his tie undone and hanging around his neck, the top button of his shirt unfastened. He looked like he needed food and sleep, and I could help with one of the two.

I stepped back and held open the door. "Want to come inside? I've got lasagna I can heat up if you're hungry."

He smiled sheepishly, and it was criminal how good the expression looked on his handsome features. "Sure," he said slowly. "If you're up for the company."

~

Robert ate three huge squares of lasagna, then attacked the ongoing puzzle. I sat cross-legged on a padded dining room table chair and watched his hands move across the board like a Mensa kid in front of a Rubik's Cube.

"Plus, there's travel." He clipped a dark piece into the border trim. "I don't want to worry about them in a crate at a kennel."

He was naming the reasons he didn't have a pet, which were all valid, if you were considering pets as sterile objects and completely discounted the joy they brought to your life.

"How much do you travel?" I swirled the wineglass and watched the dark liquid sweep around the sides.

"Not much," he admitted. "I went to Tahoe last summer. But, you know. At some point I will."

"Sure." I took a sip. "A workaholic married to his job. From one addict to another, traveling isn't actually going to happen. You know that, right?"

He grimaced.

I picked up a piece and studied the design. "I'm sorry about your son."

In the days since Robert had left my house, I had researched him online. His impressive court record and legal accolades were buried on the sixth page of results behind the national news stories, press releases, and hundreds of videos and posts looking for leads and justice for Gabe Kavin. Half the news results were from the disappearance period. The other half were after they found his son's body behind a recycling plant in Burbank, a crude heart carved into his chest, his genitals tossed into the trash. The BH Killer's signature marks, and his official sixth victim.

He looked up from the puzzle, and our eyes met. In the dim light of the bar, I hadn't seen the full extent of his sorrow. The drench of pain was haunting his eyes. Pulling at his face. Heavy in the sag of his posture.

I'd treated a few parents after the loss of a child. The grief wouldn't go away. It would dilute in his eyes. He would grow better at masking it, disguising it, but it would always be there. Losing a child was like losing a limb. You were reminded of it every time you moved, until the consistent adjustments to life became a permanent part of you.

His mouth pinched together in a flat line. "Nothing to be sorry about. The apologies don't bring him back."

No, they wouldn't. I changed the subject. "I'm assuming you're being kept abreast of the arrest."

"Yep." He picked through the pile of homeless pieces. "Are you familiar with the BH deaths?"

Killers were my obsession, and Los Angeles's most famous serial killer had been under my microscope from the beginning. I half rose from the chair and lifted the wine, pouring more in my glass. Without asking, I topped his off. "It's in my wheelhouse, so yes. I've kept a professional interest in the killings."

"You said on the night we met that you do a lot of expert testimony."

"I do."

"Psychological profiles?"

"At times." Where was he going with this?

"Done one on a serial killer before?"

"Just in med school."

He said nothing, and I waited out his thought process. Spotting a potential connection, I fit the puzzle piece in and locked it into place.

"I'd like to hire you."

"For what?"

"A psychological profile on the BH Killer, to start."

With what I already knew about his kills, I could whip up a half-decent profile within a day. But half-decent probably wasn't what Robert Kavin was looking for. "Why?"

"My son died at his hands." His glare challenged me to question the request. "Do I need another reason?"

"No," I said slowly. "But your son was found nine months ago. Why wait until now for a psych profile? They have the killer."

"I didn't know you nine months ago."

I bought a few seconds by taking a slow sip of merlot. It wasn't that I didn't want to do it. I was itching to push him out the door and sharpen my pencil. But something was off here, and I needed to put my finger on what it was. "Do you have the case file on your son?" He shouldn't. It'd be a horrible thing for him to possess. Yet something in his self-assured manner told me he did.

He nodded.

Ah, the psychological trauma that each autopsy photo, every casual case note, had to cause. I tried not to outwardly wince.

"I have his, and I can get you the others soon—in the next few days."

The others? I inhaled at the possibility of reviewing the full details of all six victims. "How are you getting those?"

"Just know I can get them."

I frowned, skeptical. "Right." If it was true, if I could look at all six of the BH victims and their circumstances . . . it'd be a psychologist's dream. And to make it all better—the killer was already behind bars. I could visit him. Talk to him. Do a proper psych analysis, assuming I could get authorization from his legal team.

I realized I was staring at him. I straightened in the chair. "Okay. I'll do it." I tried to keep the excitement out of my voice, but it still coated the words.

The corners of his mouth lifted, but it wasn't a smile. It was disappointment, and I didn't have time to process it before he spoke. "I'll bring you a copy of Gabe's file tomorrow."

"That would be great." I watched as he tossed a piece down without finding its place.

"I'm going to head home. Thanks for the food and the hospitality."

I rose. "Sure. And I appreciate the flowers. They're beautiful." Two polite people, circling a dead teenager.

"Thanks for not slamming the door in my face." He paused in the foyer, then leaned over and kissed me gently on the cheek. The stubble of his cheek brushed against my skin, and he smelled like the night we met, minus the cigarette smoke from the bar. Good. Really good.

"Night." He stepped away and moved through the door, tripping on the first step and catching himself.

"Careful. Good night." I held the door open until he was halfway down my stepping-stones, heading toward a glistening black Mercedes parked in my drive. I pushed the door shut and flipped the lock, then reached up and engaged the dead bolt.

Returning to the dining room, I collected our glasses and the empty wine bottle, then flipped off the light, leaving the rest of the puzzle for another night. Standing at the sink, I squirted lavender dish soap onto a fresh sponge and washed his plate.

He was an interesting man. Very high emotional intelligence. He could read me as well as or better than I could read him. Behind the charm, he hid his emotions well. My father would have said he played his cards flush against his chest, and he would have been right. He was a man with grief and history, but also . . . there was something deeper there. I couldn't put my finger on it, and it was driving me crazy.

Maybe it was just raw attraction. My body responded to his presence in unsettling ways, and I had struggled, when we parted, to not lean in for a kiss.

I picked up a fluffy white dish towel and ran it around the surface of the red ceramic plate. I also had to face the possibility that my attraction to Robert Kavin had increased when I'd realized his connection to the BH Killer. And now, with him hiring me for a psychological profile, my skin was practically humming with excitement.

Careers were made from opportunities like this. If Randall Thompson was the killer—and all reports seemed to indicate he was—then these events would be studied by psychology professionals for decades. Motives. History. The transition of thought into action in cyclical fashion. Randall Thompson would be compared with Lonnie Franklin Jr. and Joseph James DeAngelo, and I would have an inside look at every single detail. For Robert to give me that access . . . screw the flowers and the orgasms. This was huge, and as unbelievable as it seemed—all six case files?—I believed his confidence when he said he could get them.

That arrogance, the opportunity, the memories of our night together—sheets twisting, mouths hot and frantic—all of it had Robert Kavin stuck in my mind. A fixation, and not an entirely healthy one.

The man was grieving. Damaged. Gabe Kavin had died, along with five other innocent boys. A monster was responsible, and I shouldn't be salivating at the thought of studying him. I opened the cabinet and stacked the plate on top of the others.

Six boys had died, and soon, I would be given the keys to figuring out why.

CHAPTER 11

The next day, I walked my four thirty appointment to the lobby and paused at the sight of Robert Kavin. The tall attorney was standing at Jacob's desk, and I zeroed in on the thick file in his hand. I glanced back to my client, a Peeping Tom with unresolved mother issues. "I'll see you next week, Jeff."

Jeff Maven nodded, then beelined for the stairwell.

"Dr. Moore?" Robert ambled toward me with the confidence of an alpha male. "Do you have a moment?"

"Of course." I held the heavy office door open and nodded to Jacob. "Please hold my calls."

Robert passed into my office, and I caught the faint whiff of an expensive cologne. Inside the office, he paused, surveying the room. "Nice digs."

"We got lucky with our lease. If we signed on today, we'd be paying triple net rent." I took a seat in one of the low-slung leather chairs beside the love seat.

He noticed the breakfast bar in the corner of the room. "Mind if I get a cup of coffee?" He set the file folder on my desk.

"Not at all. In fact . . ." I leaned over and plucked my almost empty mug off the side table. "Can you top me off?"

"Sure." He reached for the cup, and his fingers brushed mine. Our eyes met, and I let go of the ceramic handle.

He turned away and stopped in front of the coffeepot. "You're a doctor, so I'm assuming our conversations are protected by doctor-patient confidentiality?"

An interesting question. "You're hiring me, so yes. But, as I'm sure you're well aware, that confidentiality is limited."

"Oh yes, I'm aware." He turned toward me, two cups in hand. "If a patient is an imminent danger to himself or others, you're obligated to tell the authorities. Right?"

It was interesting, the way he delivered questions, as if every one was accusatory. A by-product of thousands of hours on the stand or—and just as likely—a deep-rooted inclination to suspect the worst in people. I skipped the urge to point out the psychological tic and nodded. "Yes. If a patient is likely to cause himself or someone else harm, we're required to report it."

"I have a feeling, given your clients, that you've bent that rule before." He settled into the seat in front of me and lifted his cup to his lips.

Where was he going with this? I crossed my legs, but his gaze stayed on my face. Impressive focus, especially given the length of this skirt. It was one I rarely wore, and one that tiptoed on the edge of unprofessional, but it was a good card to pull out when I needed to test a man. Robert Kavin had passed. I ignored the comment and glanced at the file he'd placed on my desk. It was fat and red and had a rubber band around its midsection, pinning it closed.

"What's with the confidentiality question?" I placed my notebook down on the table between us and relaxed in the seat, hoping the new body language would ease the tension from his shoulders.

It didn't. If anything, his brow furrow deepened. "Just wondering if you're trustworthy."

I picked up the cup of coffee Robert had set before me. "It's a necessity in my line of work. If clients couldn't trust me, they wouldn't talk about their problems."

"They confess things they've done?"

I made a face, annoyed with the question, one I received frequently. "Their actions come out sometimes when we talk about guilt." I cupped my hands around the mug, comforted by the warmth of the ceramic. "Each client is different. For some, it's healing to talk."

His jaw tightened, and I studied him closely, trying to read between his questions. Some evasiveness was to be expected in his line of work. But there was more than just curiosity in his tone. And more than distrust. There was also a tight edge of . . . anger. That was interesting.

I poked the emotion. "Why all the questions?"

In response, he gestured to the folder. "That's Gabe's file. Let me know if you have any questions." He straightened the line of his tie but didn't meet my eyes. With another client, I'd consider it a deceptive tell, but this I read as pain.

This was important to him. Important enough for him to drive through rush-hour traffic and be here in person, a stiff new copy of Gabe's file in hand. I rose and went to it. Pulling the rubber band free, I opened the folder and ran my fingernail along the row of color-coded tabs that organized the contents. "How many psychologists have you given this to?"

"Shrinks? None."

"We don't really like that term," I said mildly, flipping open the tab marked "Evidence." There was a neat line of items, and my blood hummed with excitement.

"Sorry."

"There are better ways to heal than obsessing over the killer." I was dying to study the file, to read each page in detail, to find the hidden clues. I always loved clues, which was why I set down the file and turned my attention back to Robert. *He* was giving me clues—I just couldn't seem to follow them.

"Healing isn't my main objective."

"Maybe it should be. Whether you want to acknowledge it or not, this week's arrest of your son's killer is a major emotional event."

"Don't psychoanalyze me. Just read his file and tell me what you think."

I let out a half laugh. "Psychoanalyzing people is part of my job."

His gaze hardened. "Not this job."

"For a proper profile, I'd need more than just his file." I settled back onto the couch, ignoring the silent scream of the folder. "You said you could get all the other victim files?"

"Yes. But look at his first and see if you have the stomach for it."

I glanced at my watch, conscious of the fact that I had another appointment in fifteen minutes. "My stomach won't be a problem, but my time is tight. I'll need a few days to go through everything."

"You told me the night we met that you specialize in clients with violent inclinations."

"That's right."

His knee jiggled, a quick staccato beat that stilled when I looked at it. It was a tell, and I cataloged it beside the evasive eye contact and the bite of hostility in his tone. Frustration. Angst?

He leaned forward and rested his forearms on his knees, delivering the direct eye contact I wanted. It was invasive, a cross-examination level of confrontation, and I welcomed it. "Why spend your days with society's most vile individuals?"

"I don't see them as vile," I answered truthfully. "I see them as human. We all battle demons. If they're in my office, it's because they're trying to fix that part of them. I can relate to that. Can you?" I arched a brow at him in question.

He held my stare for a long moment, then rose, buttoning his suit jacket closed with a finality that came from years of practice. "I don't need you to analyze me. Just read Gabe's file and send me your initial thoughts, Gwen."

"You know . . . I think I'll pass." I stayed in place. "You can take the file with you."

It was a bitchy move and a gamble, given that I wanted the job as badly as anything in recent memory. Still, the risk was necessary. I had to see how much he really needed me. Because there were a lot of experts out there, but he was in my office, the file on my desk. Why?

He paused, and when he turned to face me, the frustration was evident. "I'm hiring you for a job. You're refusing the work?"

"There's a potential conflict of interest."

"And that—" He cleared his throat and began again. "That is what?"

"We slept together," I pointed out. "I'm not exactly an unbiased third party. You may put too much weight into my opinion, or it may be skewed on my end, based on our history."

It was a valid and excellent point, one my conscience had raised as soon as I started to get excited about the potential project.

"It was one night." He shrugged. "Not exactly history."

My ego wilted a little, and I smiled to hide the hurt. "You're also grieving."

"So?"

"The death of a loved one can eat at you," I said quietly. "Looking at crime scene photos . . . obsessing over his murderer . . . I just want to make sure it doesn't devour you."

A sardonic smile twisted across his lips. "Too late for that." He strode forward and picked up the file. "But if you don't want to do it, don't. I'll find another expert. The country's full of them."

He waited, and there was a long moment where we played a silent game of reverse psychology, and I lost.

I held out my hand. "Give me a few days, and any of the other case files you can get."

He handed it over, and then, like a lion sauntering away from a carcass, he strolled out of the room.

I looked down at the folder, then glanced again at my watch. Eight minutes before my next appointment. Just enough time for a peek.

CHAPTER 12

Los Angeles welcomed Scott back with open arms, and everyone wanted a piece. With Nita beside him, Scott appeared on the local news, then sat down with *People* magazine. His mother followed him through hair and makeup, sound checks, and on-camera interviews. With each performance, Scott's story grew smoother, and his confidence bloomed. Then the camera would turn off, and he'd retreat back to his bedroom, to his phone, uninterested in life.

Now, Nita sat in a green room, watching him on a bank of monitors, a cold diet soda in hand. Beside her, a production assistant with a diamond nose ring and a goofy headset loudly gushed over Scott.

"Your son is a hero," she mused. "To escape like that? And to be brave enough to tell his story?"

"Yes, he is." Nita watched her son on-screen, his dimple appearing as he turned his head to face the cohost. What Scott had done *was* so brave. Then again, Scott had always been brave. When he was six and there had been a giant snake in their yard, he had grabbed its tail and yanked without even thinking twice.

The camera cut to the interviewer's face. "I know it's painful to recount, but can you tell our viewers how you escaped?"

Scott looked down, as he always did when faced with a difficult question. The camera scanned across a crowd filled with concerned audience members paying rapt attention. Nita thought of the first time she'd heard his answer, in their large dining room, the silver still out on the buffet, where the housekeeper had been polishing it. The room had been dim, the curtains pulled tight, covering the impressive views of the gardens. Once it had been her dream home. Now it would always be the place where she had lost and then refound her son.

"He used to chain me up." Scott rubbed at the underside of his wrist as if remembering the restraints. "By my wrists and ankles."

Nita had heard the story a dozen times but forced herself to stay in place. If he could live through it, she could listen to it.

Naked. That was how the monster tied up her son. It was a fact Scott left out of the media interviews, and she felt guilty for appreciating the omission. The sexual torture the BH victims had experienced was something the police had kept out of the news. In awareness of that, and of the other victims' families, they had made a decision—among their family and with the police—to keep the information private.

"I had hidden a fork he had given me to eat dinner with. Normally, he watched me eat, but this time he didn't. He had a phone call or a meeting. Something."

Scott always faltered a little bit on this part of the story. Nita's sister, who was a school counselor, said some memory loss, especially in moments of high stress and trauma, was normal. Nita had asked Scott if he had any gaps in his memory, but he'd shaken his head. She'd asked him if he wanted to speak to her sister, and again, he'd shaken his head.

The only things he hadn't refused were the television interviews. There were too many of them. It wasn't healthy for him to do so much. He needed to rest, to heal, to spend time with his family and friends. But he seemed to enjoy this. The crowds of people outside each filming. The emails and letters that poured in. The social media followers. In the two weeks since his escape, Scott had grown obsessed with his follower count, checking it hourly, and seemed to find joy in each new peak his numbers hit. With the swell of followers had come offers. Scott was an influencer now, whatever that meant. He was getting packages of products, dozens of different boxes arriving each day, everything from coconut oil to protein shakes to teeth-whitening kits. And earning money, too. He'd gotten ten thousand dollars just to do a video interview at a shoe factory.

All the people and all the attention seemed to make him happy. Maybe if she'd been tied up in a basement for seven weeks, she'd crave big crowds and screaming fans, too. Maybe she'd shy away from her mother's hugs, too.

"I bent the tines of the fork and worked it into the clasp of the handcuffs. I can show you if you'd like."

This was his exhibition time. The host, like all of them, jumped on the idea, and a crew member produced a cheap set of cuffs that could probably be pulled apart by hand. Still, Scott went through the motions, his grin widening as he successfully popped open the clasp to the delights and cheers of the live audience.

"So, a fork. A fork is what took down the BH Killer," the interviewer gushed. "What happened next?"

Then, according to Scott's story, he waited behind the door until BH came in to give him his breakfast. It was then that Scott shoved him to the floor and rushed through the house and out the front door, then ran the five miles home. By the time he'd staggered through their gates, he'd been dehydrated and exhausted.

He was different now than he had been before. She wouldn't say that to anyone outside their family, but that was the truth of the matter. And who wouldn't be, after that ordeal? Underneath his new clothes, he would always carry the scars of what had been done to him. Physical abuse. Mental. Sexual.

"It's just amazing," the woman beside her said. "Unbelievable."

Nita studied Scott's wide grin, the wave he gave the crowd as he stood and exited the stage.

The stranger was right. It was amazing, but also . . . unbelievable. Scott was lying about something, and she still couldn't put her finger on what it was. Maybe it didn't matter. Maybe Scott was saying whatever he needed to in order to mentally block out the truth. The pit in her stomach grew sharper, and she pressed a hand to the pain, willing it to fade.

"Mrs. Harden?" Their handler appeared in the doorway of the room. "I can take you to Scott now."

Nita rose dutifully and waved a goodbye to the woman, moving through the rows of chairs and swallowing the mounting dread that this nightmare wasn't over yet.

CHAPTER 13

I sat at my desk and took my time with the first few pages of Gabe's file, examining the photos and screenshots taken from his social media accounts. From the looks of things, he seemed to be a nice guy. No rude responses or asshole posts. According to the file, he had no known enemies, though I was curious how hard the detectives looked at motives, given that his disappearance was casebook BH. Attractive senior. Rich family. Everything going right in his life until one day, when Robert's son was . . .

Gone.

Gabe had disappeared on a Wednesday. He'd left school around four, according to the CCTV feed by the exit gate of his expensive private school. The camera had captured video of his classic 1969 Mustang, which had pulled left without a turn signal and dropped out of view. The next sighting of the lean soccer star had been at an In-N-Out drive-through, where he'd ordered a Double-Double combo with a large 7UP.

At that point, it was unclear where he went. His Mustang was found in a back parking lot of the Beverly Center mall, in an area not covered by cameras. Its interior was useless, covered in prints from hundreds of different individuals. It was, as one detective noted, probably easier to figure out who hadn't been in his car than who had. There was no blood inside the Mustang, and the keys were left under the front seat.

Cell triangulations bounced all over the map, and his phone was finally discovered in the back of a stranger's pickup truck, the driver unaware of its presence.

Gabe had—like five teenage boys before him—just vanished into the city.

I settled back in my chair and pulled out my center drawer, retrieving the bag of gummy bears I kept there. I pulled a green one away from the others.

I didn't know a lot about Gabe's disappearance. While I had read practically every news article posted, by that point, the media was starting to tire of the deaths. They were all so similar. Good-looking, smart, athletic, and rich. And, one after another, they were dead. By the time Gabe vanished, Los Angelenos had all become a little calloused at what they knew would inevitably turn up: a naked and mutilated body.

As a city, they stopped caring because they were emotionally exhausted from the mourning. They started to look the other way, grew blind to missing-person posters and bored with the huge rewards and tearful pleas from the families.

I sucked on a red gummy bear. The city and media may have grown bored, but I never had. I'd devoured everything about the murders.

Settling back in my chair, I turned the page, surprised to find that its focus was on Gabe's family. His mother had died seven years earlier, and I hunched forward, ignoring the chime of the coffee maker. In watching the news reports, I had missed his motherless status. I thought of Robert, sans wedding ring, mentions of his late wife fleeting and detail-free. This felt like a major fact to skip over, especially given her cause of death. *Gunshot wound.* I stared at the words on the police report, blinking at it just in case my eyes were lying.

Well, *that* was interesting.

CHAPTER 14

I sat at my round breakfast table and watched Clementine stretch out on the surface, her tail curling atop a spread of photos. Digging a spoon into a large jar of peanut butter, I withdrew a heap of the creamy mixture and reviewed the report on Natasha Kavin's death.

Some family fates were cursed, others were orchestrated. The chances of Robert Kavin losing both a son and a wife reeked of suspicion, and I could see the evidence of it in these pages. Page after page of detailed notes from the detectives. Multiple interviews with Robert. A transfer of the wife's file out of cold case and back into active.

Natasha Kavin had been pretty. Hot, actually. That's how a man would describe her. Thin and blonde, with big, perky boobs that had to be fake, but who cared when they looked that good. My own fairly large breasts did a better job of making me look heavy than they did of arousing anyone.

I stuck the spoon back in the jar and set it to one side. Granted, Robert had seemed to enjoy them. I looked down and squeezed my elbows together, watching as my breasts plumped together nicely with a deep line of cleavage visible below the V-neck of my sweater.

Clem yawned and extended a paw, knocking a page to the floor. I reached down and retrieved it, then looked back at the file. Natasha Kavin had been shot in their home while Robert was out of town and

Gabe was upstairs, sleeping. One gunshot wound at close range, in the chest. A maid had found the body the next morning. Ten-year-old Gabe was still in his room, the door locked from the outside.

The door locked from the outside. Someone had underlined that sentence twice and put the words *Question Kavin* beside it.

Valid, I thought. *Who had a lock on the outside of a child's room?*

I leaned back against the wall and thought through it all. It was hard to connect the man in this file—mourning father and widower—to the one who had slid into my booth at the bar. Delivered jokes with a bashful smile. Pressed a kiss into my neck in the taxi. Pinned down my wrists and groaned into my ear when he moved on top of me. Snooped through my personal client files while cooking me breakfast. Brought me flowers and an apology and left a perfect gentleman.

There were certainly two sides to him. That of the single, romantic, and sexual male, and that of the hardened litigator—the one who stood in my office and wanted confidentiality, the one who opened John Abbott's private file without hesitation, the one who had his son's death details within easy reach.

Two sides didn't mean he was manic. I had two sides—my home and my work. Most people do.

Clem purred for attention, and I ran my fingers across her exposed belly, parting the dark-black fur.

The file had a lengthy list of potential suspects in Natasha's murder. Attorneys weren't exactly the most popular kids at the lunch table, and a criminal defense lawyer caught heat on both sides. Suspects included criminals Robert hadn't represented properly and those he'd argued against. I flipped through two pages of potential killers, most of whom had been vetted and discarded, but there were a few . . . My finger paused halfway down a list.

James Whittle. Talk about a blast from the past. James had been one of my first clients, back when I was in residency and working pro bono. He'd been a farm boy from . . . I closed my eyes, trying to remember fifteen years back. South Dakota? I couldn't remember. I wasn't advanced enough to have a specialty back then, and James had come in on court orders to work on his anger management. He hadn't been an easy client, and I had been timid and unconfident—a horrible combination that had led to another more experienced staff member taking over.

Even now, my cheeks burned at how he had rested his hands on top of his bald head and smirked at me, his lips curling upward beneath a wild red beard. He'd ignored half my questions as he had reclined back in the plastic chair, his eyes journeying over me in a lewd way that I hadn't needed a degree to understand.

I moved my finger to uncover the words next to his name. *No alibi. Have not been able to verify current whereabouts.*

It didn't mean anything. Half the names on this list had similar notes. I kept going, pushing the memory of James out of my head and scanning down the rest of the list. No other names were familiar.

On the night his wife died, Robert was in San Francisco. There was a hotel bill in his name, along with a credit card receipt showing a dinner charge at a steak house. One bone-in filet. One bottle of wine. Chocolate mousse. Pricey. He was also an exact twenty-percent tipper, down to the penny.

There was also a handful of phone records and interview logs, all citing file numbers and names that weren't included. I flipped to the end of the folder and sighed, setting it to the side and picking the jar of peanut butter back up.

So, Robert Kavin meets Natasha. Graduates from law school. Practices criminal law for three years. She gets pregnant. Has a child— Gabe. When Gabe is ten, Natasha is murdered. Case goes unsolved. Seven years pass, and Gabe is kidnapped, then killed. Nine months pass, and Robert sleeps with me, then shows up in my home, asking me to do a psychological profile on his son's killer.

I took another spoonful of peanut butter and let my mind float over the timeline. Before me was the rest of the file, the thick wedge dedicated to Gabe Kavin's kidnapping and death. I didn't have the mental fortitude to go through it tonight. I needed junk television and a long soak in a scalding-hot bath, with an extra scoop of Epsom salts dropped in.

Pushing to my feet, I twisted the lid onto the jar and returned it to the cabinet. Clem went for my sticky spoon, and I batted her away. "Stop it. Back to the floor." I took the spoon to the sink and was washing it off when I heard the faint chime of my cell phone. Returning to the table, I opened the text message from Jacob. The receptionist rarely contacted me outside office hours, so I steeled myself, expecting a note that he wouldn't be able to work in the morning.

Did u see this?

The note was followed by a link to a news article. I tapped on it, opening the page.

BLOODY HEART SUSPECT LAWYERS UP

Randall Thompson's legal woes have been solved, and the source may surprise you. The man arrested for six murders in the Los Angeles area is now represented by Robert Kavin, criminal litigator and ... wait for it ... the father of the Bloody Heart Killer's sixth victim, Gabe Kavin.

Robert Kavin's courtroom record is impressive, as are his legal fees. So, how is this high school teacher able to afford his $400 hourly rate? He can't, which is why Robert Kavin is representing him pro bono.

If you're scratching your head over this arrangement, you aren't alone. We tracked down the high-powered attorney to get some answers.

"I'm representing Randall because I believe in his innocence," Kavin said. "Trust me when I say that I want justice for my son's death. Justice will not be served if an innocent man serves time for this crime."

What in all holy . . . I scrolled back up to the top of the article and read it again, then opened a fresh browser window and did a search for Randall Thompson's attorney, hoping the first article was a spoof.

It wasn't. There were dozens of articles, all posted within the last couple of hours. Robert was representing Thompson. My psychological profile . . . it would be used by the defense, not the prosecution.

I turned the information over, examining it from all sides. There was no logical reason for Robert to protect the man who'd killed his son. Not to mention, this would turn into a giant legal tangle with *mistrial* and *appeal* stamped all over it.

I looked at the file, the open folder mocking me from its innocent place on the table, Gabe Kavin's grisly details in reach.

What was his father's game, and why was he pulling me into it?

CHAPTER 15

Robert's first meeting with Randall Thompson was supervised by four guards and lasted less than ten minutes. An offer of representation was extended, paperwork was signed, and the men parted ways. Robert dipped into his Mercedes, headed toward Beverly Hills. Randall shuffled back to his private cell, his ankle shackles clanking as he moved down the wide hall.

Now, with the appropriate permissions and protections in place, Robert returned to the Men's Central Jail. He moved through security and intake and waited for Randall Thompson in one of the private meeting rooms, his seat separated from Randall's by two-inch-thick glass. Seated at a small card table, he used the valuable time to fix the date on his watch.

Randall was considered a high-risk inmate and would be housed in solitary confinement until his trial. Solitary confinement was a blessing for someone like him. The general population welcomed violent pedophiles with a unique brand of gusto.

The door opened, and two uniforms ushered in Randall, who took the lone seat with a heavy sigh.

"When you're done, just bang on the door," the guard said.

"This room is private?" Robert confirmed.

"We'll be watching you through the glass, but there's no cameras or mikes."

Robert nodded. "Thank you."

"You've got an hour." The guard shut the door behind him with a firm click.

The science teacher, who was looking at a minimum of three life terms, surveyed Robert with distrust. "You again?"

"Me again." He unlocked his tablet. "We need to go over the initial details of your case."

Randall leaned forward and ran his hands over his white beard. "I'd like to get out of here and go home. I have a dog. I need someone to check on him."

"The local pet rescue has your dog. They'll keep it there until you are sentenced or released. If you're sentenced, they'll put it up for adoption. If there's someone you know who will take it, I can arrange that."

Randall rubbed his index fingers across the bushy white hair above his upper lip. "And you're doing that for free? That's what you said."

"Yes. Completely free."

"Doesn't seem right," the man muttered. He coughed, and something wet rattled in his throat.

"My office takes on a fair amount of pro bono cases."

"Right, sure," the man snapped. "But I'm talking about your son. He was killed by this guy, right?"

Robert removed the tablet's stylus from its holder. "Yes, he was. I disclosed that to you in our first meeting."

"Well, I was a little distracted then. But since then, I've had time to think." The man inched his chair closer to the glass and lowered his voice. "How do you know I didn't do it?"

"You don't have to whisper. No one can hear us."

His knee jiggled against the bottom of the table. "Your son—what was his name?"

"Gabe."

The man drummed his thick fingers against the top of the table. "I never had any kids, but I have a nephew I'm close to. It's, uh . . . I can't imagine how you feel."

No, he couldn't. No one could. And it wasn't a feeling you'd wish upon anyone else. The only blessing of Natasha's death was that she didn't have to experience it alongside him.

"How long ago . . ." His fingers stilled and he looked back up, meeting Robert's eyes. "Did he, um—was he taken?"

The man's ignorance of the BH Killer's history was embarrassing. Then again, if Randall were an expert on the deaths, Robert wouldn't be representing him.

"He died nine months ago."

Randall nodded. "So, uh—"

"We need to go over the evidence against you."

"Well, I don't even understand how they have evidence."

He was frustratingly obtuse. Either unwilling or unable to comprehend the fact that he was facing a lifetime behind bars. A year ago, under the prior legislation, he'd have been a candidate for lethal injection.

"Well, there are two things we have to overcome. First, Scott Harden identified you as the person who kidnapped and held him prisoner for seven weeks."

"He's lying," the man said flatly, crossing his arms over his barrel chest. "I told the detectives that."

"Any reason for him to lie about you? You ever have him as a student? Give him a failing grade? Confront him in the hall over something?"

The man sniffed, then wiped at his nose with the sleeve of his uniform. "He wasn't one of my students. Was I aware of him? Sure. He's one of those kids . . . you know the type." He met Robert's eyes through the scratched glass. "Thinks he's untouchable. Always late. Has the school sweetheart hanging on his arm. They get attention."

He may have been describing Scott, but it was a mirror to Gabe. The boyish, unapologetic smile that softened every action. The confidence that seeped from him. The gaggle of surrounding girls who called every hour, texted during dinner, and commented on every social media post.

"But . . ." Randall scratched the back of his head. "Even though I knew who the kid was, I never . . . Well, I don't think I ever interacted with him. I don't know. Maybe I yelled at him to get to class, or not to run in the halls—something like that. Maybe."

Maybe? Juries hated maybes. For now, Robert let it slide.

"The cops asked about your alibi on the night each victim was taken and when their bodies were dumped. You said, and this is a quote from your questioning, 'I don't know. I was most likely at home.'" Robert looked up at him. "We're going to have to do better than that."

Randall shifted in the hard plastic seat, and his ankle chains clanked together. "I live alone. I read at night and grade tests. I'm not sure what to tell you. Unless you can get my dog to vouch for me, they're just gonna have to believe me."

"It's hard to do that, considering the box they found." On the tablet, Robert pulled up the photo, the one that made his anger rise in almost uncontrollable ways. It was a close-up of a small wooden box filled with a brutal assortment of souvenirs. A driver's license for victim number one. The lobe of one ear. A slice of skin with a tattoo, carved out of a bicep. A watch, the inside engraved with a graduation date. A Polaroid photo of a boy, his face bruised, lip split, eyes swollen shut. *Gabe.*

"Yeah." Randall barely glanced at the photo. "They said they found that in my house."

"Underneath your bed. How'd it get there?"

The teacher raised his hands. "Who knows? I don't make a habit of looking under my bed, not unless my glasses fall under there. Do you? Anybody could have stuck it there."

"How would they get in the house?"

He shook his head in frustration. "Whose side are you on?"

"I'm playing devil's advocate. You're going to be asked all these questions during the trial."

"Look, I DIDN'T TAKE OR HURT ANYONE," Randall thundered, and if he did it just like that, there was a good chance someone on the jury would believe him. All they needed was one.

"Again, how would someone get in?"

"Someone could open the door and walk in," he said defiantly. "It's not like I own anything of value. No one's robbing me. I lock the doors some of the time, but a lot of times I don't. If the weather is nice, I open a window. So sue me."

He didn't need to be sued. Civil litigation was a moot concern when someone was behind bars for six murders. Six murders and seven kidnappings with aggravated and premeditated assault.

His life, whether he knew it or not, whether Robert got him off or not, was over.

CHAPTER 16

Nita Harden stood at Scott's door and put her ear to the wood, straining to hear what her son was saying.

She couldn't catch it. It was too low. Quiet. Almost a whisper. Scott never whispered. He blared loud music, crowed out his sentences, whooped and hollered when he leveled up or won some game, but he never whispered.

She knocked quietly on the door, and he fell silent. "Scott?" she called out.

There was the shuffle of items, steps on the wood floor, then he was opening the door and peering at her through the thin crack. "Yeah?"

"Are you okay? I thought I heard someone talking."

"It's just videos I'm watching on my phone." He gave her a shy smile. "It's late, Mom. Go to bed."

He was right. It was almost two. A couple of weeks ago, she'd have taken a sleeping pill and be drooling on her pillow, her body tucked against George's. But in this new reality, with her son back, she couldn't sleep until his light was off, the sounds of quiet snores coming from underneath his door, and that didn't seem to happen until three or four in the morning.

"Okay," she said reluctantly, wishing he would open the door and let her in. Since when did he crack the door like this? What was he hiding in there? Normally she would have suspected it was a girl, but ever since he got home, none of the girls had been around. Neither, come to think about it, had any of his friends. He used to have so many friends.

Maybe that's why the house still felt empty. She kept waiting for it to come back to life. It used to be so full of activity and noise. She would trip over Scott's baseball bag, left carelessly in the kitchen. Grumble over his books on the counter, the empty soda cans littering every surface in the media room, and the open bags of chips attracting ants in the pantry. And, oh, the kids. It had been normal for her to wake up on Sunday morning to find a half dozen of them zonked out in her living room. That Ralph kid had spent two months in their guest room, and the entire football and baseball teams seemed to have their gate code and the green light to help themselves to anything in their fridge, including the beer.

Where had they all gone? Those first few days, they had all called and stopped by, but Scott had begged off seeing them. He'd said he was busy, and tired, and she had let it go because *of course* he wouldn't feel like seeing anyone right after all that—but what about now? It had been two weeks, and Scott felt fine enough to go in front of TV cameras, or chat with new followers on social media, yet he hadn't returned a single message from his real friends.

George kept telling her to mind her own business, and maybe he was right. So what if Scott was being distant? He was home and he was safe. She was looking for problems instead of counting her blessings.

She said good night and headed down the stairs to the bedroom she shared with George, vowing not to think about it anymore. But Scott had been talking to someone. She knew it. Even with the heavy door between them, even with his voice muffled, she would swear that he'd been begging someone to call him back.

CHAPTER 17

In my last decade of counseling, I'd given out over a thousand business cards. Never had any been such a pain as this one. I stared down at the business card from John Abbott's wallet, which had made it back onto my desk, still in its evidence bag. Underneath it, and without a protective sleeve, was the one thing I really hated to see. A warrant.

"What's with the coffee? It got mint in it?" Detective Saxe peered down into a pale-blue mug, which must have been poured by Jacob.

"If it's from the lobby, yes. You can dump it out if you don't like it." I flipped over the top page of the warrant and scanned the appropriate sections, hoping for a miracle in the short and precise descriptions. According to the warrant, I was required to answer questions about Mr. Abbott's state of mind and any criminal activity I was aware of, but I didn't have to surrender his client file. *Thank God.*

"Nah. It's fine. Not bad, actually." He pulled one of my chairs loose of its cluster and faced it toward my desk. "You can keep that warrant. It's your copy."

"Thanks," I said smartly.

He sat down and opened his notepad. "We've been looking a little more closely into John Abbott." He glanced at me. "Interesting guy."

"In what way?"

He grinned. "Come on now, Doc. Let's not play games. I got your warrant. Now let's talk openly, okay? I got a lot of bad guys out there I still need to catch."

Yes, and I had a business I needed to protect. If Brooke Abbott's family sued me for negligence, I could be ruined, both financially and professionally.

"I don't want to play games," I said. "But you can't make a random observation and just expect me to gush information. Ask me a question and I'll answer it."

His expression soured. "We have three Peeping Tom reports that were filed against Mr. Abbott. What can you tell me about his sexual perversions?"

"What?" If it was possible for a jaw to drop open, mine did. Twelve months of sessions, and this was an absolute surprise. "Who was he spying on?"

"Various wealthy women. Was caught on security cameras most of the time. Are you telling me you didn't know anything about this?"

I raised my hands in innocence. "I'd swear to it in court. And to be honest, it shocks me. I—" I paused, not wanting to violate John's privacy any more than I had to.

"What?"

"Are you certain it was him?"

"Three separate reports from three different women over seven years?" He nodded. "Yeah. Why?"

I grimaced. "It just doesn't match his personality type. John was a very precise, organized individual. He thought things through, sometimes obsessively. And sexually? First of all, this warrant is focused on the deaths of Brooke and John Abbott, so I don't see how an outside sexual obsession or deviance would be relevant, but I don't mind answering the question, because the answer is simple. John Abbott didn't have sexual perversions, as you put it. At least, none that he shared with me."

"Never hit on you? Said anything inappropriate? Made you feel uncomfortable?"

I shook my head. "I'm shocked that he was stalking women. If anything, his focus was completely on his wife. He was practically asexual toward me."

"Did you ever feel unsafe around him? Get the sense he was taking an unnatural interest in your personal life?"

"Absolutely not."

"So, no sexual perversions." He eyed me as if he didn't believe it.

I spread my hands in ignorance. "Not that I had any knowledge or hint of." I kept my voice mild and the rest of my opinion to myself. In John's continual suspicions of his wife and other men, I'd often suspected a latent homo- or bisexuality. But that was pure speculation on my part, and would never hold up in court. It would be both easy and reckless to say that a man who wanted to kill his wife was doing so out of a growing frustration of his own inability to be attracted to or sexually perform with her. To share that hypothesis now would do a disservice to John, as well as Detective Saxe's investigation, which still seemed muddy in scope and focus.

I dipped a toe into dangerous waters. "What exactly are you investigating?"

He studied me. "I'm not entirely sure. Something's off. With the scene in the kitchen, with him receiving psychological treatment . . . and then the other stuff."

I frowned. "What other stuff?"

He shrugged, and it was his turn to skirt the question. "I've got one last question, at least for now."

Here it was. The moment it would all fall apart. The beginning of the end. I forced myself not to stiffen or flinch.

"Last time I was here, I asked if I should look at this as anything other than a suicide." He glanced at me. "And you said, and I quote, 'Not that I'm aware of.'"

I nodded. "Right."

"You'd still stand by that statement?"

"Of course." Was he still hung up on this? Questioning John Abbott's death and ignoring Brooke's supposed heart attack?

"Let me change the question a bit. If I told you that John Abbott was found dead of a knife wound, would you have suspected a suicide?"

Well, that was an interesting question. I smiled at him, enjoying the mental game. "His wife was dead beside him, right?"

"Ignoring that."

I scoffed. "You can't exactly ignore that."

"Most husbands, when their wife dies of a heart attack, don't kill themselves."

Excellent point. "To clarify," I countered, "most emotionally stable husbands don't kill themselves when their wife dies." *Unless he was the one who killed her.* "But John Abbott wasn't emotionally stable. I'm not saying he was a sexual predator," I hastened to clarify, "but he wasn't emotionally . . ." I paused. "Maybe *stable* isn't the right word. Let me return to your question. If you told me that John Abbott was found dead of a knife wound, my first inclination would be what anyone's would be—that someone stabbed him." I leaned forward. "But if you told me that Brooke Abbott died first, I would immediately suspect suicide. One hundred percent, without hesitation."

I leaned forward and put my forearms on my desk, appreciating the hypothetical exercise. "For one, because what scenario could exist? Brooke died and then a random person showed up and murdered John?" I made a skeptical face. "Not likely. But also, and what you should really care about"—I chose my next words carefully—"is that John had an unhealthy emotional connection with Brooke. Her death would affect him differently than a normal husband. I agree, the standard response for a husband wouldn't be to kill himself. But with John?" I sat back in the chair. "Absolutely likely."

"Huh."

All that brilliant insight, that complex chess game of words and delivery, and he responded with a word that was one step above a grunt. Not that I expected a standing ovation and a round of cheers, but come on.

"Let me toss something crazy in your lap." He set down the coffee cup.

I waited, my pulse spiking.

"Brooke *kills* John, then has a heart attack."

I let out an awkward laugh. "No."

"No?" He raised one dark brow.

"No." I shook my head, then paused, making sure that the knee-jerk reaction was valid. *Was* it possible that John told her about his dark fantasies, or he tried to kill her and she fought back and killed him in self-defense?

It was a mild possibility, but faint in the face of the much more certain truth—John had poisoned her and then killed himself. And there was no way I would allow them to drag a dead Brooke Abbott's name through the mud. I'd break John's confidence and risk my own reputation if need be. I shook my head. "Absolutely not."

"Okay." He rose. "Like I said, it was just a crazy theory. Thanks. I'll be back in touch if I have any more questions."

I plucked up my business card, still in the plastic baggie, and held it out to him. "Here."

He took it, then extended his hand. "Thank you for your time, Dr. Moore."

"Anytime."

I watched him exit and silently begged him not to come back.

CHAPTER 18

"Something's different about you." Meredith studied me over the Thai-restaurant menu.

"I cut my hair." I flipped the giant laminated board over. "I don't even know what half of this stuff is."

"Just get the shrimp fried rice." She sat back as a bowl of steamed pork dumplings was delivered, then rattled off her order to the waitress.

I followed suit, then watched as the waitress retreated. "I wanted to get bangs but chickened out and did something different with the layers."

"It's not your hair that's different. It's your aura."

I swallowed the urge to tell her what I thought of her New Age bullshit. That might work on Calabasas housewives, but if I told any of my clients to rub a positivity rock, I'd get laughed out of practice in a week.

"I'm serious. What's wrong?"

"I'm a little stressed," I managed.

"Over your dead wife killer?" She tapped a trio of faux sweetener packets against her palm.

I glanced around the outdoor courtyard, making sure no one was in earshot. "Easy, Meredith."

"No one's listening." She waved off my concern. "Talk to me. Are you still feeling guilt over the suicide?"

"Yes, but that's not the main source of it." I watched a couple rise from their seats. "I'm doing a psych profile for a new client."

She plucked up a dumpling and dipped it into the sauce. "Prosecution or defense?"

"Defense." I walked her through Robert's initial request of my services, leaving out our drunken night of passion.

Meredith's eyes widened as I moved through the story. "Hold up." She quickly swallowed the full mouthful before speaking. "He hires you, gives you the file, and you haven't talked to him since?"

"No."

"Why?"

"I left a message for him at his office, but he hasn't called me back."

"I saw a news story on this guy . . . ," she said slowly. "His son was one of the BH Killer's victims, right? Like, number five?"

"Six," I confirmed.

Her eyes widened as she connected the pieces. "And he's hot, right?"

"He is very good-looking," I allowed.

"No," she argued. "He's smoking hot. You need to push aside the doom and gloom and saddle him up like a prize stallion."

I struggled to maintain a casual air. "Anyway, I'm—"

"Oh, this just gets better and better." She pushed the dumplings away and hunched forward, her green eyes glowing with interest. "You already did, didn't you?"

"I did not saddle him up and ride him like a prize stallion," I said wryly. "It was more like an arthritic grandma on the Tilt-A-Whirl."

She crowed with laughter and clapped her hands together. "Oh my word, you dirty slut."

I blushed despite myself. This had been, after all, my crowning sexual achievement of the decade. I couldn't believe I'd kept it to myself this long. Meredith normally sniffed out an indiscretion the minute someone's panties hit the ground.

"So it's not stress," she said, picking her chopsticks back up. "It's the glow of sexual satisfaction. Unless it was a disappointment?" She glanced at me for confirmation.

I colored, trying not to think of the sexual peaks the night had delivered. "Very satisfying," I assured her. "But I think it's still stress. I haven't had a solid night's sleep in weeks."

Her response was cut off by her phone. As she answered the call, I lifted the teakettle and poured myself a small cup.

It was a little annoying that I hadn't heard from Robert. Our sex history aside, I'd been hired for a job and was waiting on the rest of the victim files he had promised me. Granted, in the last five days, he had retained the most high-profile killer in California history. His office must be flooded with press calls, discovery requests, and prehearing prep. My voice mail was probably buried in a mountain of other messages.

"So, what's in the file?" Meredith ended her call and moved on from my sexual exploits as easily as she did the dumplings. "Have you started the psychological profile yet?"

"I don't have enough to go on. I need to see all the victims' files, which I should be able to get." No wonder he'd been so confident about getting them. He'd have a mountain of information if he'd secured Randall Thompson as a client.

"Girl, that's like gold for you. The Bloody Heart files?"

"I know. Six murders." I smiled.

"Try not to look so gleeful about it."

I shrugged. It *was* exciting, especially since he was behind bars. I said as much, and she nodded slowly, something clearly on her mind.

"Why do you think he's representing him? I mean, I watched the news bit. You believe what he says, that he thinks Randall is innocent?"

It was the question of the hour, and I sighed. "I don't know. If someone killed my child, I couldn't be in the same room without clawing their eyes out, so that part of me says that he must believe in Thompson's innocence. But then again, how would he know?"

"Unless he's the real killer," she pointed out.

"He killed his own son?" I shook my head. A decade of studying habitual killers had taught me that they didn't get around to their own children on the sixth victim, then continue on.

"Don't look at me like that. First off, people kill their kids. And Robert could be the BH Killer and not kill his son. Maybe Gavin—"

"Gabe," I corrected her.

"Gabe died some other way. And everyone assumed it was the BH Killer because the kid was a hot young stud, and his dad disposed of his body in the same way."

I pulled my gaze off a couple who had entered the restaurant, the man's hand clamped on his girlfriend's shoulder. She was going to have a problem with him, if she didn't already. I mused over Meredith's hypothesis, which could have legs. "That's a stretch."

She shrugged. "Why? Because he was good in bed? Trust me, the better the motion, the more screwed up the ocean."

I laughed. "Okay," I mused, going down her path of reasoning. "So you're saying that Gabe Kavin dies from some other cause. And Robert Kavin is the real BH Killer, but Scott Harden points the finger at Randall Thompson for some reason, and then Robert Kavin defends him because he may kill teenagers for a hobby, but he has a conscience and doesn't want an innocent man to go down for his crimes."

"Or, he killed his son, staged it to look like the BH Killer, though that would have required him to hold him prisoner for over a month . . ." She frowned. "Okay, so there are a few gaps in the logic," she allowed.

"Lots of gaps in the logic. Pretty much no logic at all." I moved my tea to the side as our entrées arrived.

For the next half hour, we ate, discussed bad TV and industry politics, and didn't mention dead teenagers at all.

It was a nice reprieve—one that ended as soon as I stepped from the restaurant and glanced at my phone.

I had a missed call and a voice mail. Robert Kavin had finally called me back.

CHAPTER 19

The voice mail had been from Robert's secretary, who requested that I meet with him the following morning at the ungodly hour of 7:00 a.m. I returned her call with a stiff refusal in place, then yielded at her dignified and maternal tone and agreed to a 7:30 a.m. meeting.

After another fitful night, I paired a conservative high-neck wrap dress with my tallest heels and spent an extra ten minutes wrestling my thick hair into a French twist. I made quick time to Beverly Hills and entered the sleek and intimidating entrance of Robert's building fifteen minutes early. After riding up in the elevator, I exited to find a statuesque older woman waiting for me at the entrance to Cluster & Kavin.

"Dr. Moore," she said warmly, "Robert is expecting you in our conference room."

Robert was seated at the far end of a long table, his cell to his ear, his gaze immediately latching on to me. He didn't smile, didn't react, and I placed my purse in the first seat, then sat in the second. I crossed my legs, and this time, his attention traveled down the length of them and lingered.

I could feel the heat of his gaze as it caressed its way down my calf and around my ankle. I folded my arms over my chest and adopted an aloof air. Despite our history, we were in a business relationship, which drew a very clear line in the sand in the eyes of my profession and his.

He ended the call. "In case you haven't heard, I'm now representing Randall Thompson. I have copies of the remaining six case files available for your review, including Scott Harden's. Are you done with Gabe's?"

And, just like that, he skipped past the elephant in the room. I considered the evasion and decided to let it slide for the meantime.

"I am." I reached over and pulled the file from my purse. "Your wife's was in there, also."

"And?" His face was blank, and I realized that he would be hell to face at a poker table.

"I reviewed it."

"I expected you would." He rose from his chair and walked down the length of the table until he was at my seat. He rested his weight against the table. "You look tired."

I grimaced, annoyed with myself for putting extra effort in my appearance this morning. "Thanks."

"I didn't mean it as an insult." His voice deepened a little, and I was reminded of when he had leaned into me in the cab, his chest warm, cologne faint, voice husky. He'd kissed the side of my neck, and I had been instantly done for.

I forced the memory away. "Well, I am tired. Meetings at the crack of dawn will do that to you."

The edge of his mouth twitched, but the smile didn't break. Picking up Gabe's file, he slowly flipped through it, verifying its contents. He looked at me over the top of the file. "Any insight?"

I gave him my honest opinion. "Given the loss you've experienced, I'm not sure I'd be able to function if I were you."

He looked down at the file, then slowly placed it on the surface beside him. "Work, Dr. Moore, has been the only thing that has kept me functioning." His attention returned to me, and there was no confusing the look in his eyes. "Work, and a few rare distractions."

I didn't trust myself to speak. I'd never been tempted by a client before, but this was new and dangerous territory. We already knew how our bodies fit together. Knew the sound of our pants, the groan of our orgasms, the rough yet tender heartbeat between our bodies.

In a normal scenario, he'd be stepping closer, and I would be leaning in. Yielding to him. Surrendering. Instead, I cleared my throat and circled back to the elephant. "Why are you defending Randall Thompson?"

He gripped the sharp edge of the table. "I believe he's innocent."

"Why?"

"That's what I need you to prove." He nodded to the folder. "Other than concern for my psychological well-being, do you have any insights into Gabe's killer?"

"You're not answering the question. I'm not asking how you're going to convince a jury of his innocence, I'm questioning why you believe it."

"I read people for a living, Dr. Moore. Much like you do." He smiled, but the gesture didn't reach his eyes.

"No." I shook my head. "You manipulate people for a living. Manipulation to fit and believe your narrative. You play with emotions and, sometimes, facts."

He chuckled. "You have a low opinion of lawyers. Fine. I'm used to that. To be honest, shrinks aren't my favorite people in the world, either. I'll do my job, you do yours. Right now, you're the one avoiding my questions. What do you know about my son's killer?"

His voice was steel, and maybe he was right. I'd sat here for ten minutes and hadn't told him anything. I had theories, but it was hard to be secure in anything when you were just looking at one-sixth of the evidence.

"I need to see the other files. Identify patterns. I don't know much now, other than that he's smart and patient. Someone who plans things out and doesn't act on impulse." A new thought occurred to me, one I should have considered as soon as I heard about his role on the defense. "Are you going to put me on the stand?"

"It depends on what you think, after seeing the evidence. If your conclusions match my suspicions, then yes." His eye contact was a drug, one that stayed with me longer than was appropriate.

"And if I think that Randall Thompson is guilty?"

He let out a half laugh, and if there was a joke, I had missed it. "I won't put you on the stand if you think he's guilty." He pushed Gabe's file back toward me. "Keep this. I'll send over copies of the rest. Once you have a chance to review them, I'll set up an interview with you and Randall." He stood, and the material of his suit pants brushed against my bare knees as he passed.

I rose and turned to face him. "Why me?"

He paused. "That's the second time you've asked me that."

"The last time I asked, it was with the understanding that you wanted a psychological profile on your son's killer. This is something else. Something bigger. You could be fighting to free a killer. Lives are at stake."

"My son's life was at stake, and I will spend every day I am breathing on this earth to make sure that anyone who could have prevented or who caused his death answers for what they did." He glowered at me with a look so hateful, I took a step back.

"We slept together," I reminded him. "A cross-examiner could use that to discredit my testimony. There are other psychiatrists you could use who wouldn't expose you to that risk."

"No one's going to find out about that. I didn't tell anyone." He studied me. "Did you?"

"Yes. I told a colleague." I flushed, embarrassed by the admission.

"You trust them?"

"I do."

He shrugged. "Then we're fine."

We weren't fine. This wasn't right. This was a broken equation. Him defending Randall. Gabe only dead nine months. Me, battling attraction while digging through the most intimate details of his life.

We were a wrecked car, barreling down the highway without lights, our steering locked into place. I could put a seat belt on. I could reach out and jab the hazard lights on. But I couldn't turn off the car, and I couldn't seem to open the door and fling myself out.

There was calamity ahead—I just had no idea what it would look like.

CHAPTER 20

Scott was halfway onto the side porch when Nita spotted him carefully pulling the door closed, his hand keeping it from hitting against the frame.

"Scott!" she called.

A guilty look flitted across his face. Just as quickly, it was replaced with a bored teenage stare. "Hey."

"Where are you going?"

"Just for a drive. Thought I'd go by the school."

Beverly High. The scene of his abduction. The private school where he no longer attended classes, his assignments now delivered each week with offers of tutoring and special assistance steeped in apologetic guilt. One of their own was responsible for this. The man who ate doughnuts in the faculty break room had pressed lit cigarettes into her son's ribs. He had forced objects into him. He had tied him down, naked on his bed, for days at a time.

"I'll drive you," Nita offered, looping her purse over her shoulder and pulling the door open so she could squeeze through.

"Oh no. You said Susan was coming over." He blocked her path.

"I don't need to be here for that." She waved off the concern. Susan had been cleaning their home for the better part of a decade. She could figure out what to focus on without Nita's help, though Nita did make a mental note to text her a reminder to dust the fan blades in the loft.

"Mom, I can drive myself." Scott held up his truck keys, which she would have sworn were locked in their safe.

"The battery isn't charged," she protested. "You haven't driven it in months."

"Dad put in a new one yesterday."

Damn George. He knew she didn't want Scott driving. She wasn't ready for this, couldn't stand to watch him drive away and potentially never come back.

"I need to go by the grocery store anyway." She elbowed her way through the door. "I'm making fruit pizza tonight. The one you like, with the strawberries and mangoes. We can swing by the grocery store after we go to the school."

"Mom. Stop."

She met his eyes and silently pleaded with him to let her come. He didn't have to go to the school. He could go next week. Or the next. She needed just a few more days to conquer the fear that was closing its fist around her heart.

"I love you, but I need to get out of this house and be normal for a few hours, okay? I don't need a chaperone."

"Promise me you won't get out of the truck," she said desperately. "Just drive around. And if you get a flat tire, or break down—"

"I won't." He carefully steered her back inside. "I'll be back in a couple of hours."

"One hour," she countered. "The school's ten minutes away. One hour is plenty."

He groaned. "Fine."

"I love you."

He grinned, and it was almost like it used to be. "You, too, Ma."

She watched as he turned and strode toward their garage, the far door lifting to reveal his truck. They should have gotten him the Volvo sedan. Five stars on every single safety rating. It wasn't too late. She was looking at them just yesterday. His truck was a rollover waiting to happen. Those giant tires? The center of gravity was dangerous. The visibility was horrible. And he played the radio way too loud. It wasn't safe, having the music that loud. He couldn't hear a horn, or if someone shouted out a warning.

The noisy diesel engine rumbled to life, and she wondered if George had put gas in it. Stations in this area were safe, but if he took a scenic route home and stopped in a questionable area . . .

"Stop fretting." George came up behind her and wrapped an arm around her waist. "I know that look on your face."

She stayed in place, watching as Scott's truck pulled forward. "I can't believe you put a new battery in his truck. He can't be out there driving, all by himself—"

"Would you rather him sneak out and then get stuck somewhere with a dead battery?" he asked gruffly. "Nita, you've got to trust that he's going to be okay."

She pulled out of his arms and headed for her study, quickening her pace as Scott's truck rumbled down their drive.

"Nita?" George called.

Settling at her desk, she opened her laptop and powered it on. Pulling her hair into a tight ponytail, she watched the screen with impatience, then opened a web browser and logged in on a tracking software's website. Blue, red, and green dots appeared on the map, and she let out a sigh of relief.

There was a tracking device in Scott's truck and an app installed on his phone. The phone was a new one, purchased after his return, the original uselessly left in his football bag on the night of his abduction. She had spared no expense with the replacement phone, or the tracking disks that were now affixed to the soles of his favorite shoes, underneath the seat of his bike, and in his backpack and wallet.

She would not lose him again. Counting slowly to ten and inhaling deeply to relax her tension, she watched the cluster of dots as it moved down their street in the direction of the high school.

One hour was manageable. She could watch him from here, call the police if anything happened, and take enough Xanax upon his return to drown this stressful event in a sea of pharmaceutical bliss.

"Nita." George appeared in the open doorway of the office. He had been at his mistress's apartment the morning that Scott had returned home. She had dealt with their son's disappearance by falling apart; George had weathered it by falling into someone else's arms. She didn't blame him for it. Someone had needed to keep their life running, keep the money coming in, the bills paid, the staff maintained, and he had done all that. And ever since Scott had come home, George had been right by her side. No scent of another woman on his clothing, no mysterious errands that took him out in the middle of the night. "Let's go sit in the garden. It's beautiful outside."

"I can't." She clicked a button to switch to satellite view, and a pinwheel slowly turned in the center.

"He'll be fine. He's just—"

"Why, George?" She looked up at him. "Why will he be fine? Because he's a grown man? Guess what, he was still taken. Because he's in a nice area? So was his school!"

"Randall Thompson was arrested," he said gently. "He's in jail. Scott is safe."

What a stupid statement. Scott was not safe, and the most maddening thing about it was that she didn't have any way to protect him. He wasn't safe here in the house, and he wasn't safe out there, and life had been so much easier when she was blissfully unaware of that.

George mumbled something, then left, the office falling silent as she watched the satellite image fill the screen. The dots had moved, and she zoomed in. Her eyes narrowed. Why was he driving south on Santa Monica? The school was in the opposite direction. She started to call him but stopped herself. While Scott was aware of her paranoia and fears, he would freak out at the idea that she was tracking his movements.

Instead, she checked his phone through the software. Battery full. Location services on. *He'll be fine,* she told herself. He was driving around. He didn't have a good reason to go by the school anyway. He was probably heading to that burger drive-through, the one past Westwood Boulevard. Kicking off her wedge heels, she put her bare feet on the small footstool she kept underneath her desk and forced herself to let go of the death grip she had on her mouse.

Her worry was unhealthy. That was what George and her therapist said. Her obsession with what-ifs and dangers was emotionally depleting her. Plus, according to Nan Singletary, who had become a visualization guru after watching a Netflix documentary, continually envisioning and expecting something risked bringing that event about. Hearing that, Nita had promptly cut off contact with Nan, because now it was impossible not to think of all the dangers facing Scott, and she wasn't about to feel guilty for potentially triggering a future event with her thoughts.

Scott's journey continued as he moved in an odd path south, then east. Nita watched as he drove down Sepulveda, then Venice, then turned onto a residential side street, where he finally curved around and came to a stop about halfway down the block. She stared at the blinking dots, expecting the phone to separate from the truck as Scott left the vehicle. The dots stayed in place. A minute passed. Then two.

She glanced at the clock, noting the time. Maybe he'd stopped to return a text. Maybe to call her. Maybe to flip through the GPS and figure out where he was and how to get back to home.

She let out a slow, controlled breath. This was no reason to panic, she reminded herself. If he sat there long enough, she could always call him.

The green dot turned purple, and she frowned, hovering over it to see what the change was.

Location services disabled during call.

He was on the phone. A burst of relief hit her. He was on the phone and he'd pulled over to be safe. For years, she'd been telling him not to drive and talk on the phone, but had always assumed the advice had been ignored, especially since both she and George frequently bucked the rule.

The purple dot turned green again, then moved, separating itself from the others as Scott's phone moved away from the truck. The dot moved in an erratic fashion to the left, then right on the street, almost as if he were pacing. It was still for a long moment, then returned to the truck.

She frowned, then switched screens, pulling up his cell phone records.

Today's activity was sadly empty, except for the most recent call, to an unfamiliar number, with a call duration of less than a minute.

She considered calling the number but opted to put it in the search engine first. As the results loaded, his truck finally moved, the group of dots pulling a U-turn in the middle of the residential street.

This was odd. The number was for a San Diego real estate company. Seized by a sudden burst of insight, she searched for the addresses near his parked location. Sure enough, one across the street from his parking spot—22 Terrace Drive—was one of their listings. Scott must have seen their sign in the yard and called.

She nodded, feeling a burst of triumph for putting so much of this together.

Except . . . why? Was this a random drive that had sparked a curious call? Or was Scott looking to buy a house?

The second option seemed absurd. He was seventeen and—if she had any input into it—would live under their roof for another three or four years, at minimum. And he didn't have a job—he certainly would never be approved for a mortgage, not without her or George signing on.

Okay, so a random drive-by was the only solution, though the theory had its own plot holes. Unless there was a hot girl in the front yard, Scott didn't pay attention to homes and had certainly never called a number on a real estate sign. She glanced at the tracking software, her son's truck following a return route back to her house.

"Here." George stepped into the office, a chilled glass of wine in hand. He came around her desk, and she closed the window before he could see the screen. He held out the flute, and she took it with a grateful smile.

"Thank you." She took a sip.

"I'm sorry for going behind your back with Scott's truck."

"Just tell me you put gas in it."

"I did." He gave her shoulder a reassuring squeeze. "He'll be okay, Nita."

She nodded and let him put his arm around her. He didn't need to know about the Realtor call. Not now. Not until she could figure out what was really going on with their son.

CHAPTER 21

I had spent two days immersed in the files, surrounded by death.

Randall Thompson, if he was the Bloody Heart Killer, had killed six boys. Six deaths and one escape. My job was to do an independent assessment based on the information I had about BH, which meant discarding anything I knew about Randall Thompson and approaching the profile without bias.

It should be easy, given how much information I had at my disposal. Full case files on each crime? I hadn't had this much data since my doctoral days.

I stood in my office and stared at the wall between my office and Meredith's. The two framed prints had been taken down and leaned against the love seat, giving me a large landscape to work with. I'd used a piece of chalk and divided the dark-green wall into three columns, each about six feet wide. The first column was labeled "Crime Scenes." The second was labeled "Victims." The third was "Possible Suspects." I stared at the interior of each column.

Every serial killer is fed by a reason.

Some can't handle their violent impulses. Each interaction with a person is a risk, and they control themselves through those risks until they break. After they break, they experience a reset of sorts and continue on. The kill is like a meal, one that satisfies their hunger for a period of time before they need to eat again. That type of killer is often sloppy, engages in crimes of convenience, and can be unpredictable in their choice of victim.

Others are sociopaths who see other people as dispensable. Killing isn't done for enjoyment but as a solution. If a person is in the way or causing an annoyance in their lives, they handle them the same way they'd handle a mosquito—kill it, flick it to the side, and move on. They don't grieve, regret, savor, or think about the killing again unless that action causes consequences or requires cleanup.

Then you have the attention seekers. They enjoy the power rush that comes from killing and want the media splash, the tearful families, the fear. They embrace the notoriety, the cat-and-mouse game with the police, the belief that they are outsmarting everyone. These killers are often the kind and helpful neighbors everyone loves, the ones no one believed would ever hurt anyone. They display their kills in public and make decisions based on the amount of media impact and legend status.

My initial steps were simple. First, gather all the information. Done. Then, establish the common characteristics and details of the killings.

There were a lot of commonalities, especially in the "victim" category. As I went through each file, I wrote details and pinned photos into the columns, building a sea of neat white fonts and images. The victims were practically cookie-cutter in nature. Seven high school seniors, all athletic, with thin builds and moderate muscle tone. Handsome and Caucasian. They were all popular, wealthy, and well liked—the studs of their respective high schools. As far as criminal profiles were concerned, these were low-risk victims who lived in safe areas and didn't engage in dangerous activities. These weren't the hazers or assholes of their schools. They didn't deal drugs on the side, weren't active in gangs, and had few to no enemies.

Each was taken from a different school, which indicated planning. The killer had probably stalked the victims prior to the kidnappings and carefully selected each from his peers.

I scanned over all the information. It looked organized—until you read it all and realized how disjointed it sounded. Still, I was making progress. I had done a superficial sweep and was now doing a deep dive of each kill, in chronological order. I was on the third boy, and patterns were beginning to emerge. I took a long sip of tea and stared at an image of Travis Patterson, victim number two.

The boys were taken from public places. Always outside, normally in parking lots. The kills never happened at the snatch point. Instead—and this was the most disturbing piece of the puzzle—BH took them to a separate site, where he held them for six to eight weeks before killing them and dumping their bodies in a third location.

Three locations was risky. It was three locations for possible DNA transfer. Three locations where he could be caught. Two times he'd have to transport a body and risk being captured on camera, having car trouble, or losing his victim to an escape.

And there was something deeply personal about the archetype of the boys that triggered something in the killer. My hypothesis was that the killer's high school years had been traumatic with respect to his mental growth. The likeliest and easiest theory was that he was bullied by a boy very similar to the victim profile. Given the sexual nature of the torture BH inflicted, he was probably molested or raped by this bully or had struggled with a crush or sexual attraction to the boy—an attraction that could have been nurtured or rejected. Either could have led to hatred or inadequacy, which had festered and eventually sparked this series of killings.

My office door eased open, and Meredith stuck her head in. "You busy?"

"Just in my own thoughts." I sat on the couch and tucked my feet under me.

"Well, I come bearing chocolates."

"In that case, pull up a chair and settle in." I patted the cushion beside me. "Close the door behind you."

"Hush-hush stuff, huh?" She entered, stopping short when she saw my wall of notes. "Wow. How are clients reacting to this?" She gestured to the wall and offered the bag of M&M's to me.

"I'm meeting them in the conference room this week." I took it and shook out a handful of brightly colored chocolates.

"Good move. This is a little scary," she said, nodding to the notes.

"Tell me about it." I stretched out my arms and rolled my head to the side to ease a kink. "I'm cross-eyed from looking at this stuff."

"Oh, please," she scoffed. "You love it. Full case files?" She glanced over the stacks of green folders. "I'm surprised I'm not hearing you orgasm through the walls."

I laughed at the crude analogy. "I'm not that ecstatic over them. But, yes. This is historic. Getting to be involved and having this glimpse into the cases . . ." I shook my head. "It makes me want to quit private practice and join the police force."

"Seriously?" She gave me a skeptical look. "Do I need to remind you what you make in a year?"

I groaned. "Money isn't everything. Though . . ." I yielded. "Yes, you're right. I said it was tempting, not a serious possibility."

"You're in the right place," she said. "Being hired by counsel is the best of both worlds." She studied the wall. "What's the crime scene column?"

"Everything I know from the evidence and autopsies. Normally it wouldn't be so much, but in this case, the autopsies are giving us a timeline of the boys' captivity."

"What do you mean?"

I leaned forward and snagged Noah Watkins's file from the stack. "Here." I paused. "Have you eaten lunch?"

"Just an energy bar. But don't worry." She patted her belly. "Stomach of steel."

I opened the file. "From drug tests on his hair, we can see that he was exposed to drugs on an almost continual basis during the eight weeks he was in captivity. Speaking of time, he was held the longest. The killer started shortening the lengths. Either he was growing more anxious for the kill, or he was getting whatever he wanted sooner."

"Jesus." She reached over and pulled the crime scene photo of Noah. "This is how they're all found?"

"Yeah." I looked away, still not conditioned to see the humiliating position of Noah's body, one designed for maximum visual impact.

"He's the same with every kill?"

"Pretty much. Body spread-eagled, the genitals removed, a heart carved into his chest." I tucked a lock of hair behind my ear. "And there's always a pinkie finger missing. Sometimes other digits, too, but always a pinkie."

"So why isn't he called the Pinkie Finger Killer?" Meredith asked.

"It's a detail they've intentionally kept from the media."

She absorbed the information. "So, the guy keeps a finger and his penis?"

I shook my head. "The genitals are always somewhere else on the scene. Discarded as if they've just been dropped, without thought."

"Ouch." She handed back the photo. "What does that mean?"

"You're the sex therapist. You tell me."

"Are the mutilations done while the boy is still alive?"

"The amputations are postdeath. The heart carving, that's done while they're alive."

"And how do they die?"

"Strangulation. The deaths show a bit of mercy, though it's a little late, given everything else the victims have been through." I walked her through the road map of torture on the bodies. Cigarette burns. Bruises. Anal tears that indicated penetration. Handcuffs and restraint marks.

She frowned. "How sexually experienced were the victims before they were taken?"

I paused. "I don't know. I haven't seen a mention of that in the files I've gone through so far. Why?"

She shook her head. "I don't know. Just wondering if it's part of the pattern."

"It's worth looking into." I returned my attention to the board. "Any other insights?"

She let out a breath. "Genital mutilation postdeath, torture and anal penetration during an extended period of captivity . . . I don't know. I'd be really curious to see what the escaped kid . . . Seth? Scott?"

"Scott. Scott Harden."

She nodded. "You need to see what he says. Was the abductor molding him? Nurturing him? Was there aftercare? Wait . . ." She shook her head regretfully.

"What?"

"I forgot that you've been hired by the defense. You can't cherry-pick what you use from Scott's testimony. If he fingered this guy as the killer, and your guy is saying he's innocent, then why does it matter what else Scott says? He's either credible and your guy is guilty, or he's not credible and it's a waste of time to listen to him."

She was right. Almost everything I had on Scott had to be ignored. "Sounds like I'm wasting my time either way."

"Yeah, but you're getting paid the big bucks and loving every minute." She shrugged. "Autopsy photos and psych profiles? Please. You're in heaven."

I grinned. "Okay, you caught me. How terrible is it that I'm enjoying this?"

"It's terrible. But I spent last night masturbating to thoughts of my new client, so we're going to hell together." She returned her attention to the wall. "Okay, so what do you think?"

"I don't know . . . ," I said slowly. "Whoever this is, he's got enough issues for three people. I also have to consider the fact that he's staging the deaths and intentionally placing red herrings to catch attention or throw us all off."

She considered the idea. "You think the genital mutilation and heart carving could all be for show?" She angled herself on the sofa to face me.

"The carving is most definitely a calling card," I confirmed. "He wants to be famous, and he wants credit for each kill. As far as the rest . . ." I sighed. "There are inconsistencies."

I tried to sort my thoughts into logical order. "There are standard psychological reinforcements and intrinsic motives for crimes." I pointed to the chocolate. "It's like the chocolate. Why do you want the chocolate?"

"Because it tastes good." She played along.

"That's why you think you want the chocolate. That's everyone's reaction when they're asked that question, but when—"

"I understand hidden triggers," she cut me off. "I eat it because my body craves sugar. You eat it because you like the way it tastes. Jacob eats it because putting something in his mouth is a habit, and my mother eats it because her anxiety requires dopamine."

"Right," I confirmed. "Well, people kill for different reasons. Mostly pleasure, but varied types of pleasure. The duration of captivity reeks of a control-oriented type, someone who derives enjoyment from exerting their dominance over the victim. The bindings, the rape, the naked bodies . . . it sounds sexual, but it's more about making the victim feel helpless, which causes the killer to feel more in control."

"I'm missing the chocolate connection."

"I'm getting there. With the BH kills, the death itself is almost merciful. Quick. Strangling them until they black out and die. The means to the end versus a pleasurable activity. I eat chocolate because I'm hungry and I like the taste of it better than my second option." I nodded to the granola bar sitting half-eaten on the side table. "They kill because they like the idea of it more than the alternative. But in the timeline of all this . . ." I waved my hand around the sea of files, notes, and images. "The death is short and quick. Almost a non-event. There is little, if any, pleasure in that specific act. Which leads me to assume that the trigger is that they're bored of the victim and ready to move on to the next stage—the body staging and the media attention."

"Or maybe they're just an asshole." She smiled.

I ignored the comment. "The death event changed with the last kill. While the others were quick and kind, Gabe Kavin's was not."

Her smile dropped. "What do you mean?"

I leaned forward. "The first five—strangled. But Gabe Kavin, though he did die of asphyxiation, wasn't strangled."

"What? Drowned?"

"Waterboarded."

She flinched. "Like, CIA-type waterboarding?"

"Yes. It's an extremely painful way to die. Long. Probably slow. So? Why?" I looked across the room, studying the wall, his photo tacked beside Noah Watkins. "What made Gabe Kavin different?"

A loud rap sounded on my door, and we both jumped at the sound. It eased open, and Jacob stuck his head inside. "Meredith, your four o'clock is here."

"I'll be right out." She rose to her feet and glanced over the stack of files. "At least I know what you've been doing for the last two days. When are you meeting with the attorney again?"

"Tonight." I turned my watch so I could see the oyster face. "At five. His office is downtown, so I'll need to leave soon if I'm going to beat traffic."

"Uh-huh." She gave me a not-so-subtle once-over. "Chanel suit, no pantyhose. My mother would be proud."

Meredith's mother had been one of Los Angeles's most notorious madams, so I took the comment as it was intended. "It's not that sort of meeting."

She popped a red chocolate in her mouth. "Still, easy access up the skirt . . . Does that bra unclip in the front?"

I ignored the insinuation and picked up my empty teacup. "Remind me to never tell you about my sex life again."

"Ha!" She laughed. "Honey, it's not a life. It was a fart in a silent room. That's why it made a big stink. Trust me, if you had my sex life, you wouldn't still be thinking about this guy. You'd move on to another muscular pogo stick and be done."

"Please don't compare a night of passion to a fart. And I'm not still thinking about him. At least, not in the romantic sense."

She gave me a knowing grin. "Oh, honey. You know killers, I know sexually deprived clients. You're definitely thinking of him, and there isn't anything wrong with that." She pointed a stern finger at me. "Just don't separate starvation from good food."

Robert Kavin was good food. I may have been starved, but the man had been a master chef of pleasure. I swallowed a response and circled the end of my desk. "Will you tell Jacob I'm heading out soon? Just in case he needs me for anything."

"Will do." She crumpled the empty candy bag and surveyed my pile of files. "Good luck."

I waited until she left, then opened up my side drawer and considered the extra pack of pantyhose I kept there, in case I got a run. I stared at the shrink-wrapped package for a long moment, then closed the drawer, leaving it there.

It had *not* been a loud fart. That was just ridiculous.

CHAPTER 22

While my office looked like the inside of a psych ward, Robert's was perfectly in order. I set my purse down on his private conference table and surveyed the room. Very masculine. Dark wood accents, powerful and rich colors in the art. All it was missing was a stuffed animal head on the wall. I fought not to psychoanalyze it, but the decor was a dog pissing on the walls, marking the territory and asserting Robert's dominance.

He was on the phone, his voice low, his chair swiveled toward the window, and I took the opportunity to wander around the space. It was huge, a clear status play, big enough for the conference table, a seating cluster, and his massive desk. There was a bookshelf, and I paused beside it, surprised to find novels instead of legal journals. On the second shelf was a small fishbowl with a bubbler. A goldfish stared at me blankly as a treasure chest slowly opened behind him.

A goldfish. That was interesting.

"Dr. Moore."

I turned. Robert had ended the call and was facing me.

"How is the good doctor today?"

"I'm okay." I looked back at the aquarium. "You have a fish."

"That I do. A beautiful woman told me that I should have a pet, so . . . there you go."

He was smooth, I'd give him that. How many women had he delivered similar lines to? Dozens? Hundreds?

I turned back to him. "You always do what 'beautiful' women tell you to?"

"Depends on the woman." The words were light, but I could see the fatigue in his features. He stood and came around the desk. "Take a seat. Those heels have to be killing you." He settled into one of the big leather club chairs, and I followed suit. "How's your profile going so far?"

"I'm not sure," I admitted. "I did a quick sweep of the kills and am now going through each in detail, chronologically. I'm about halfway through. I'm on the third victim now."

"Noah."

"Yes." I watched his features, reading the rigid tension in them. He didn't need a psychological profile. He needed a grief counselor. That and a vacation a million miles away from blood and gore and photos of dead teenage boys. "Have you been through all the files?"

"Yes."

"You know, you can't desensitize yourself to it. Looking at photos of the other boys doesn't make Gabe's death any easier."

"It helps me." He sighed. "I wasn't the only parent who failed."

"None of you failed. You know that."

"Yeah, well. So many small decisions might have changed it. If he had never seen Gabe, he wouldn't have taken him."

I shook my head. "You can't go down that rabbit hole. For every action and decision that you beat yourself up over, look at your intentions. You did and continue to—even now—do the best you can to protect him."

He forced a smile. "I don't need a counselor, Gwen. I need to know what you've learned."

He didn't know what he needed, but it wasn't my place to force treatment on him. I switched to business mode. "Well, I've reviewed the files enough to give a rough sketch of the killer, but it's likely to change as I finish reviewing things."

He relaxed slightly at the change in topic. "Go ahead."

"Are you familiar with grounded theory methodology?"

"No."

"It's the discovery of emerging patterns in data and the generation of theories from that data. With each victim, I create a list of factors. Factors about the victim, the circumstances, the kill, and the treatment of the victim from the moment of capture to the moment of death. Also, the disposal of the body." I watched him carefully, wondering if I needed to be more sensitive with my language.

He nodded, his brows pinching together in interest, and I continued on.

"Once I have exhaustive lists on each crime, I can find the commonalities among them and establish patterns. Both in the killer's consistencies, but also his inconsistencies. Is he changing his MO of victims? Growing older or younger in age, more innocent or less in experience . . ." I shrugged. "So far, these victims are eerily similar. That's the pattern, and it points strongly to the killer personifying either himself at a younger age or someone in his past."

"Which is more likely?"

"Someone in his past," I said immediately. "Most likely someone who hurt him in a very traumatic way. Given the length of the victims' captivity, the abuse was probably extended. It could have lasted for years."

"Okay. What else?" he asked.

"The crime scenes are staged and extremely clean. No fingerprints, DNA, tire tracks, or evidence. They're clearly planned and executed in careful fashion. Between that, and the preparation of the body, we're dealing with a very detailed and organized individual. Someone who is patient and who enjoys mental mind games. The killers who display their victims are seeking attention from the onset and probably planned the series of murders from the beginning. They are very proud of their kills, proud of their intellect, and confident in their ability to evade the police."

I paused. "Even without finishing the research, I'm confident in those aspects of the killer."

He gave a dismissive nod, unimpressed. "Okay, so? A cocky, organized individual who likes mental mind games. You just described half of this floor, including me. Tell me there's more."

The next part required me to go into the murder details. It would be a light dip, but I was very aware of the fact that I was dealing with a grieving father. "I'm considering the possibility that the killer is bisexual or gay but is living life as a straight man, and he feels deep shame and self-loathing over his orientation."

"You're basing that on the sexual activity with the victims?" Robert didn't flinch at the question, but he also couched it as *sexual activity* versus *rape*, which was an emotional tell in itself.

"Yes." I hesitated. "What was Gabe's sexual orientation?"

His brow furrowed. "Straight."

"Are you sure?"

He shifted in his chair, his annoyance flaring, and I could see the moment he intentionally calmed himself. It was impressive, a complete shuttering of emotion. If I could package the action and teach it to my clients, I'd be hailed as a genius. Then again, such emotional control wasn't particularly healthy. A quick burst of steam kept a kettle from boiling over. He folded one hand over the other. "Why are you asking?"

"If all the victims were gay or had homosexual potential, it would tell us a lot about BH and why he selected those boys in particular." I paused. "And, also, I'm trying to figure out why Gabe's death was different from the others."

He rubbed his index fingers over his mouth, then straightened in his seat. "You're talking about the dry drowning."

"Yes." I wanted to apologize, hated the path of the conversation, but he started this journey. If he was going to represent Thompson, there were going to be a lot more of these discussions in his future. "It's a significant ramp-up in aggression. Much more violent and painful. More emotion fueled. It indicates a loss of control. The question is, why? Why Gabe?"

"Well, it wasn't because Gabe was gay," Robert said wryly. "I couldn't keep him away from girls. We had a pregnancy scare with his girlfriend just two weeks before he was taken. Now . . ." He sighed. "I keep thinking about if she had been pregnant. We'd have a baby right now. One with his eyes, his smile—" His voice cracked, and he cleared his throat.

I quickly moved on. "Did Gabe drink? Use drugs?"

"He drank. Not a lot. High school parties, that sort of thing. Drugs . . ." He grimaced. "I'm sure he smoked weed at some point in his life. Anything harder than that—I kept a close eye on him. He didn't have a habit."

"Okay, that helps." I thought of the piles of handwritten notes in my office, many with giant question marks beside them, and considered how much more to share. "There's . . . something off. I'm not sure what it is yet."

His attention piqued, and I shouldn't have said anything until I knew more. "What's off?"

"Like I said, I don't know yet. It's just a feeling. I don't know if it's a manipulation of evidence or if it's a missing piece, but there's something, and I can't put my finger on it." I shrugged. "It could be nothing. I could be wrong."

"Or you could be right."

Yes. I could be right. Hell, I *was* right. Something was wrong. Every time I tried to draw a line between two ideas, it was slightly off. I was missing something, and it had better emerge soon, or I wasn't going to have any hair left on my head.

~

A half hour later, I sucked Diet Coke through a paper straw and glanced across the conference room table at Robert. "How do you want me to use Scott Harden's case in my profile?"

"Disregard it completely," he said, wiping at his mouth with a napkin, an Italian sub from the lobby deli in hand. "He's lying."

"Lying about what?" I countered. "You don't think he was kidnapped?"

"No, I think he was kidnapped. But he's lying about Randall Thompson."

"Why?"

"Why wouldn't he?" he countered. "California's most vicious serial killer in recent history is out there. Who knows what he's threatened this kid with? And everyone's assuming the kid escaped. But what if he didn't? What if the killer let him go?"

"Let him go?" I made a face. "Why would he let him go?"

"You're the shrink." He set down his sandwich and picked up his soda. "Let's say you knew he let him go. Why would he? What would be your psychological reasoning behind that motivation?"

I sighed, taking a bite of my sandwich and thinking over the idea. I chewed slowly, then washed it down with a long sip of soda. "He wouldn't. He grew more violent with the sixth death, and then he releases the seventh? It doesn't—" I paused as a possibility, though remote, came to mind. "Wait. *If* he released him . . . ," I allowed, "and that's a big if, then it was planned. There was a purpose for it and—if I had to guess—it was part of an exit strategy. He needed Scott Harden to be free so that . . ." I closed my eyes and tried to figure out why the BH Killer would intentionally create a loose thread. Part of the game with authorities?

"So that Scott could point to someone else." The resolution in Robert's voice made me open my eyes. The attorney was nodding, warming to the idea. "A scapegoat."

"Whoa." I held up my palm. "That's a stretch. Let's not forget about the trophies in Randall Thompson's house."

"Could have been planted there. Plus, they haven't found the fingers yet."

I frowned. "The pinkies from the victims?"

"Yeah. Went through Randall's house with a fine-toothed comb, and there isn't a fleck of DNA evidence from any victim, and no pinkies. Now, you said the BH Killer is organized. Planned every part of his crimes. So he planned this—to release Scott Harden and have him ID someone else." He pulled open a bag of chips and raised his brows at me, challenging me to contest the thought.

As much as I hated to admit it, it wasn't a horrible theory. I hesitated. "Eyewitnesses are convincing," I allowed.

"Convincing?" He shook his head. "Screw that. They're gold. Trust me. I'm in front of juries every day. If Scott Harden points his finger across that courtroom and says Randall Thompson stripped off his clothes and tied him down to a bed, that trumps hair fibers at a dump site. At that point in time, the cops stop looking, and lack of evidence ceases to matter."

"So that's going to be your defense?" I gathered my trash and stuffed it into the bag, then reached across the corner of the table to get his. Our knees brushed. "Scott Harden is lying?"

"You ever open a pair of handcuffs with a fork?"

"No," I replied. "Have you?"

"No one has. It's impossible." He held up his hand. "Okay, not impossible. But you aren't doing it one-handed, and look at the autopsy photos. Rope burns, not handcuffs. These boys were spread out on the bed, not chained to radiators with their hands in close proximity."

"It's a stretch," I argued. "You're making a lot of stretches."

"Gwen." His use of my name caught my attention and held it. "What if I'm right?"

If he was right, then this killer was still out there. Laughing at us. Free, while Scott Harden ate up the press and Randall Thompson was locked away in solitary confinement. It was a sobering and terrifying thought, because he was correct about one thing—the cops weren't out looking right now. They were sitting back and congratulating themselves on a case well solved.

"If you're wrong, and you get Randall Thompson off—then what?"

"I'm not wrong." He met my eyes, and for a moment, I saw his pain. Raw and unfiltered, the weight of his grief was right there, etched in the hunch of his shoulders and the tight knots in his neck.

Maybe he was wrong, but he was a father and he was hurting, and I couldn't argue with that.

CHAPTER 23

Three days later, I perched on the counter of the break room and watched Scott Harden speak into a fuzzy mic with a Channel 27 logo on it.

"It's a second chance at life," the seventeen-year-old said. "It makes me want to be a better person, to deserve the life I've been given." He flashed a smile to the camera, and there was no disputing that the kid was cute. He had all the attributes that would make a teenage girl swoon, which was evidenced by his blooming celebrity. Last night, I checked his social media followers and was shocked to see the number approaching a million fans.

Jacob let out a boo, then drained his can of Mello Yello. "He's such a camera hog. I bet he practices these lines each night in front of the mirror."

I didn't disagree, but it seemed wrong to talk crap about the one teenager who had avoided the gruesome end the other six had received. "Whether it's cheesy or not, he's right," I pointed out as I dug into a bag of microwave popcorn. "He did escape death. That causes people to approach life in a different way."

From her spot at the table, Meredith looked up from her phone. "Have you noticed he never really says anything in these interviews?"

I had. In the last day, I'd watched every television and radio piece I could find of him. And Meredith was right. He skimmed over his time in captivity and said little to nothing about the man who had supposedly held him prisoner.

The interviewer continued. "How much interaction did you have with Randall Thompson prior to him kidnapping you?"

"Mr. Harden won't be speaking on that." Juan Melendez, Scott Harden's attorney, stepped forward, and Jacob let out another boo. I grinned, appreciating the lighthearted moment after a day spent in the death files.

I'd made it through the fourth victim, then had to take a break. It was all so incredibly sad. Six smart and talented lives taken. Six families—parents, siblings, grandparents—whose lives were irrevocably destroyed. And all for what? One sick individual's twisted pleasure. Was that one person Randall Thompson? I was dying to research him, to see if he fit my profile so far, but I'd behaved. I couldn't have his reality alter my analysis, so I was mentally compartmentalizing what I already knew about the man and locking it away for later.

"I don't get the media tour," Meredith mused. "He's on TV every time I turn it on. Shouldn't he be at home with his parents?"

"He's a teenage kid who has a chance to be famous." I chewed a handful of popcorn. "Plus, he's probably avoiding the emotion dump. It'll hit him at some point, and he'll break down. But right now, he's distracting himself with all this."

We watched as the camera cut to a montage of shots of the victims. I watched the faces of the teenagers I now knew by heart. Gabe Kavin's photo appeared, and my heart sank at how much he resembled Robert. Same dark hair. Same knowing eyes. He would have grown up to be a heartbreaker, just like his dad.

I pushed off the counter before the show turned its coverage to Randall Thompson. "I'm going to get back to work. Jacob, I've got Luke Attens coming in at one."

He made a face and squeezed the empty soda can, crinkling it. "Right, *if* he shows up. That guy's a dick."

I had no comeback for that. Luke *was* a dick, and the most volatile of my clients. He'd been a no-show on his last two appointments, which was common for him. He'd be regular for a while, then go out of town or miss appointments for a month, then pop back up as if everything were fine.

I didn't mind. His appointments were exhausting, and he paid the no-show invoices without complaint. I'd made just as much in penalties as I'd made in billable time.

"Well, he called me this morning, so I'm expecting him to come in." His early-morning call had been textbook Luke. Terse and demanding. Thirty seconds in which he'd barked at me to tell him his appointment time, then abruptly hung up.

"You're meeting him in the conference room, right?"

"Yeah." I stuffed the bag of popcorn into the trash and downed the remaining swallow of soda. Meredith grunted out a goodbye, her attention still on the television.

~

Luke Attens sat in front of me in bright-red pants and a paisley-print silk shirt. He was a walking contradiction, and if I ever had to create a psychological profile on him, it would involve a lot of question marks and blank lines.

Luke suffered from insecurity and abandonment, with a triple helping of uncontrollable rage. When his sister had gotten engaged two years earlier, it had spurred Luke to set fire to her car with both of them inside. Luke did not handle stress or heightened emotions well, which was why he was mid-hyperventilation right now.

"Breathe," I instructed firmly. "Cup your hands in front of your mouth and breathe into your belly, not your chest."

He gasped.

"Now, hold your breath for ten seconds."

He shook his head, his hands still cupped over his mouth, and I raised my eyebrows at him. "Trust me, Luke. Hold your breath for ten seconds. It'll reset you. Come on. I'll do it with you." I made a big show of inhaling and holding my breath. He hesitated, then followed.

I held up one finger, then two, holding my breath along with him as I counted to ten. Then I slowly exhaled and reminded myself that Jacob was right on the other side of the door, and if Luke tackled me across the table, it would take at least a minute for him to strangle me to death.

His panic attack had started after I'd refused to meet him in our standard location: my office. He accused me of bugging the conference room, and I'd offered to postpone our meeting until next week, when my office would be back in order, but he refused, stating that he had to talk to me now because SOMETHING HAD HAPPENED. When I asked what had happened . . . well, here we were.

His gasps were starting to come back under control. I stayed in place and watched as he dropped his head back on the swivel chair and gulped for air. He always had a flair for the dramatic. During my first appointment with him, he had pounded his fist on my desk so hard that my pen cup fell over. I think his fury had been over my rates, which was amusing, given his level of wealth. Luke Attens was the eldest son of *the* Attens family, creator of the mega-slice pizza, forty-two thousand delivery and take-out locations worldwide. I didn't know that stat initially, but Luke liked to scream it at random moments if he felt his manhood or authority were being questioned, which was often.

It was good for Luke that he was an Attens, because any normal individual would be in jail after what had happened with his sister. It had taken a team of attorneys to convince a judge that the fire had been an "accident," and another team of plastic surgeons to repair the damage from the fire. Even two years later, I could see the skin grafts along the edge of his jaw and the scar around his left eye. His sister, whom he had doused with gasoline prior to lighting the match, had it worse. I had never spoken to Laura, who had moved to Florida with her fiancé and taken out a restraining order against Luke, one he'd already broken twice.

His breathing quieted, and I waited.

We were already twenty-five minutes into the session. I was still ignorant of what inciting event had occurred, but hopefully it could be wrapped up and solved in our remaining thirty-five minutes.

Another three minutes passed, and Luke wasn't known for drawing things out. Any minute and he would—

"You know this serial killer that was caught?"

I looped my fingers together. "Yes."

"What's your take on it?"

I chose my next words carefully. "I don't have a take. He's in custody."

"He a client of yours?" His breathing was starting to get more labored, his eyes widening, and he was losing control. This wasn't good, and it especially wasn't good with someone like Luke.

"No, he wasn't a client of mine." *And still isn't,* I told myself. I was hired by Robert, not Randall.

"You know, he was my *teacher.*" He sneered the word.

I blinked. "He was? At Beverly High?"

That wasn't a huge surprise. All the rich kids went to Beverly High or Montbrier. Luke was a decade older than Scott, but Randall Thompson had taught science there for almost twenty years.

Luke rose from his seat and moved toward me. I glanced through the glass walls of the conference room to find Jacob watching us. I held his gaze for a moment, then returned my attention to Luke.

He stopped before me, the buckle of his belt scraping against the conference room table as he leaned in so close that I could smell the stale odor of his breath.

"The receptionist said his name, so is he your patient?" he hissed, and spittle from his mouth peppered my jaw.

Maybe I should have just let this guy hyperventilate to death.

"Luke, you need to step away from me," I said calmly.

"That pervert," he said coldly, "put his—"

The door to the conference room swung open. "Everything okay?" Jacob asked. Luke turned toward him, and I took the opportunity to roll my seat back and stand.

In my peripheral vision, I saw Luke's hands balled into fists. Escalation had begun, and while I didn't think he would hurt me, Jacob was a different story.

"Luke, let's finish this up another day." I walked around the end of the table, keeping it between me and Luke as I all but shoved Jacob into the hall.

I glanced back at Luke and gave my best calm and comforting smile. "Call me if you need to continue this session today. You have my cell number, Luke."

An angry breath hissed through his lips, and I was reminded of the press coverage after the car fire. The video of his sister, screaming out from the stretcher. I turned and walked straight through the reception area, beelining for Meredith's office and motioning Jacob along with me. She was on the phone, and I closed her door behind us and locked it.

She immediately ended the call. "What's wrong?"

"Potentially nothing. Still, call security and send them up here."

She dialed the downstairs desk and relayed the message. I pressed my ear to the door and tried to hear what was happening in the hall. There was a shout and then the slam of wood. A door. I straightened, my alarm growing as I heard a louder crash. This one hadn't been out in the lobby. It had been on the other side of Meredith's wall.

Luke was in my office.

CHAPTER 24

My first concern was for Matthew, our third partner. The tiny psychologist had the physical presence of a field mouse. I hissed at Meredith to call his cell and hoped the man was tucked inside his office, the door locked. Luke shouldn't go after him. If anything, as soon as he saw my wall of BH Killer notes, he'd misunderstand them and come for me.

"What's wrong?" Meredith asked, coming to stand beside me. "I mean, aside from the obvious. You look pale."

"He's in my office."

"So?"

"He's got something against Randall Thompson. Just now, he asked if I represented him."

"Which you don't."

"Yeah, but—" I waved a hand in the direction of my office. "That's not what he's going to think when he sees all my work in there." The victims' names, in chalk on the wall. The columns. The notes. Crime scene photos, pinned up in a neat grid. It'd be impossible to miss. I lifted my head, listening. Luke was quiet, probably standing in place, staring at it all.

What was taking security so long?

"Do I want to know what this guy's kink is?" Meredith asked softly.

"I wish I had an easy answer for that." In layman's terms, Luke was a walking train wreck. In non-layman's terms, he was best conceptualized as recurring patterns of covariant traits rather than a single diagnostic category.

"But he's violent?"

"He has a temper, which he loses often." But it wasn't just a temper. There was premeditation behind his outbursts. The incident with his sister occurred after Luke bought two cans, filled them with gas, and then sat for two hours outside her work, waiting for her to get off. Two hours where his anger built and solidified into a firm and deadly resolution. "Yes," I amended. "He's violent."

A knock rattled against the door, and we both jumped. "Don't say anything," Meredith whispered.

"Dr. Moore? Dr. Blankner? It's Bart, from the front desk."

I immediately flipped open the lock and cracked the door for the security guard. "Do you have him?"

"They stopped him just off the elevators and have him at the desk." Bart ran a hand over his smooth head, then scratched the back of it. "He's saying he didn't do anything wrong, other than breaking a lamp, which he said you can bill him for."

"Okay." I straightened my blouse, a little embarrassed that we'd been cowering in the office like babies. "Dr. Reeker—our psychologist. Is he okay?"

"I'm fine." A sheepish Matthew peeked around the corner. "I was making contingency plans if Mr. Attens decided to break my door down. He didn't."

"I almost wish he had," Bart said, unclipping a walkie-talkie from his belt. "Then we could call the police and file an assault charge. As it is, we have to let him go." He brought the radio up to his mouth and relayed the instructions.

"That's fine." I hugged myself. "I just want him out of here. Can you keep him from coming back?"

"Yeah, they'll add him to the list now. Don't worry, Doc. We'll keep you guys safe."

We'll keep you guys safe. That was impossible. Bart's team was great, and their presence was why I'd chosen this building, but they could only do so much, and their protection ended at the building's doors.

"You okay?" Meredith asked as the security guard headed for the elevators.

"Yeah." Frustrated, I ran a hand through my hair. "I don't like putting any of you in danger."

"Meh." She brushed it off. "You have to deal with my perverts checking you out from the waiting room, and we both have to suffer through Matthew's mopey clients. You ever chatted one of them up in the elevator? I swear, their depression is contagious."

Perverts. I flashed back to Luke's dark face. *"That pervert,"* he had seethed, *"put his—"*

What had Randall done to him? Luke's temper wasn't a new behavior. It had been present his entire life. If Randall had molested him as a teenager, he would have fought back.

Meredith poked me, and I struggled to return to the conversation. "You're right. Who cares about getting your throat slit when we have to deal with your clients using up all the hand lotion in the bathroom?"

Her eyes crinkled at the corners when she smiled. "Exactly. See?"

"I'm going to see how bad my office is." I gave the group a grateful smile and left Meredith's office, stepping into what I had previously thought of as my sanctuary.

It was almost in order, aside from the rose gold–and–glass lamp that was now shattered beside my desk. Judging from the impact and outward spray of glass shards, it had been dropped straight down. Probably heaved over his head and toward the dark wood floors.

I had loved that lamp. It had been a gift from my mother when I first moved into the office and would be impossible to replace. I crouched beside the exposed interior and cupped my hand, picking up the pieces and collecting them.

"Here." Jacob held out the small silver trash can that was normally by my coffee maker. "Why don't you let me get that?"

"No, no." I dumped the handful into the trash can and took it from him. "I got it. You've got to get back to the desk."

He hesitated, then nodded. I continued the cleanup as best I could, leaving a small amount of glass powder for the maids to catch in their biweekly rounds. Rising to my feet, I did a slow 180, seeing the office through Luke's eyes. The wall of details. The photos. The files spread out everywhere. A forgotten coffee cup by the chair I was sitting in. I moved behind my desk, examining the contents with a critical eye. My calendar was closed, computer locked and asleep. There was a legal pad filled with doodles and a few lines of notes that wouldn't mean anything to anyone but me. By the phone, Robert's business card was propped up against my paperweight. I frowned and picked it up. Had Luke seen it? If he had, would it have meant anything to him?

Before I could second-guess the decision, I picked up the receiver and dialed Robert's office line.

"Cluster and Kavin."

"Mr. Kavin, please."

"May I ask what it's regarding?"

"It's Dr. Gwen Moore, about Randall Thompson."

"Please hold."

A gentle cadence played, and I pulled my chair up to the desk and sat down. Closing my eyes, I let out a slow breath, reminding myself of the same things I had told Luke. Breathe from my stomach. Relax. He wasn't the first client who had lost his temper with me, and he wouldn't be the last.

"Hey."

Robert's familiar greeting did something foolish in my chest. "I'm sorry to bother you. I know you're busy."

"It's no bother. What's up?"

"This is probably nothing, but I wanted to mention it to you just in case. A client just left my office. His name is Luke Attens. He's a little fixated on the Randall Thompson arrest. He asked me a lot of questions, wanted to know if he was a client of mine." I paused.

"He's not. He's my client. You're a consultant for me," he responded.

"I know. I didn't go into that with him, I just denied it. He pressed the issue, didn't believe me, and got a little heated."

"Is he a violent individual?" Robert's tone was calm, his words measured and almost deadly cool.

"He has been in the past." I twisted the coil of the phone cord around my finger. "He forced his way into my office and saw my notes and files. Just briefly, but if he suspected Randall of being my client before, I'm sure he's convinced of the fact now."

"Are you worried he'll come after you again?"

"I had your business card on my desk. I'm worried he saw it and might come to your office next. If you put me in touch with your building's security desk, I can give them a physical description of him."

"I just pulled him up online. There's a photo. Is this right? He lit his sister on fire?"

"Unfortunately, yes." I cleared my throat. "He said Randall was his teacher—"

"This isn't a secure line," he cut me off. "Let's continue this conversation tomorrow, at our two o'clock."

I glanced down at the floor and stilled, catching sight of my purse in its spot against the leg of my desk. The neck of it was open, and I reached down and plucked it off the floor.

I'd never been a big purse stuffer. I don't carry Band-Aids and medicines, checkbooks or phone chargers. My purse mimicked my house—the bare necessities, in neat order. Inside the Chanel bag were my lipstick, powder, a travel-size Kleenex pack, a pen, and a small tin of peppermints.

My wallet was missing, as were my keys.

I didn't have to retrace my steps or figure out if I had forgotten my wallet. I hadn't. And I'd used my keys to unlock my office this morning. If they both weren't in here, they'd been taken. I thought of my driver's license, with my home address on it.

"Gwen? Are you there?"

"I have to go," I said faintly.

"What happened?"

"He took my wallet and keys. I need to go." I'd need to change my locks. Was he headed there now? If so, why? I thought of him shaking out a can of gasoline on his sister, of his obsession with fires. He brought it up frequently. My beautiful house. All the pieces I worked so hard to collect. Clem was inside, the lock on her cat door securely in place. "I'll talk to you later." I stood and grabbed my purse, then realized I didn't have my car keys.

"Where are you going?" he demanded.

"I've got my cat at home. If he goes in—"

"My office is closer. I'm leaving now. Call the police and meet me there."

He hung up before I could respond.

CHAPTER 25

In my driveway, a squad car was next to Robert's sleek Mercedes. The knot of anxiety in my chest relaxed as Jacob's car pulled up to the curb to let me out. He stared through the windshield at the two men who stood on my lawn. "That the lawyer?"

"Yeah." I unbuckled my seat belt. "That's him."

"Handsome guy."

It was the first time Jacob had ever commented on a man, and I swallowed my surprise. "Yes, he is."

"You want me to come in?"

I reached over and squeezed his forearm. "You've done more than enough today. Go home, and I want you to take tomorrow off. I'll email my appointments and cancel them. Meredith and Matthew can handle themselves for a day."

"Nah," he protested. "I'm okay."

"No. Seriously. Take it off and enjoy a three-day weekend." I opened my door and stared at him until he relented.

"Okay, okay." He grinned. "Thanks, Doc."

"Thanks for the ride." I stepped out of the dented Toyota and closed the door. Checking the road for oncoming traffic, I crossed the street and climbed the small incline of my lawn.

"Hey." I nodded to the cop and Robert. "I'm Gwen Moore, the homeowner."

"Officer Kitt." He offered his hand, and I shook it. "We did a perimeter sweep, but the doors are locked. No sign of anyone."

"Thank you. I have a hidden key. If you don't mind, I'd really appreciate it if you came inside with me and checked the house."

"Of course." The cop nodded, as did Robert. I met his concerned look and gave him a grateful smile, moving past them and up the drive to the side entrance.

Robert followed me closely. "Are you okay? You're white as a sheet."

"I'm fine. Just a crazy afternoon." I paused by the side door. "Turn away."

"What?"

"I don't want you seeing where I hide my key. Turn away."

The corner of his mouth twitched. "It's a pretty small porch. I could just figure it out."

Under the weight of the stress, there was a crack—one that allowed a brief moment of levity. "I'm a master key hider. You would not figure it out."

He held up his hands in surrender and turned, waiting as I pulled the key from the top of the porch light and unlocked the door. The cop, who had been on his radio in the carport, stepped forward, his hand resting on the butt of his gun. "Let me check the house first, Ms. Moore."

"Sure."

Clem streaked out the door and into the yard. I relaxed in relief as she skidded to a stop and examined a new tulip bud sprouting in the carport planter. "That's my cat," I said. "There shouldn't be anyone else in the house." The officer nodded and stepped inside.

An awkward silence fell, and I leaned against the pillar. "You didn't have to come here."

"It's my fault he went after you." He threaded the watch's band through its clasp. "I feel responsible."

I snorted. "Don't. I have high-risk clients. Sometimes they're triggered by obscure things."

He took the opposite column and smoothed his hand down the front of his tie. "How did you end up with that specialty? It seems a bit . . ." He glanced at the house, searching for the right word. "Macabre."

I watched as Clem stalked after a lizard. "People have always fascinated me. Their motivations. Decisions. I like figuring out how their brains work."

"That doesn't answer the question."

"Yes, it does."

"You could figure out a normal person's brain. Why focus on violent individuals?"

"Why defend criminals?"

He gave a humorless smile. "Gwen."

I folded my arms across my chest. "It's not a short answer."

"I can respect that." He met my eyes. "Why don't you tell it to me over dinner?"

"Ahh . . ." I wrinkled my nose. "I don't know. Given everything that we're working on, maybe we should maintain a line of professional boundaries."

"Maybe I want to jump over that line."

I smiled. "Another night, maybe."

The rejection bounced off him like rubber. "I won't give up."

"Spoken like every stalker I've ever treated."

He winced. "Excellent point. Still, you have to eat. I could bring something over tonight. It'd be safer to have company, just in case this asshole shows up."

There were so many red flags. The confident eye contact. The playful crook of his mouth. The paper-thin layer of control over his guilt. If he was going through a roster of women in an attempt to distract himself from his guilt, he could use someone else. I'd been there. Enjoyed that. While one night with Robert Kavin had been fun, a second might kick-start a risky game with my heart.

Then again, he was a handsome, intelligent man. A skilled and generous lover. Was I an idiot for not embracing this opportunity? Wasn't he exactly what every woman in this city was looking for?

Plus, I had finished my first-draft psychological profile. All that was left were tweaks and polishes, as well as a few days to allow my final determinations to properly marinate in my mind. It would be good to talk through some of my sticky points with him and get his feedback.

"Why do I feel like you're making a pros-and-cons list in your head?" he asked.

"Because I am." I glanced at the open door to the kitchen, wondering how much longer the officer would be.

"I know the pros. What are the cons?"

"Ego, for one." I gave him a knowing look, one he brushed off.

"What else?"

"I'm just not in the market for heartbreak. You may date around a lot, but I don't."

His attention shifted past me and to the street. I turned to see a dark sedan stop at the curb. Robert moved in front of me. "That wouldn't be your patient, would it?"

"Not unless his Ferrari is in the shop." I squinted at the car, my concern easing as I saw a tall Black man step out. "Oh, I know him."

I skirted around Robert and met Detective Saxe halfway down the drive. "Everything okay?"

"You tell me, Dr. Moore. I heard your name and address over the radio. You kill off another client?" He gave me a mirthless smile.

"Funny," I said flatly. "I just called the police as a precaution. Someone stole my wallet and keys."

He rested his hands on his hips. "You going to change the locks?"

"Yeah. Locksmith is on his way."

His gaze moved to Robert, who approached from behind me. "What are you doing here?"

Robert stuck his hand out. "Robert Kavin. I'm working with Dr. Moore on a case."

The detective considered the hand, then dismissed it. "I know you, Mr. Kavin. You got Nelson Anderson off after he killed his wife."

"If I'd gotten him off, he wouldn't be behind bars." Robert's expression was pleasant, a sharp contrast to Detective Saxe's rigid scowl.

"On a bullshit plea deal. He'll be out within five years." The detective's attention returned to me. "You could do better with your friends, Dr. Moore."

I ignored the dig. "Any updates on John Abbott?"

He squinted at me, and it wasn't that sunny out. "Nothing to share."

Nothing to share? What did that mean?

His gaze swept across my yard. "Well, looks like things are pretty calm here. If no one needs me, I'll head on out."

No one needs you, I thought, and delivered a thank-you through gritted teeth as he opened his car door, gave me a final, measuring look, then disappeared inside. I waved.

"Cheery guy," Robert said. "I think he trusts you about as much as he trusts me."

I turned to look at him. "He was joking."

"Was he?" There was a moment of heightened tension, then he cracked a smile. I gave an awkward and uncomfortable laugh, then craned my head to the side, catching a glimpse of Officer Kitt in the doorway of my house.

"The house is clear," he said, holding the door open.

"Thanks." I moved past him and into the house, glancing around to find everything in order, my kitchen spotless.

"You have a locksmith coming?" The officer spoke from behind me.

"Yes." I turned to him. "They should be here any minute."

"I can wait until they arrive."

"No, I'll be fine, thank you."

"I'll stay with her." Robert stepped in.

The officer looked between us, then nodded. We said our goodbyes, and I took his business card. Between his and Detective Saxe's, I was starting to build a collection.

Once we were alone, Robert arched a brow at me. "So, it's settled. Dinner tonight, say . . . seven o'clock?"

I hesitated, self-aware enough to realize that my biggest problem with Robert Kavin was my attraction to him. Even now, with my nerves still frayed from Luke Attens, and with a police officer backing out of my driveway, my body was responding to his presence. If he strode forward, if his hand cupped around my waist and pulled me against him . . . I wouldn't be able to resist. And what then?

What if I slept with him again? Not as two strangers drunk off cheap beer, but as Dr. Gwen Moore and attorney Robert Kavin—business associates with a mess of secrets between us. What then?

CHAPTER 26

At three minutes before seven, my doorbell rang. I looked through the glass panes of the front door and let out a frustrated sigh.

Robert had brought flowers. Again. The last ones hadn't even died yet. I swung open the door before I had a chance to rethink the action. "More flowers?" I gave the bouquet a questioning look.

He swatted at a mosquito. "I was raised to bring a gift when you visit someone's home. I bring men scotch and women flowers. Don't take it personally."

"How sexist of you." I smirked. "For the record, I like scotch, also."

"I'll remember that." He pulled the door shut the minute he was inside and flipped the dead bolt. "The bugs are terrible."

I tried not to stare at the locked door, the hardware new and shiny. He was here to protect me, I reminded myself. A bit of added muscle power in addition to the baseball bat I kept in the coat closet.

He paused in the foyer and sniffed. "It smells delicious in here. I'm sorry you had to cook, but I'm dying for more of your cooking."

I didn't respond, still emotionally opposed to this dinner. I had protested, he had countered, and it wasn't easy to debate an attorney. In part because I couldn't share the true reasons for my trepidation, which had less to do with my legal reputation and more to do with the vulnerable swell of hope and attraction that appeared whenever our eye contact held.

There had been a lot of eye contact, which was another something I needed to pull the reins on.

"I'm going to put these in water." He headed for the sink, and I eyed the dining room table, grateful that I had skipped the candles and real china and stuck out some paper plates and disposable silverware. If that didn't send out enough of an unromantic vibe, the sweatpants and baggy T-shirt I was wearing would complete the facade.

The water started to run, and I cracked my knuckles, a nervous habit I'd never been able to break.

"I'm assuming you haven't heard anything from the client? The one who has your wallet?" He turned his head so I could hear him more clearly. He was still in his suit, and I pulled at the bottom of my T-shirt. Maybe I had overdone it with the casualness. There was the whole "Doth protest too much" angle to consider.

What had he asked me? About Luke? I cleared my throat. "No." The police had gone to his house and questioned his housekeeper, but they hadn't found the pizza heir.

"What's your opinion on his state of mind?"

"I'm not sure," I said honestly. "I need to talk to him and explain what he saw in my office. That's the easiest solution to the problem. I've tried his cell, but he isn't answering my calls."

Luke's final words, his fury over Randall, hung on my lips. I was dying to share them with Robert, but doing so would violate Luke's client confidentiality.

He turned off the water, and I moved closer, watching as he combined the new lilies with the tulips he had brought earlier. "So you'll tell him that you're working for me?"

"I'll tell him I'm looking at the deaths and creating a profile."

He set the flowers on the windowsill above the sink and turned to me. "You mentioned that your profile is done."

"My first draft, yes. I'm missing the application or nonapplication of it as it relates to the subject."

"Randall," he clarified.

"Yes. I'll be ready to talk to him this week, if you can set that up."

"Absolutely. Just let me know what day. I'll make it happen."

This week, I would sit across from the alleged Bloody Heart Killer. I had tossed out the interview mention as if I didn't care, but the idea of it was constant. Would he fit my profile? How high was his emotional intelligence? How would he respond to me—and which questions should I ask?

"I'd like to see the profile so far."

I opened the oven and peeked at the pot roast, which had another four minutes, according to my timer. "I just need to think through a few pieces of it. I can email it over tomorrow."

He leaned against the counter and loosened the knot of his tie. "Do you still feel like something is off?"

"Yes," I admitted. "But there's another thing I want to make sure you're clear on."

He raised his eyebrows, waiting.

"I'm going to be honest with my assessment. If you put me on the stand, I'll deliver the truth, including how Randall Thompson might fit the profile."

He held up his hand, palm facing out. "Whoa. If I expected a jury puppet, I wouldn't have wasted your time in giving you the files. I would have just told you what I wanted you to say."

"Okay." That was valid. "I just wanted to make sure that was clear."

He dropped his hand. "Why are you certain that Randall fits your profile? Have you been researching him? Because you were the one who told me—"

"I haven't done any research on Randall," I snapped. The timer shrieked, and I silenced it, then worked my hands into two thick

Garfield oven mitts. "But I know the basics of his arrest. You've got a victim's testimony and evidence."

"You're referring to the box of souvenirs." He rubbed along the side of his jaw, scraping his fingers through the short hair, and I cataloged the movement in case it was a tell.

"Yes. You're stuck on the innocence of a man who had pieces of the victims in his home and Scott Harden pegging him by name." I pulled off the oven mitts. "You're wasting money in hiring me. It doesn't matter what psychological theories I give on the stand. They're going to convict him." *Because he's guilty.*

As my first logic and reasoning professor liked to say, if something smelled like shit and tasted like shit, you didn't have to see it come out of a horse's butt. I had raised my hand and asked him how we would accurately recognize what shit was supposed to taste like.

Looking at this logically, Randall was guilty. So, why was Robert defending him? To get close to the man who killed his son? To punish him in some other way?

He picked up a hand towel and slowly wiped off his hands. "I can't tell if you're intentionally frustrating me or just being obtuse."

"What?" I sputtered.

He looked at me in silence, like he was waiting for something, like I had hidden a puzzle piece behind my back, and this time, the eye contact didn't cause my knees to quiver or my heart to race. This time, I felt guilty—and maybe that's why his win record was so impressive. The sheer force of guilt admission via glare.

The timer went off again, this time for the rice, and I jabbed at the touch screen and pulled the pot off the burner. When I turned back to Robert, his expression had darkened into distrust. I had failed a test.

But what test?

~

We ate in stony silence, our plastic silverware scraping quietly against the paper plates, and I was reminded why I was single. Men were idiots. Frustrating, unreadable idiots. To think that I was worried about seduction.

He broke the silence as he was sopping up the final bite of beef sauce with his bread. "This is delicious." He took a sip of wine, which I had opened when it became obvious that neither of us was going to make conversation. "Where'd you learn to cook? Your mom?"

I folded my napkin longways in my lap and chuckled at the sexist assumption. "No, neither of my parents knew how to cook." Every meal, regardless of the day, date, holiday, or occasion, was spent the same way—staring at a crisp menu as the waiter hovered, pen raised in expectation.

"Private chef or TV dinners?" he asked with a cautious smile.

I made a face. "When I was young, we just ate out." Back then, the restaurants were always trademarked by white tablecloths and snooty staff. I cleared my throat. "As I grew older and money grew tighter, the restaurant meals were soon out of our budget." The bone-in filets and wine flights were slowly replaced with grilled chicken breasts and salads, the downward spiral coming to a dramatic low point when my father announced that we were going to have to start eating at home.

It didn't go over well and was almost immediately followed up by another announcement: my father was going to have to get a job.

My mother had flung herself onto the couch, Scarlett O'Hara–style, and started to sob. After all, she had married a phone-booth king, one with 172 booths in two airports, fourteen bus stations, five malls, and countless gas stations, each earning almost fifty dollars per week. She wasn't prepared for her new reality, one with mounting credit card debt and 172 booths that didn't cover their own real estate rent.

Cell phones were the death of our livelihood and, eventually, their marriage.

Our transition to at-home meals was painful. Mom seemed to be punishing him with every meal. Everything was too bland, too spicy, too raw, or burned. I couldn't tell if it was intentional or she was just that horrifically bad of a cook. After a few weeks, I took over the kitchen and learned as I went. To my surprise and the enormous gratitude of my father, I was a natural and was soon fixing us stuffed peppers with melted cheese, seafood fettuccine, and his personal favorite, fried pork chops.

"Thank goodness I enjoyed it. It was the one positive to come from what eventually led to Mom's alcoholism and Dad's emotional withdrawal." I took my own large sip of wine.

Robert, who had remained quiet during the story, rose and reached for my empty plate. "I wasn't close with my parents, either." He moved through the arched doorway into the kitchen and spooned a second helping onto his plate. "But I had two brothers, so I had someone else to bond with."

"I had an older brother, but he's seven years older than me, so I was a bit of an only child when things got really bad." I picked a piece of bread out of the basket and tore it in half. "Being the only child left at home taught me to be more independent. To emotionally take care of myself. It was good for my character." I glanced at him. "It was probably good for Gabe's."

He groaned. "No counseling, please. Gabe is the last thing I want to talk about."

Grieving parents often spoke constantly about their children, or not at all. It seemed that Robert was the latter. Still, a resistance to conversation wasn't an indicator that the subject should be avoided. Quite the opposite.

"You know, all the BH victims were sibling-free."

That caught his attention. "You're right." He looked at me, surprised. "Why is that?"

"It could be convenience," I remarked. "It's easier to take a teenager who travels back and forth to school alone, for instance."

He was silent for a moment. "My wife"—he cleared his throat—"wanted another child. I didn't. Gabe . . ." He sighed. "Gabe was a handful. He'd have temper tantrums over anything. It started when he was two, and I didn't have the patience for it, much less a second baby. He got better as he got older. Maybe if Natasha had brought it up again, when he was six or seven, I might have said yes, but—" He broke off. "She didn't. And then it was too late."

I tucked my foot under my thigh. "Gabe was ten when she died?"

"Yes."

"Did he push you away or cling closer to you?"

He sectioned off a piece of meat with the edge of his fork. "Both. Each day was different. Initially there was more pushing, then more clinging. I took a year off work, and that was the most he'd ever seen of me. We grew a lot closer during that year." He smoothed down the back of his hair. "Now I wish I'd never gone back to work."

I pulled my wineglass closer to me. "There are very few parents who could have taken a year off to spend time with him, or who would have. Focus on the positives of that. And as far as taking off another six years to spend with him . . ." I shook my head. "You both needed a return to normalcy. If I had been your doctor, I would have strongly recommended a return to work, for both of your sakes."

He finished chewing and swallowed, taking a sip of wine before he spoke. "What does it say that I took a year off when she died but kept working when he did?"

"It says that you haven't given yourself permission to mourn. And . . . that year off was focused on his healing and not your own."

"You know, I don't need a shrink, Gwen. All the questions, the prodding, the exploration of feelings—I've done all that before. I hired the best doctors in the country to help Gabe, and I was right there beside him as they made everything better."

The reaction rolled off me. I was used to anger and resentment from clients. My first four years in the business had been dominated by court-ordered sessions with disgruntled rage machines who didn't want any help.

"You seem like you have your life together," I said mildly. "But keep in mind that any grief techniques you learned with Natasha's death were designed for a spouse or a son. With Gabe, your grief is that of a father. It's a different scenario and carries its own and unique mountain of pain."

"One I'm handling," he said, his voice rasping.

"Well, you're defending his alleged murderer," I pointed out. "So you've veered down a rather unorthodox path of healing, if that's what you want to call it."

"It's working for me."

"Okay." I poured the final amount from the bottle of wine.

"So, the boys were all only children." He changed the subject. "What other commonalities did they have?"

I rolled with the new topic, eager to talk it through. "There's the obvious—they all fit a certain mold. Rich, good-looking, popular, seventeen years old, male. Are you familiar with the psychodynamic theory of criminology?"

"Vaguely. It has to do with unconscious personalities, right?"

I nodded. "Specifically, the development of those unconscious personalities by negative experiences. The unconscious personality, which we call the id, is the primitive drive that most of us are unaware of. The drive to eat. Sleep. Protect our loved ones. Have sex." I colored slightly and continued on. "That id is normally kept in line by your ego and superego, which are the other pieces of your personality that govern your morals and societal expectations. It tells a man that though he wants to screw his wife, he shouldn't do it in the middle of the grocery store. Or, in a less crude analogy, though you may hate your boss, killing him isn't the solution that makes the most sense, given the consequences and moral turpitude of the act."

I had his full attention, his gaze on mine. His breathing slowed, senses fully engaged, food forgotten. It was intoxicating, and I struggled to maintain my momentum.

"Serial killers are often overtaken by their id, due to a weak ego and superego. The psychodynamic theory blames those weak egos on a lack of proper development—typically during adolescence, and often from trauma. In this case . . ." I searched for the right way to explain it. "If the killer was bullied during his formative middle or high school years, it could have stunted his personal development of his ego and superego, which makes him at much higher risk for his id to manifest latent feelings of oppression toward an individual who reminds him of that bully."

"Wait." He held up his hand. "So the killer was bullied by someone who fits this mold—rich, good-looking, popular."

"*Maybe* bullied. *Maybe* molested. *Maybe* manipulated. This is just a theory," I stressed. "A possibility. But it would explain the resemblances between the boys, and the abuse. He's not just killing them. He's toying with them. He's building a relationship with them. He's fighting for their attention in every way he can get it. And then, either he loses control and they die, or he grows bored with the boy and he ends it. My profile points to the latter." I paused and took a sip of wine.

"He grows bored and kills them," he confirmed flatly.

"Yes." It was my turn to change the subject. "Can I ask you something about Randall?" At his nod, I continued. "Have any other students come forward and said anything? Male or female?"

He paused. "Not particularly. I mean, in the last twenty years? A few complaints from disgruntled students, but nothing major."

"Male or female students?" I thought of Luke, his eyes red, face trembling in rage. He couldn't have been the only one. Surely there had been more.

"All female." He picked up his fork. "Now, can the inquisition stop long enough for me to enjoy these last few bites of home cooking?"

I smiled. "Sure. Go ahead."

~

At the sink, Robert ran hot water as I packaged up the leftovers for him to take home. I glanced at him as I snapped a lid into place. He had abandoned the jacket and lost the tie, his stiff shirtsleeves now rolled up to the elbows, his posture relaxed. The change was nice.

He reached past me for a dish towel, and our sides brushed.

"So, the detective who came by earlier . . ." He picked up a sponge and began to scrub it against a pot. "What was that about?"

I put the rest of the bread in a ziplock bag and sealed it closed. "I think he's just keeping an eye on me."

"Why did you ask about John Abbott's death? They're investigating it?"

"I think they investigate all deaths, especially when it's a situation like that where two people are involved."

"Is it suspicious?"

I hesitated. *He's a defense attorney,* I reminded myself. Someone used to picking apart cases and looking at them from all sides. Still, my unease grew. What exactly had he seen in John's file? I stacked the containers and put them into a bag with the bread. "I don't think so," I said carefully. "People have heart attacks all the time. Even though Brooke was fairly young, I think she had a family history of that." John had said that to me once, hadn't he? He'd said something about her medicine, something about her mother . . . I would have made a notation if he had, especially because poisoning had always been a common method in the laundry list of ways that John wanted to kill her. As a pharmacist, it had been one of the most logical paths for him to take, but also one of the most risky in terms of drawing suspicion.

It was another reminder that I needed to do a full overview of John's file. I should have looked already, but I'd been putting it off due to guilt and the newer, more exciting distraction on my time—the BH case.

"Oh, so Brooke's death is the one they find suspicious?"

Too late, I realized the error in my response. I had replied to him while knowing the most likely true sequence of events: John kills Brooke, kills himself. Outside observers—both he and Detective Saxe—would put the bulk of attention and suspicion on the stabbing death, not the heart attack. It was why Detective Saxe had asked whether Brooke might have killed him, and what Robert had been referring to when he had asked about the case.

So, maybe he hadn't read John's file. Maybe he hadn't seen more than a line or two. Maybe all my paranoia was completely off base.

"No," I quickly amended. "They don't find her death suspicious. I was just saying that heart problems ran in her family. And John was very close to her. People handle grief in strange ways."

"So, you think it's possible that he killed himself?"

"Yeah." I turned to meet his eyes. "I do."

He nodded, returning his attention to the pot, and inside, my unease bloomed.

CHAPTER 27

I woke up alone, with the taste of regret, or potentially sour wine, in my mouth. Robert had left without incident or anything as bold as a kiss on the cheek. Now my body felt cheated. I stared up at the ceiling and realized, with a strong dose of self-loathing, that I had expected to have sex with him.

So much for my stern stance on professional distance. Thank God I hadn't made a move, though the conversation had certainly stuck to topics that doused any thoughts of romance.

My unresolved libido aside, it had been a productive meal. We had journeyed into a few light conversations about Gabe, but not enough to appease my concerns about his grief management. Instead of focusing on healing, Robert was picking up loose women after funerals and constructing what, from all outward appearances, seemed to be a very strong defense for his son's killer.

And that was the other thing keeping me up at night. The victims. The agonized faces of the parents on the news. Was I helping to free their murderer?

I wouldn't do that. I had told Robert that I would speak the truth, and he seemed to accept it, but with this sly half-amused expression that indicated he knew my game. I wished I felt so confident. I was lost, in the middle of the board, with no idea if I was ahead in the score or behind. Probably behind. Most likely, I'd fallen off the board entirely.

Clem was on my bedside table, lying on top of my cell, and I eased my hand under her belly and slid it out, prompting a hiss. Ignoring her, I unlocked my phone and checked the security alerts.

No unauthorized entry. No security-cam motion alerts. A quiet night. I let out a sigh of relief and then, before I forgot, rearmed it. Normally I left the system off for the day, often keeping the doors open for a breeze, but until I spoke to Luke, or until the police did, I needed to be smart.

Rolling out of bed, I took a hot shower, then dressed in cream khaki pants and a ribbed red tank top. Pulling out a new gray hair that had sprung onto the scene, I plaited my wet hair into a braid, then picked up Clem and headed downstairs, inhaling the smell of her. She spent most of her days in my laundry basket, and she smelled like the linen-scented dryer sheets.

On his way to the door, Robert had pressed again to see the profile. I needed to send it to him by early afternoon if I was going to stick to my timeline. There was no point in sitting on it any longer. My core avatar—an organized, control-oriented killer who had been molested or raped during his teenage or adolescent years by a wealthy and popular teenager—had cemented. I needed to get the draft off my desk and into his hands so I could focus on a more urgent task—re-reviewing John Abbott's client file. The questions about Brooke's death had made me second-guess his mention of her family history of heart trouble. I wanted to pin down the possibility and was due for a re-review anyway. With Detective Saxe still lurking around, the possibility of my client file being subpoenaed was a plausible concern. I needed to copy the file and study every moment of it, from first appointment to last.

Before diving in, I poured a bowl of cereal and watched a reality show on matchmaking. On the screen, a big-breasted blonde giggled at the male contestant. My mom loved this dumb show. On our last call, she'd spent ten minutes in a full recap of the most recent episode. That had been painful enough, but then it had segued into a critical dissection of my life. A childless, single woman in her late thirties was grounds for maternal panic, and she had bleated her concern at top volume for the bulk of the call. My job, in her opinion, was my biggest barrier to love. After all, where was I going to meet a man? The morgue?

Life would be easier without my brother, whose wife was popping out kids like a toaster on Sunday morning. You'd think all those babies would keep my mother happy, but somehow it just increased the expectation that I perform.

I ate a spoonful of cinnamon-flavored cereal. Maybe my love prospects *were* hampered by my job. While Robert's eyes had lit up in the bar when I'd mentioned my occupation, the typical response was more of a wary shudder. A very nice-looking man at a speed-dating event had once asked if I'd ever killed anyone. Another had asked if I planned to "do the counselor thing" forever.

Maybe I should start going back to church. According to my sister-in-law, that was a hotbed of eligible men. And I needed an eligible man—or a fresh batch of batteries—something to take my mind off the one bachelor I should be staying far, far away from.

Robert Kavin was hiding something. I'd felt a few seeds of suspicion early on and was growing more convinced of the possibility as time progressed. And the weird thing was—the more certain I grew that he was hiding something from me, the more certain I grew that he suspected me of something.

Initially, I thought his suspicion was around Brooke's death, given that he'd seen at least part of John Abbott's file. But which part? That was the big question. My second question was how well Robert had known John. He'd attended his funeral, so there had to have been at least an acquaintance relationship. I couldn't tell you my pharmacist's first name, let alone attend their funeral—but I also didn't have a diabetic son. Had he and John grown close enough that he'd protect the dead man's reputation and not come forward with suspicions about Brooke's death? It was possible, maybe even probable, given that I should be under investigation by the Code of Ethics board right now.

And I couldn't ignore the possibility that Robert hadn't seen anything at all. Maybe I had left open the file in an innocent place that hadn't meant anything to him, and my fears were bred from paranoia and absolutely nothing else.

I rinsed my cereal bowl under hot water and placed it in the dishwasher. Before I worked myself even further into knots, I needed to look at where I'd left John's file open on my desk. I wouldn't be able to remember the exact spot, but I had a general sense of where my review had ended and when the wine and sleepiness had won over.

I dried my hands and moved to the study, pulling on the lamp's stiff chain and illuminating the wide surface. It was clear of files, my lesson learned, my confidential documents now locked in one of the two sliding drawers of my desk. I moved the gold elephant beside the lamp to one side, revealing the small key. My security still had room for improvement.

Settling into my chair, I opened up John Abbott's thick file and flipped through the session notes until I found the area where I had last stopped. Pulling my chair tighter to the desk, I began to read.

JA is testy and irritable. Suffering from VT about wife. Worse with temper. Incident with guest—air-conditioning.

I remembered this. They'd had a guest staying with them, and the air-conditioning had gone out. John had tried to fix it himself and couldn't.

"I have a Mensa-level IQ." He'd pinned me with a look that dared argument. "I'm better educated than ninety-nine percent of people in this city. I can kill or save someone with the knowledge right here." He tapped his temple. "And she wants to call someone to fix it, doesn't think I'm smart enough. And so what if the air is out? It's not like he's paying us to stay there! Let him sweat."

I hadn't been able to figure out if his solution was to let the poor guest sweat, or if he had plans to try again with the repair. I nudged the conversation back to Brooke. "At what point did you feel like you were losing control?"

"She just wouldn't stop. Pecking at me, that's what she was doing. Continually wiping her brow so I would understand she was sweating. Asking when I was going to go outside and take a look at it. Bringing up articles on her phone and making 'helpful suggestions.'" He put air quotes around the words. "I just looked at her, sitting there on the couch, and I pictured her stomach cut open."

His words had drilled into me, as if it had been my own stomach at risk. So calm. So matter-of-fact. As if he cut into flesh on an everyday basis.

"She's getting fat," he'd added. "It bounces when she moves. I thought about that, wondered if it'd make it harder to cut or easier." He had looked at me. "What do you think?"

I'd met his gaze without flinching, because most of my clients wanted a reaction. For some, that's why they kill, because they're standing there, screaming at the ones they love, and aren't getting the feedback they want. I wasn't going to give him a reaction. "I think we need to work on you not having that visual."

Now, I ran my finger down to the next handwritten line of the notes, and my heart sank at what it said.

Not just looking for attention from me—he is a serious threat to her. High risk.

CHAPTER 28

Nita watched as her husband put their Range Rover in park, the movement deliberately slow, all of them dreading this moment. She twisted to unlock her belt and glanced into the back seat, where Scott sat, his body slumped against the window, his gaze out on the police parking lot.

"I don't want to go back in there," he said quietly. "You know what they did to me last time."

She closed her eyes, blocking out the memory. The medical examiner had told her that it would be quick—a DNA swab of his genitals and a rape exam kit. It had just taken fifteen minutes, and Scott hadn't met her eyes when he'd come back to the waiting room. He'd even walked differently. She thought of college, when her roommate had gotten drunk and blacked out and Nita had taken her the following day to the women's crisis center to see if she had been raped. Her roommate had sobbed the entire way home and said that she would have rather not known than undergone that exam.

"They're just going to ask you questions." Their attorney, who had gone to college with George, spoke up from behind her. "And I'll be right there."

"But I have to answer all their questions?"

"I'll step in if they ask you anything that is inappropriate. But we need you to be honest with them, Scott. It'll help with their case against Mr. Thompson."

Scott limply pulled on the door release handle and slowly stepped out of the car. Nita met her husband's eyes.

George gave her a reassuring smile. "It'll be okay," he said quietly.

But would it? How could it ever be okay again?

~

As they moved down the hall of the police station, the heel of Nita's sandal caught on an uneven piece of flooring, and she stumbled forward. George caught her, helping her back upright, and she smiled at him in gratitude. She should have worn flats. After months in her pajamas and slippers, she felt off-balance in high heels. Assuming she didn't fall flat on her face, they just needed to get through this questioning so they could get back home. They weren't criminals, and Scott wasn't under suspicion. While there would eventually be a trial, for now, they could knock out these inquiries, then get back in their Range Rover and go to lunch. She could sip an ice-cold mimosa and they could discuss college. Not Vanderbilt, not anymore. He should be closer to home, given everything that had happened. Pepperdine would be perfect. Small, private, and safe.

Crowding into the small viewing room, she looked through the glass at Scott, who was seated, their attorney right beside him. Juan was good, though criminal law wasn't his specialty. Still, he'd known Scott his entire life, and this questioning, as the detectives had assured them, was mostly fact-finding. Fifteen or twenty minutes, tops.

Detective Erica Petts cleared her throat. "Scott, I need you to tell me about the place where you were kept."

Nita shifted on her heels. Scott had already told them that he didn't know, that he'd been blindfolded. *Blindfolded for seven weeks?* they had asked. Seven weeks of darkness—no wonder he couldn't sleep. It was amazing he didn't need a lamp left on in his room.

"I don't know anything about it," he mumbled. "I was blindfolded."

Look up, Nita wanted to shout. *Look into their eyes so they believe you.*

"Well, you were blindfolded in the room. But then you escaped, right? So we need to know what you saw when you got your hands loose. You took off the blindfold then, right?"

"It was dark," Scott said. "I felt my way to the door and then down the hall. I was running. I didn't really see anything until I got outside."

"And you didn't have to go down or up any stairs to get outside?"

He hesitated. "No."

"Was he in the house? Did he live there?"

"I—I don't know."

But they did know, didn't they? The police had searched Randall Thompson's house top to bottom and decided he hadn't kept Scott there, but at some other location. And the morning that Scott had escaped, he'd been at school, teaching. Nita had learned that not from the detectives but from the news. The detectives had kept them in the dark on everything.

The pair grilled him on the neighborhood he'd run through on his way out. What he described—quiet streets with run-down homes—could have matched a hundred Los Angeles neighborhoods. What she hadn't understood, what she *still* didn't understand, was why he hadn't stopped at one of those houses for help. Why hadn't he flagged down a car? Why had he run for miles, all the way home?

"Let's go back to the room where you were kept. We understand that you didn't see anything, but let's talk about what you could hear, what you could smell. Could you hear any activity in the house?" This was the other officer, the chubby male, who stood in the corner, one foot crossed over the other.

Scott paused. "I don't think so."

"When he came into the room, would he open a door? Did you hear him coming down the hall? Think about how you knew he was there."

Scott rubbed at his forehead. "I don't know. I guess I heard a door open. I don't remember any stairs."

"Take your time," Detective Harvey urged. "In the room, was it carpet or solid floor? Could you hear his footsteps?"

"Solid floor." He swallowed. This was ridiculous. They knew who the killer was. Why did these details matter? It wasn't fair to make Scott relive all this.

"Okay, so you couldn't hear any noise from other rooms? What about a TV, maybe playing nearby?"

"Uh, I don't think so."

"Road noise? Trucks? Horns?"

"No."

"What about the temperature in the room?" The male detective crossed in front of the glass. "Was it hot?"

"Sometimes."

"Was the space air-conditioned? Did you hear the air-conditioning coming on and off?"

"I don't know."

Nita could sense their frustration, could hear it in the way their questions were beginning to clip at the ends. Maybe they'd stop. Throw up their hands and let Scott leave.

"Okay, so no sound. What about smell?" Detective Petts leaned back in her chair. "Maybe must or mildew?"

Scott inhaled, like he was smelling it all over again. "Maybe a little like mothballs."

"So, you picked the lock open on your handcuffs, is that right?"

The abrupt shift in questioning caught her son off guard. His gaze darted to their attorney, then he nodded. "Yeah."

"Not an easy thing to do with a fork." Detective Petts looked at Harvey, who nodded in agreement. Nita straightened, her hackles rising at the woman's tone.

"Well, I didn't really pick it," Scott hedged. "It wasn't locked in place right. Normally it was tight, but this time it wasn't, so I could pull my hand out."

This was new. Nita frowned, her gaze catching with her husband's. They'd both heard the story a dozen times. Scott loved to talk about how he had popped open the cuffs.

"Ah, now, see—that makes more sense. Because we were beginning to wonder," Harvey said.

There was that tone again. Like they were playing with him.

"You said you were blindfolded in the room, and you don't know how you got in the room, right?"

"Yeah." Scott looked miserable, and she needed to get him out of here.

"So, how do you know it was Mr. Thompson? If you couldn't see, it could have been anyone."

"I saw him when I was taken. He was next to my truck. He was the one who stabbed me with something."

A sedative of some sort. That's what they'd said. The police had long suspected the BH Killer had drugged the boys with something, but Scott had given them the confirmation—it had been a shot, not anything put in his food or drink.

"And you recognized his voice? In the room? Because he might have taken you but then passed you off to someone else."

Scott wavered. "No," he said finally. "It was him. He would talk to me." He nodded, his gaze glued to the table. "Yeah. Him. He was a pervert. He told me about things he'd done. Girl students he raped."

There was a moment of silence as the room absorbed the new information. George put his arm around Nita and squeezed her to his side.

"Any girls you know? Names you could give us?"

He shook his head and crossed his arms over his chest, and she knew a stubborn streak when it was coming. He was about to clam up. To get defiant.

"Did he tell you why he was doing this?"

Scott didn't move, didn't speak, didn't acknowledge the question. Hot under George's arm, Nita pushed free and mentally begged her son to respond.

"He just said he needed to put me in my place." He tucked his chin against his chest, and the next words were soft, almost so soft that she couldn't hear it.

"What was that, Scott?"

"He said it was fun. That he liked to hurt me. And he liked to watch."

"Watch what?"

She held her breath, almost afraid to hear the answer.

Her son shrugged. "All of it." He ran a hand through his shaggy blond hair, pulling it forward over his face, and stood. "I need a break." He looked at his attorney. "Can I take a break?"

"Sure," Detective Harvey said. "Take your time."

Nita thought he'd come to her, but he didn't. He walked out of the police station and to their SUV, where he sat for almost twenty minutes, just staring out the windshield. Motionless. Still. The boy who couldn't go a few minutes without looking at his phone sat there, like a zombie, before finally opening the vehicle door and stepping out, his gait slow and laborious as he walked back to her and George and Juan.

When he sat back down with the detectives, it was a different version of her son. One with a straighter back and a slower, more confident voice. And this time, he told a new story.

CHAPTER 29

I couldn't get the dead boys out of my mind. Pushing the grocery cart, I moved past a display of strawberries and tried not to compare the bright-red hue of the fruit with the crime scene photos of the bloodied flesh.

I had seen plenty of evil in my life, had studied countless individuals who killed without reason or intent, but these deaths were sticking to me with a clawlike intensity. These deaths weren't random. The careful and consistent structure of kills . . . the ramp-up. Even Scott Harden's escape . . . it all meant something.

I paused at the meat counter and picked up a package of chicken thighs and a rack of lamb. Pushing forward, I almost bumped my cart into the woman in front of me. She turned, and I gave an apologetic smile, then started in recognition.

"Lela! Hello."

Her eyes lit up. "Dr. Moore," she purred. "How are you?"

"I'm good." I pushed my cart out of the main aisle. "I'm sorry about rescheduling our appointment next week. I've got a court case I have to prep for."

She waved off the apology. "Does it have anything to do with the BH Killer? I saw that handsome attorney at your office last week. The one on the news, whose son died."

"No, it's about something unrelated." Just what I needed—Lela Grant blabbing all over town about Robert.

"You know, my daughter is at Beverly High. She knows Scott Harden, almost went on a date with him once!" She beamed, like it would be wonderful if her daughter could have been connected with a boy who was kidnapped, tortured, and almost died.

I picked up a glass bottle of almonds that I didn't need and looked for a way to exit the conversation. "How are things at home?"

"Oh, they're okay." A younger version of her came around the corner and tossed a family-size box of marshmallow cereal in the end of her cart. "Maggie, can you say hi to Dr. Moore?"

The teenager examined my red ballet slippers with a sneer. "Can I say hi? Of course I can."

I ignored her entirely.

"Maggie," Lela pleaded, and I wondered if her inability to control her child was one of the reasons she manifested violent fantasies about her sister-in-law, a woman who seemed to have flawless control over her life.

The teenager pushed her hair out of her eyes, and I saw the scars on the insides of her arms. Old and new. Crisscrosses of pain and depression. My eyes met Lela's.

"Maggie, will you grab us some ice cream?" she suggested brightly. "Whatever flavor you want."

The girl turned without responding and slunk down the aisle.

I waited until she was out of sight, then spoke. "How long has she been cutting herself?"

She sighed. "About two months. I try and keep up with Neosporin, but as soon as the wounds heal, she opens them up again."

Something about the statement snagged in my brain. What was it? I nodded politely as I tried to chase it down. "Have you taken her to see anyone?"

"It's just teenage heartbreak. You know, boys." She dismissed the cuttings with a shrug. "But, yeah—we're taking her to Dr. Febber at the Banyon Clinic. They specialize in teenagers. In fact, you'll never guess who we once saw there." She leaned in closer, and her wheels squeaked.

"Please don't tell me." I forced a polite smile. "Patient confidentiality is one of our pet peeves as doctors. Especially in mental health areas."

Her face fell in disappointment. "Oh. Yeah. Sure."

"Anyway, I'll see you week after next? Back on our normal schedule?"

"Uh-huh," she said listlessly. "Sure."

Lela turned her cart around and lifted her hand in parting. I echoed the action. Poor Maggie. I'd had six sessions with Lela, and she'd never mentioned her daughter's struggles.

I turned down the dairy aisle and picked up a gallon of milk, then a box of salted butter. What was it about our conversation that had jabbed at me? I moved back through it in my head.

Her daughter . . . Beverly High . . . Scott . . .

I stopped at the chilled wines and picked up a bottle of sauvignon blanc. I wedged it into an open space beside the milk and pushed the cart forward. Ahead of me, the line at the pharmacy thinned, and I quickened my pace, hoping to get in while there wasn't a wait. I was coming down with something and needed to get a nasal spray before it got too bad.

I parked my cart, grabbed my purse, and stood in line. Maybe I shouldn't have rushed the conversation with Lela, especially since I wasn't meeting with her this week. The line inched up, and I made a mental note to continue our conversation about her daughter in future sessions.

Bored, I studied an end display of bandages, antibiotic creams, and other first-aid supplies.

I try and keep up with Neosporin, but as soon as the wounds heal, she opens them up again.

Was that what had stuck in my mind? If so, why? I closed my eyes, focusing on the image of Lela putting Neosporin on Maggie's cuts. While it was an interesting visual, my mind stubbornly refused to cooperate. Behind me, someone cleared their throat. I opened my eyes and stepped forward.

Neosporin . . . Neosporin . . . Wounds heal.

The images from the BH files snapped into view. Close-ups of wounds. Cigarette burns. Cuts. Some healed, others fresh. I undid the top clasp of my purse and pulled out my phone. Checking the time on it, I called the office and hoped Jacob was still there.

His calm greeting brought a smile to my face.

"Jacob, it's Gwen. Can you go in my office? I need you to take a picture of something."

I waited as he found his keys and unlocked my office. Giving him directions, I led him to the area of the wall where I had pinned photos of all the wounds.

He made a noise of discomfort.

"I know, they're gory. Can you take pictures of the entire section? Close enough so I can zoom in on the photos, please."

"All of them?"

"Yes, you can get three or four in each photo."

"Okay. I'll text them to you."

"Thank you. Please be sure to lock the door when you're done."

I ended the call and moved up, now only second in line. I was swiping my credit card and accepting the nasal spray when my phone began to buzz with incoming texts. Returning to my cart, I opened the group of images and began to scroll through them.

It was a good thing I hadn't eaten. The photos were a horror show of pain, the worst being the penectomy close-ups. I swiped quickly through those and zoomed in when I found the image that had jogged my memory.

It was a neat line of cigarette burns down the center of a back. Unremarkable, except for the sheen that covered them. Almost like a snail had traveled across the wounds. It was ointment or aloe vera, and applied on an area that the victim could never have reached himself.

The BH Killer was doctoring them. Hurting them, then patching them back up. Why? Remorse? Guilt? Or was it something else, something deeper?

I looked up from my phone and thought through the implications of this. This was wrong—in complete conflict with the psychological profile I had created. An organized control-oriented killer didn't provide first aid, not unless it was to keep his victim alive for a specific purpose. These wounds weren't life threatening, so they didn't require first aid. This was almost . . . I thought of Meredith, her question of aftercare. Yes. This was potentially aftercare, which, again, didn't match my profile. While there were no absolutes in human psychology, there were patterns, and this would be breaking every pattern of human behavior.

I stuffed my phone in my bag and gripped the handles of the cart, spinning it to the left and heading toward the checkout, skipping the rest of my shopping list as I beelined for the shortest queue.

I had known that something was off. Maybe this was the key to figuring out what that was.

CHAPTER 30

I dropped the groceries off at the house and drove to the office. It was dark, Jacob's computer powered off, the only illumination coming from an **EMERGENCY EXIT** sign above the stairwell. I flipped on the lights in my office and powered up my iMac. As it hummed to life, I cleared off my desk and withdrew the stack of case files.

I undid the thick rubber bands around each file and spaced them out around the large surface of my desk, putting Gabe Kavin's in the middle.

My computer chimed, and I logged in, then pulled up the twenty-two-page psychological profile I had sent to Robert. I printed out two copies of the document and grabbed a red pen. Flipping on the desk lamp, I curved the neck so it shone down on the folders.

My first order of business was to determine if there was actually aftercare involved, or if the photo Jacob had sent me was an exception to the rule.

I opened the first file.

Trey Winkle was seventeen, a lacrosse player from Serra Retreat. He was found in a ditch along the entrance road to the Griffith Observatory. I flipped to the autopsy section and scanned the findings.

Some adhesive residue along a deep cut in his thigh. The wound was clean and looked cared for. A Band-Aid would be the likely explanation for the residue.

My killer wouldn't use a Band-Aid.

I flipped to the next victim. Travis Patterson. Well fed. His hair was clean. Partially healed wounds.

I pulled out a pad of paper and took notes, moving through all five files before getting to Gabe Kavin's.

I took a deep breath. A pattern was already established, but Gabe had been an anomaly from the start. His death was more brutal—maybe his care had been skipped.

But it hadn't. Like the others, he was healthy at the time of his death. Also well fed and cared for, if you ignored the torture and rape every couple of days.

I set down the pen and rubbed my temple. If guilt and regret were responsible for the kindnesses, but the individual was still engaging in habitual violence, then we were talking about a disorder. This wasn't bipolar disorder or borderline personality disorder. That would be characterized by manic swings or episodes, and there was no way that a manic individual would be able to execute this level of evidence-free and precise pattern kills.

I leaned back in my chair with a groan and looked up at the tray ceiling.

If the aftercare was an established pattern, which it was . . .

If the abductions, captivity, and kills had been well planned and executed with careful timing, which they were . . .

If signs pointed to a killer's history of personal trauma, which they did . . .

Paranoid schizophrenia—PS—or dissociative identity disorder—DID—were the most likely culprits.

Paranoid schizophrenia was the most common mental disorder diagnosed among any criminal, but especially serial killers. David Berkowitz, Ed Gein, Richard Chase, Jared Lee Loughner . . . Randall Thompson could easily be joining their ranks. The disorder was characterized by delusions, and typically, in a case like this, voices or visions that dictated a person's actions. An imaginary individual might be orchestrating and ordering the violent actions, and the killer's true personality is the one caring for and comforting the patient in the aftermath. Or—and more likely—vice versa.

Dissociative identity disorder was commonly known as multiple personality disorder. If accurate, it would mean that the BH Killer was acting in separate personas. Maybe two, maybe more.

I'd had a client with DID before. It was one of psychology's more complicated diagnoses, and every case was different. Often it was triggered by a severe emotional or physical trauma. Sometimes it could be "cured" by therapy; often it could not. In the more publicized cases, the secondary personalities could be quite violent.

As impossible as it probably was, I needed to talk to Scott Harden. His interactions with the killer would help me understand if it was a clear switch from one personality to another, or a mental communication with a delusion. There was a big difference, one that he should have been able to distinguish, especially after seven weeks as a prisoner.

While PS was practically a given, DID was a big criminological jump to take. If I was wrong, it'd be a huge blow to my credibility and reputation. And once the press caught word of it, the media coverage would flare like a California brush fire in September.

I tapped the pen against the page. Simply put, I didn't have enough to go on and should keep all this to myself until I knew more.

My interview with Randall was set for Wednesday. In that first impression, I should get at least a general sense of the sort of individual I was dealing with. And Robert's office had to have private investigators they could hire. DID-affected individuals left clues that an investigator could unearth. Missed appointments. Forgetfulness. Unexplained outbursts.

The elevator dinged, and I glanced through my open office door, my tension easing as a woman and a cleaning cart exited the car and rolled into the reception area.

Luke had been eerily quiet. The police had finally found him, questioned him, and gotten bubkes in answers. According to Luke, he hadn't taken my wallet or keys. I reported all my cards stolen and wasted my entire Sunday afternoon ordering new IDs, club cards, and a replacement fob for my car. The police had nothing to charge Luke with, so he left. Since then, he hadn't made any effort to contact me, which should have been reassuring, but it wasn't. Instead, the silence felt like the pregnant pause in a horror movie, right before the chain saw–wielding villain springs out.

I closed the file and stood, leaning over and gathering each folder into place, then stacking them all in the middle of my desk. Moving my mouse, I disrupted the screen saver, then shut down my computer.

I needed to get home and, for the rest of the evening, try not to think about death.

CHAPTER 31

Robert's door was ajar, his attention on his monitor, and I rapped my knuckles lightly against the wood, then ventured a step in. "Hey."

He looked up and raised his eyebrows, surprised. "Hey. Come on in. You could have just called me back."

"I was in the area. My tailor is three blocks down."

"Frank and Pat?"

I smiled. "Yeah. Best needles in Los Angeles."

He gestured to the chairs before his desk. "Please, sit. I just wanted to talk about your profile."

I took the left seat and glanced over at the goldfish. Still alive. "Sure."

"It's great work. Good stuff."

I sighed. "But?"

He tented his hands before his face and studied me. "It feels like you're holding something back. What is it?"

Damn attorneys. The good ones were way too good at reading between the lines and finding holes. I had barely had the chance for my new theories to solidify in my mind and wasn't ready to present or defend them. Not yet, and not before talking to Randall Thompson. I cleared my throat and evaded the question. "I'm holding something back?" I countered. "What are *you* holding back?"

He ignored the response. "Tell me who this psychological profile fits."

"I don't know," I said exasperatedly. "I haven't interviewed Randall yet."

"Fuck Randall."

The harsh verb caused me to flinch.

"Who else?" He stared me down as if I were the one on the stand. "Does it fit any of your clients?"

"Is that why you hired me? For access to my clients?"

"Answer the question, Gwen."

"No," I sputtered. "This profile isn't like any of my clients." I said it without going through my roster, because SCREW HIM. It wouldn't matter if one of my clients was an identical match to this profile. I paused. I couldn't say in good faith that I wouldn't tell someone, because I would. But I'd go to the police. I'd tell Detective Saxe, not this prick. "You know what?" I rose from my seat and snatched my purse off the floor. "I'm done here. I don't have time to play games."

"He killed my son."

And just like that, with those four cracked words, my anger deflated. He was allowed to play games. He was allowed to get dirty. Someone had stolen his son, raped him of his innocence, dry drowned him, then dropped his body in a drainage ditch behind a recycling plant. Who was I to be mad at him for something, anything, that he did in an attempt to catch his son's killer?

"What aren't you telling me?" he asked tightly.

I turned back to face him. "It's just a theory," I managed.

"About the killer?"

I gripped the top of the leather chair. "Yes."

"Tell me."

I sighed. "It's not confirmed, and needs some research. A private investigator would help. And I need to speak with Randall. Multiple times, if possible. I could share my ideas with you now, but it'll only be a distraction. What's in my report is more solid. Much more solid."

I met his eyes, and the pain in them was raw and flaring. It'd only been nine months since he had buried his son. Too soon.

"It could be wrong," I pointed out quietly.

"Just tell me," he bit out.

"There are contrasting actions on the part of the killer. He hurts them and then puts salve on their wounds. Tortures them but feeds them well. His actions show dramatic swings in his compassion levels. Some actions are almost loving, then you have the barbaric act of removing their genitalia."

I inhaled, prepared for ridicule the moment my next words came out. "It's *possible* that the swings are consistent with someone with either paranoid schizophrenia or dissociative identity disorder."

Robert looked down at the printed profile before him and let out a quiet snort. It wasn't quite a laugh, but it wasn't the intelligent reception of the idea that I was hoping for.

"Like I said," I told him stiffly, "it's not something I could stand by in court."

"But you believe it. If your child was the one who had died, you would pursue this path of thinking?" He looked back up at me.

No. It was too risky. I swallowed. "I'd keep it in the back of my mind, but I wouldn't commit to it."

He held his stare on me for a long time, and it was the sort of look you put on a Where's Waldo board. An intent focus, looking for the one piece that doesn't match the rest. I shifted, uncomfortable under the scrutiny.

"What?" I finally asked.

"I'm just trying to figure out if you're really smart or really dumb."

"That's funny," I said dryly. "I spend most of my time trying to figure out if you've lost your mind or can somehow see the future."

He chuckled. "Okay, let's talk in arguable ideas for a moment." He tapped the top of a stack of pages, and I glanced at it, recognizing the cover page of my profile. "You've given me a potential psychological picture of the killer." He shook his head. "I'm going to ignore the possibility of a psychological disorder for now. Let's assume he's a single male, likely sexually abused or seduced by a popular teenage peer when he was young. Highly organized, control freak, intelligent, and analytical."

"Yes."

"So let's go." He scooped up a small ring of keys from his desk. "Let's see if Randall fits the bill."

I glanced at my watch. "Right now? I have an appointment on Wednesday to meet with him." It seemed reckless to head to the jail without planning and emotional preparation, especially given my new potential diagnoses. This was big, the biggest moment of my career. What if I asked the wrong question? What if he said something historic and I wasn't prepared?

"Why not? You can go Wednesday, also." He held open his office door, his brows rising in question. "I thought talking to killers was what you did."

"I thought he wasn't a killer," I countered.

A grin pulled at the corner of his mouth. "Well, let's find out."

CHAPTER 32

"You don't seem nervous." Robert emptied out his pockets into a small bowl held out by the security guard.

"I'm not nervous. A little excited."

He chuckled. "Excited . . . that's an interesting emotion to have."

We moved through the metal detectors, then waited for our items to pass through the conveyor belt. I looked down. "Cute socks." They were a gray argyle with small flamingos printed across them.

He moved his toes in response. "Cute polish. Would you call that magenta?"

"I was thinking plum."

He grabbed my heels off the belt and passed them to me. We sat in the metal folding chairs against the wall and put our shoes back on. I glanced at the security guards, who were laughing at something. "How often have you visited him?"

"Randall? Every other day."

"Really?" I stood and waited for him to finish tying his shoes. "That seems like a lot. You have that much to talk about?"

"Not really. Most of them are more of a pep-talk visit." He stood and retucked the back of his shirt in. "He's not doing too well."

"Does anyone do well in prison?" I asked.

His hand gently rested on the small of my back as he guided me to the left hall. "I'm worried about him. I'll be curious what you think about his mental fortitude after talking to him."

"He's still maintaining his innocence?"

He sighed. "Yes." He pressed an elevator call button, and we paused, waiting.

I glanced at a camera that pointed down at us. "You know it's weird, right? That you're defending a man who is on trial for murdering your son?"

We stepped into the elevator.

"I wouldn't defend him if I thought he was guilty."

"Have you defended guilty people before?"

"Sure." He selected the third floor. "But I wouldn't in this situation, for obvious reasons."

"So, you're willing to overlook morality, unless it involves your family."

He let out an irritated huff. "I wouldn't put it that way." He turned his gaze to me. "But sure, my moral compass can be off at times. Same as yours."

I folded my arms across my chest. "In what way is mine off?"

"Well, I defend the guilty. You protect them." The elevator doors opened, and I waited for him to get out. He didn't.

I followed his lead and stayed in place. "How do I protect the guilty?"

His face hardened. "Pop quiz, Dr. Gwen. What do you do when a patient confesses their secrets to you?"

I paused, and the elevator doors closed, isolating us in the small space. "Depends on the secret."

He gave an unamused chuckle. "Ah, depends on the secret. Okay, I'll play. Have you *ever* turned in one of your clients or reported anything that was told to you in a session?"

Something in the way he asked the question made it seem like it was wrong that I'd never broken a client's confidence. "No," I said carefully.

"Have any ever confessed to a crime?"

I hesitated. Yes, of course they had. That was why a lot of them were clients. To sort out guilt and regret and learn from their pasts and how to prevent future violence from occurring. "Yes," I said flatly.

"Have any of them told you about a future crime they were planning?"

On this one, I stayed silent. I wasn't the one on trial here. I didn't have to answer to him. I had doctor-patient confidentiality on my side and—if you pretended that John Abbott didn't exist—I had a spotless track record in deciding which confidences to keep.

A spotless track record, assuming your clients tell you everything, a little voice inside my head whispered, and it was the same one that kept me awake on the bad nights. The truth of the matter was, I didn't know everything my clients did. I knew what they told me. They shared a lot, but they kept secrets from me, too. Did Louis really stop beating his wife? I wouldn't know. Did Carlos still kill stray animals? Had he ever hurt a person?

All I knew was what they chose to tell me. That was it.

Robert rested his weight against the far wall, giving me plenty of room. "You got quiet all of a sudden, Doc."

I reached out and pressed the "3" button, grateful when the doors immediately opened. Stepping out into the hall, I plowed forward, hoping I was heading in the right direction.

"It's this direction," Robert called out.

Of course it was. I pulled a tight 180 and forced a breezy smile. "Please, lead the way."

He studied me for a moment, then started down the hall. Shaking his head, he mumbled something under his breath.

I didn't ask him to speak up. Right then, I didn't really want to know what he had to say.

~

Randall Thompson sat in a folding chair in the center of a glassed-in room. We were led to the adjacent room, and I frowned as the door was shut behind us. "Why aren't we in with him?" I'd done this before, multiple times, and even with violent offenders, I was always in the same room as them.

"Safety," Robert said.

The guard pulled aside a curtain, and we were exposed to the man through a large window of glass. The older man seemed half-asleep, his wrists and ankles both secured by handcuffs, the latter of which were linked through a ring on the floor. "I think we'll be fine."

"They aren't worried about us." He scratched the back of his neck. "They're worried about me."

"You?" It took a moment to process, then was absurdly obvious. Of course. There was no way they'd allow the parent of a victim in the same room with his alleged killer. "Oh." I let out an awkward laugh. "Well, let me go in with him."

"He can hear and see us," Robert said. "You can just press the button, and it'll open up the microphone so you can talk to him."

"No." I knocked on the glass window between us and the guard. "I want to be in the room with him."

"But—" Robert's comment was cut off by the guard, who opened the door.

"Everything okay?"

"I'd like to meet with Mr. Thompson in his meeting room." I pulled out my credentials. "I'm on the approved list."

The guard glanced from me to Robert. "Just you?"

"Yes."

Robert stayed silent, but I could feel the irritation radiating from him.

The guard shrugged. "Okay."

～

It took them five minutes to counsel me on the safety protocol, make sure I didn't have any weapons or contraband on me, and do a rigorous pat-down. I verified and reverified that I would have privacy inside the room, then I was stepping into the bare area. Randall Thompson turned his head and looked at me.

"Who are you?" he asked warily.

"I'm Dr. Gwen Moore." I walked to the center of the window and turned my back to it, aware that Robert and the guards were watching each move I took. "I'm a psychiatrist who specializes in clients with violent tendencies."

"Let me guess. You're here to decide if I'm crazy?"

"Actually . . ." I dragged a chair over from the corner, its feet shrieking against the floor in protest. "I'm here to see if Robert Kavin is crazy."

It was an intentional move, one designed to pull the focus off him and lighten up the mood. An attention seeker would immediately react in a way that would yank the conversation back to him. Randall found the comment amusing. The change was visible, his shoulders losing some of their defeated slump, his spine stiffening back to life. "Are you serious?"

"Completely." I sat down in the chair. "A grieving father defending his son's killer?" I made a face. "Come on."

"I'm not a killer." His voice was quiet but firm. Resolute, with no attempt at eye contact and no fidgeting or change in his breathing. Either he was a good liar, or he was telling the truth.

Could he be telling the truth? I frowned, worried at the implications of that possibility, which would mean that the Bloody Heart Killer was still out there.

"Okay," I said simply. "But how does Robert Kavin know that?"

He glanced at the window. "Is he out there?"

"Yes. But he can't hear us. I'm a doctor, so you and I have our own form of confidentiality."

He shifted in the chair, uncomfortable with the conversation. The chain between his ankles clanked against the floor hook and seemed to remind him of his position. He sobered, glancing at the floor restraint, then back at me. "I don't know why he's defending me, but he's the only person who believes me. If you're here for me to throw dirt on him, you're barking up the wrong tree."

"I can respect that." I leaned forward and rested my forearms on my knees. "Got any questions for me?"

This surprised him, and it was a method I used a lot with new clients. They were always so on guard, so used to defending and protecting themselves that they normally jumped on the chance to ask me something. And no matter what they asked, I was honest with them. You couldn't earn trust without giving it.

"Is that why you're really here? To ask me about him?" He nodded to the window, and Robert was probably beside himself trying to figure out what we were talking about.

I tucked a loose piece of hair back into my bun. "I was brought on your legal team to write a psychological profile. Not on *you*—but to give my impression of what type of person the Bloody Heart Killer is."

His nails were bitten to the quick, dried blood around the outside of one cuticle. His beard was overgrown and unkempt, his eyebrows bushy instead of tamed. The overgrown beard could be a product of his time in prison, but the bitten nails were a sign of poor self-control. The eyebrows were indicative of long-term physical negligence. Neither matched the BH Killer, though poor personal hygiene was one of the symptoms of paranoid schizophrenia. So were slow movements, and if Randall Thompson moved less, he'd be asleep.

I cleared my throat. "I created a psychological profile and need to compare you to that profile and see if it's a match. That's why I'm here, and why I was hired by Robert. Who, by the way, seems convinced of your innocence." I stared at him until he lifted his eyes and met mine. "How'd he end up as your attorney?"

"He showed up shortly after I was arrested and offered to represent me." He cleared his throat. "I'm not exactly in a position to be choosy."

No, he wasn't. After sending my profile to Robert, I had caught up on the television reports and the news articles on Randall. The media had done an excellent job of dissecting and documenting his unimpressive life. He lived in a run-down home that had belonged to his parents, earned a menial wage from teaching, and was a strip-mall Santa each holiday season. He kept the beard and belly year-round and had the pallor of someone who rarely saw sunlight.

I didn't like it. It didn't feel right for the BH Killer. I switched tactics. "We know someone in common." I clipped my pen into the top of my binder. "Luke Attens." I watched him closely, waiting for a reaction to the mention.

He stared at me blankly, and unless this guy grew a personality when he drank coffee, I didn't know how he'd ever earned a nomination for Teacher of the Year.

"Luke Attens," I repeated. "He was a student of yours."

"Oh." He nodded, but there was nothing there. "Okay. How long ago?"

"I'm not sure exactly. Probably ten years ago."

He lifted his shoulders in a half shrug. "Lots of kids come through my classroom. Two hundred a year. It's hard to keep track of them all."

I thought of Luke, of the raw rage trembling through his features, and how he would react if he knew that Randall Thompson didn't remember him.

I took a risk and lied, filling in the blanks that Luke Attens had given me and hoping it would goad Randall Thompson into revealing something. "He says that you acted inappropriately toward him. Sexually."

His features immediately shuttered, a door closing in my face. "No. Absolutely not."

"Maybe you don't remember it," I suggested.

He looked me right in the eye, and it was the most energy he'd given me so far. "I'm not a fag," he said emphatically, and the corner of his lip lifted in a sneer.

Hmm. One key that fit into place. Strong disdain toward homosexuality. And there was something in those eyes, in the flare of emotion, that read *predator.* I'd been around too many dangerous individuals to not recognize one in the flesh. This one was slow and old—would probably wheeze over and die while chasing you through the woods—but there was still something rotten behind that wary stare.

My impressions of him clicked through my mind. What matched my profile, what didn't. My instincts on his character versus my clinical opinion and the profile. He wasn't an innocent man, despite what Robert protested. Had mild signs of paranoid schizophrenia, but poor hygiene and slow movements weren't unique identifiers.

The big question was, was he the BH Killer?

~

Robert waited until we were out of the jail and halfway across the parking lot before asking my thoughts.

"I don't know yet. Let me go through my notes." I noticed a news van at the far end of the lot, a camera pointed our way, and increased my speed.

"Gwen . . ." It was more of a warning than a plea. He unlocked his car, and the lights on the Mercedes flashed.

I met his eyes over the roof of the car and fished in my purse for my own keys. "These aren't building blocks, Robert. I can't just tell you if a round peg fits in a hole. I need to absorb everything he said."

"Fine. Let's talk later tonight. Drinks at my house."

I glanced toward the cameras, aware that one was headed our way. "What about tomorrow? I'll call your office and schedule an appointment."

His grin was almost wolfish when it unfurled across that mouth. "Oh, come on. If I spend any more time in my office, I'll go batty. We can relax at the house. Sit by the outdoor fire. Trust me, I'll be a perfect gentleman."

And he always had been. The issue was on my end. I had never been to his house, but I was assuming it was like the rest of him. Smooth. Tempting. A siren's call to slip off your heels, unbutton your blouse, and guzzle wine like a cheap whore. "Tomorrow," I tried again. "I'm free in the afternoon."

He opened his car door and prepared to step inside, his final words tossed over the roof of the car as he disappeared inside. "Come by the house at eight. I'll text you the address."

No, I thought. *No.* His engine purred to life, and I took a step back, then glanced around for my car. Spotting it three rows over, I headed toward it. As Robert's Mercedes swung past me, I didn't turn my head and didn't acknowledge it.

No, I thought. *I will not be at your house at eight.* I needed a desk between us. Papers and folders and staples and desk lamps. A receptionist in the background. Order applied to the chaos.

The stance sounded good, but I was already picking out lingerie and shaving my legs, my body humming in anticipation of what the night might bring.

I stepped into the warmth of my car and unlocked the roof, needing as much fresh air as I could get. I had a bigger problem than my libido, and that was that both men inside that jail—Robert and Randall—had been lying to me. I would face one of them again in a courtroom, and the other in just a few hours in his home.

Both were lying, but were both of them dangerous?

CHAPTER 33

Nita flipped through a catalog of patio furniture at the kitchen counter. Beside her, Beth, their chef, started the mixer on a large batch of brownies.

"Would you like me to turn off the television, Mrs. Harden?"

Nita glanced at the screen that hung above the stainless double ovens. The news had moved off their discussion of restaurant regulations and was now showing an aerial view of the jail where Randall Thompson was being kept. "No, it's okay." She set down the catalog and watched as the camera showed a close-up of the jail's sign. Was this the moment that they would share the update on Scott? Ever since he'd changed his story and admitted he'd lied . . . she'd been tense, waiting for the media to sniff out the news and explode into action.

It hadn't happened yet, but it would. Any minute, any day, the story would break, and they would become instant villains. Accused of obstructing justice. Lying. Scott's hero status would immediately be stripped, his reputation forever tarnished.

The newscaster spoke. "Randall Thompson's legal defense team has grown to include Dr. Gwen Moore, a psychiatrist who specializes in criminal behavior."

The camera zoomed in on the entry doors, where Randall's attorney ushered out a tall brunette in a black suit. Nita's stomach instinctively rolled at the sight of Robert Kavin. When Scott had first gone missing, Kavin had been one of the first to reach out. It had been nice, speaking to someone who had gone through the same thing she and her husband had, someone who could truly understand the horrible roller coaster of emotions involved in losing a son and being helpless to find him.

But he'd been a snake, one with a handsome smile and a sharp knife hidden behind his back. As soon as Scott had identified the killer, he had reemerged, offering free legal services to Randall Thompson and building a case to discredit Scott.

George's theory was that Robert Kavin was bitter that Scott had lived and his son had died. He thought Kavin was punishing them because he'd lost Gabe, so he wanted to make Scott's life hell.

Nita refused to believe that a parent would be that selfish. Even in her darkest moments, she had never wished ill on a child. Even the BH Killer's own, if he had one. Randall Thompson did not.

"Dr. Gwen Moore is known for her work with the Los Angeles Police Department on the Red River shooter." The camera flipped to show a close-up of Gwen, who was striding through the parking lot. She was a beautiful woman. Dark hair, pale porcelain skin. She had a slightly upturned nose, which gave her a sense of youthfulness. Her eyes caught the camera, and she stared at it coolly, then continued walking.

She looked like a woman who had all the answers, which must be nice. At the moment, Nita was swimming in questions, all of which concerned her son. She glanced toward the ceiling, in the direction of Scott's room. It had been a week since he'd confessed the truth to the police, and she had barely seen him during that time. He stayed in his room, the door locked, and ignored any offers for food or attempts to get him out of the house. Their interior security cameras had caught him sneaking downstairs in the middle of the night to eat, then quickly retreating back to his room.

Maybe she should get him to a doctor. This was probably PTSD. There were programs they could get him into, mental exercises that would help his emotional fortitude. And protection dogs—huge, intimidating creatures that could crawl in car windows and keep his fears of attack at bay. She had already found one in Germany, which could be here within two weeks.

Attack dogs and counseling sessions—was that what her parenting options had come to? Earlier this morning, she had researched obstruction-of-justice laws and criminal attorneys, in case the LAPD pressed charges against Scott. And last night, she had logged in to their cell phone billing system and looked at his call and text activity.

She didn't recognize herself. Spying on her son. Tracking his movements, monitoring his calls, watching him on their home security cams. Six months ago, her concerns would have been centered on drugs and girls. Now she was afraid of losing him mentally, physically, and emotionally. When faced with those possibilities, she had to break boundaries and invade his privacy. She wouldn't apologize for that, even if he hated her for it one day.

She climbed off the stool. "I'm going to head upstairs, see if I can get Scott to eat something."

Beth set down a spoon and moved to the oven. "Wait, I'll prepare a plate for him." Opening the door, she pulled out the tray of cheeseburgers she'd kept warm in hopes he would come downstairs.

Nita waited as she assembled one with bacon strips and a bun, half wrapped it in foil, and placed it on a tray with a handful of crispy fries and a bottle of ketchup.

"He want mustard or pickles?" Beth asked.

"No, this is fine. Thank you."

Nita skipped the stairs and took the elevator, juggling the tray with one hand as she closed the gate and pressed the button for the second floor. Scott's phone records had been alarming, so much so that she had woken up George to get his take on them. There had been almost constant activity until the day he was taken—then, as expected, complete silence for seven weeks. Then, upon his return, almost nothing.

Almost.

With the exception of his single call to the Realtor, all his calls and texts had been to a single number. Just one. No calls to Kyle or Lamar or Andy. No back-and-forth messages with the dozens of girls who had always hung around, hoping for his attention. This had been just one number, and dozens of calls and texts to it. The calls had been short, less than a minute in length. And all the texts outgoing, with none incoming.

Then, a couple of weeks ago, he stopped, and his cell phone usage ceased to nothing. As if he were gone again.

George had told her to call the number, which she had. It had gone straight to an automated voice mail, one that repeated back the number but gave no hint to its owner.

The elevator chimed, and she stepped off. At Scott's door, she knocked, then jiggled the heavy chrome handle. "Scott, it's Mom."

Music played from inside the room, and this was how suicides happened. Emotional withdrawal was always the first sign, according to the articles she was reading online. And Scott had been sulking ever since they'd returned from the police station and he and George had had that fight.

God, she would almost rather take the screaming over the silence. Though, later, George had agreed—yelling at Scott hadn't been the right move. Yes, he had lied to police. Yes, he could be facing an obstruction-of-justice charge—but he was alive. Home. Safe. The other details didn't matter.

"Scott, Beth just made bacon cheeseburgers," she tried again. "I've got one hot and ready for you, with those crispy fries you like. Please open up." She put her ear to the door and listened. Nothing. Could he even hear her?

At the end of the hall, the door to their study opened, and George emerged. He was in pale-green golf shorts and a white polo and looked as successful and put together as he had the very first time she'd seen him, twenty-two years ago.

"The door still locked?" George asked.

"Yes." She used the flat end of her fist to pound on the door. It created a soft thud, and if she'd hit her childhood bedroom door that hard, it would have cracked the cheap plywood.

George spoke from behind her. "Just let me kick the door in. He's not going to open it."

A week ago, she would have argued with him, but her concern for Scott was beginning to border on panic. "You shouldn't have been so hard on him," she said quietly, though she had been right there beside him, both of their voices raised in frustration during the drive home from the station.

"Scott," George called out, "open the door or I'm going to break it down."

The music turned down, and Nita held her breath. A few moments later, Scott opened the door.

At the sight of her son, she put a hand on her husband's arm and gently pushed him away. Navigating into the room with the tray of food, she gave George a warning look and pulled the door closed behind her.

"Come on, Mom," Scott groaned, his shoulders slumping. "I just want to be alone."

She set the tray on his desk and made her way to his minifridge. Opening the door, she tsked over the almost empty contents. All sugary soda. Her son, who had once been so health conscious, was now just like every other American teen. Half-opened bag of Cheetos on the top of the fridge, an overflowing trash can with candy bars and empty soda cans. She pulled an orange soda from the fridge and brought it to him. He already had his butt in the desk chair, the burger to his mouth. Fast, ravenous bites.

He was shirtless, and her gaze traced over the heart outline that Randall Thompson had cut into his chest. He cleared his throat, and she realized he was watching her.

She averted her gaze. "Sorry."

"It's okay." He stuffed a fry in his mouth.

"I can put some ointment on that," she offered. "I have a scar-repair cream I used after my knee surgery that really worked . . ." Her offer dropped off as he shifted away, almost shielding the wound from her.

"I don't want to put anything on it."

She frowned. "It'll leave a scar, Scott. Surely you don't want to—"

"No!"

The ferocity in his tone shut her up. She swallowed and sat on the edge of his bed. "I was just trying to help."

His face softened. "I know, Mom. I just—I don't want to lose the scar. This happened to me. I'm not going to forget it."

Of course he wasn't. And she wasn't trying to make him forget anything. She just wanted to heal him. Inside and out. "We miss you, Scott. You don't have to lock yourself away up here."

"I don't want to talk to anyone."

"I know, but Scott—" She swallowed the urge to ask him a dozen questions and settled for one. "Why'd you tell us that you escaped? Why didn't you just tell us that he let you go?"

He took a bite of the burger and chewed, his eyes on the wall before him, his shoulders stiff with tension. By the time he wiped his mouth— he never wiped his mouth—she was ready to reach out and shake him. "I don't know. No one else was let go."

In Scott's newest statement to the police, he said Randall had unlocked his handcuffs and put him in the trunk of his car, then drove him out to a gas station a couple of miles from their house, where he pulled him out and told him that he'd let him go, but only if he ran straight home.

"I was different," he'd said, his voice thick with emotion. "Special. It's why I was set free."

Special? Something about the way Scott said it had unnerved Nita. There was gratitude in his voice, a spark of pride in his eyes. Even now, he placed his hand on his chest, almost as if to protect the wound.

"So, you thought we wouldn't believe you? That's why you lied?"

He swallowed the bite he was chewing and reached for the soda. "Yeah."

Her motherly intuition flared, as it had been doing since the moment he got home. He was lying. Had the first time, and still was. The conflicting evidence, previously dismissed by her, was starting to stack up. Just this morning, the attorney reminded them that they hadn't found any of his DNA in Mr. Thompson's trunk. Her patience snapped. "Scott, look at me."

He turned his head, and his eyes found hers, but there wasn't a connection there.

"Right now, I need you to tell me the truth. Without your father listening, without the cops around. Just talk to me."

He blinked.

"Scott?" she pressed. "What else are you keeping from me?"

He turned back to his cheeseburger and picked it up. Studying it, he slowly dipped his head and took another bite.

Her frustration rose. Yes, he had been through a traumatic ordeal. Yes, she was grateful that he was home. But a man was in jail based off his testimony. Police and county resources had been used to prepare a court case based off what he had said—what he had lied about. His new story was causing countless hours of work in shifting evidence, reports, and defense strategies. And yet he didn't want to talk about it. He'd been more than happy to tell his fake story of escape to anyone who wanted to listen, but now—with the truth out—he was clamming up.

She reached out and slammed a hand on his desk, then immediately regretted the action when her son flinched in response. "I'm sorry," she said quickly. "But talk to me, for shit's sake."

"Can't I just eat?"

His cell phone was on the desk. She grabbed it before he could stop her, her haste unneeded as he ignored the action. She pressed the screen, but nothing happened. It was dead. No wonder he was ignoring her texts. "How long has your phone been dead?"

"I don't know." He put a few fries in his mouth.

"I looked at your call records, Scott. Why haven't you been talking to any of your friends?"

He turned to face her. "Don't look at my calls."

"We pay for your phone. We have the right to know who you're talking to." God, when had she become her mother?

"So I have no privacy? Is that what you're telling me? I've traded one prison for another?"

She flinched. "I wouldn't call this a prison, Scott. You can—"

"I can what? I can't drive anywhere without you freaking out on me. And I can't leave my room without you and Dad screaming at me, and now you're in here, yelling at me—"

"Who have you been calling?" She interrupted him before he got worked up. "What's this number you kept calling?"

His gaze darted to the side. "No one."

She folded her arms over her chest. "Fine. Don't tell me. I'll just find out on my own."

The threat worked. He dropped his head in his hands. "Мом," he groaned.

She waited.

"It's a girl." He sighed, his head still in his hands. "Someone I dated."

"When?"

"Earlier this year. I called her when I got my phone back, but she didn't answer."

"Is it Jennifer?"

"You don't know her."

"Does she go to Beverly High?"

He let out a frustrated growl. "She doesn't live here anymore, so it doesn't matter."

"When did she move?"

"She's gone, Mom."

"What do you mean, gone?"

"She moved while we . . . while I was gone. I drove by her house, and she doesn't live there anymore."

The house for sale. The call to the Realtor. Relief rushed through her. Was that what all this was—the moping, the staying in his room and refusing to talk to them . . . Was it teenage heartbreak?

"Oh, Scott." She held out her hands and wrapped him in a hug. Startled, he sat there, unresponsive, then awkwardly patted her shoulder. "I'm sorry," she whispered. He had probably thought of this girl during all that time at Randall Thompson's house, then finally gotten free only to call her and call her, with no answer. "She must have changed her number when she moved," she said.

"Yeah." He pulled free. "Are there any more burgers?"

She smiled. "Sure. Come downstairs with me. I promise"—she held up her hands in surrender—"we won't ask you any questions about anything. Just lie on the couch and watch some television while Beth makes brownies."

Brownies were his weakness, and she watched a bit of life enter his eyes. He nodded, and even though it was a small victory, it felt monumental.

They were going to be okay.

CHAPTER 34

Robert's home was annoyingly perfect. Clean contemporary lines, rich dark walls, and sleek gleaming surfaces, with just enough leather and fabric to warm everything up. He had two bottles of wine breathing and a fire crackling in an outdoor hearth. I took it all in with a raised brow. "Why do I feel like you do this often?"

"I don't." He brought a beer bottle to his lips, then nodded at the wine. "Pick your poison."

I chose the chardonnay over the pinot and poured a glass, then took in the view. His home was in the Hollywood Hills, perched high enough to show off the city, and a rainbow of lights was beginning to glow out of the dusk. A half hour earlier and I'd have caught the sunset. Still, it was impressive. I turned back and caught a tendril of hair before it whipped across my face. "I miss the smell of a fire."

He smiled. "My contractor wanted to put in propane, but I like the smell of the wood, even if it does stick to your clothes."

"Same here."

In front of the fire was a half-circle sectional with dark-blue cushions and big white pillows. I took a spot on one side and slipped my sandals off, then tucked my feet underneath me.

He sat in the middle, six feet between us. "How was the rest of your day?"

"Quiet." I had gone straight home and filled up my bathtub with lavender-scented bubbles. Soaked in the hot water and thought through every piece of the case and how Randall Thompson fit into it.

I still—even with a thousand pages of case files and a personal interview with the accused—didn't have enough to go on. I didn't know what Randall had done to Luke. I didn't know if he exhibited characteristics of secondary identities. He certainly hadn't in my time with him. If I had interviewed Randall Thompson as part of a lineup of potential suspects, I would have put him in the "unlikely" category. He wasn't precise. Emphatic and unwavering in his innocence. Psychologically, he was wrong for this crime.

But then there was the evidence side of things. He had been identified by Scott Harden. There was the box of keepsakes from all six victims in his house. And there was something inherently dark in his soul. I recognized it, I just couldn't take a pulse on how deep the depravity went.

Robert rolled the beer bottle between his palms. "Before I ask you your impressions of Randall, there's something you should know about Scott Harden."

Oh no. My fingers tightened on the stem of the wineglass. Scott was so young. Surely he hadn't—

"He changed his story."

The alarm whooshed out of me in a single breath. "In what way?"

"Originally, he said he escaped. Now he's saying that he was let go and dropped off a few miles from his house."

"Let go?" That was strange, and my heart beat faster. That lent itself to DID, which I was starting to lean toward over paranoid schizophrenia. "When did you find that out?" This was huge.

"About fifteen minutes ago."

I set my glass on the arm of the couch, needing my full wits. "Wow. That's interesting."

He gave a bitter laugh. "Yeah. It surprised me, too. If only Gabe could have been so lucky."

I turned the new information over in my mind. "Do you believe him?"

He tilted his head to one side. "That's an interesting question. What are you getting at?"

"There are two things at play here. First, why would Scott Harden have lied initially, then told the truth? I have to work through that in my head. How does it affect the validity of his identification? What motivations prompted the first action, then the reversal of fact?"

"And the second thing?"

"Well, that's about the killer. If Scott is telling the truth, why let him go? What made Scott different? What happened during those seven weeks?" I sighed. "If he really did let him go, then it lends credence to your theory that Scott is lying about Randall's involvement. He could be protecting the real killer. He could have developed a loyalty or almost a love for the man."

"Like Stockholm syndrome."

"Yes." The syndrome wasn't an official diagnosis but a mental coping strategy, one exploited by Hollywood and novelists but still very real. I had dismissed Robert's initial scenario as unrealistic, but now . . . with my opinion of Randall Thompson already shaky and Scott's validity as a witness in question . . . it was starting to look like a valid possibility.

I tucked the end of my dark-purple maxi dress under my knees. "You didn't answer my question."

He looked at me, and the firelight flicked over his features. "Remind me of it."

"Do you believe Scott's new story?"

"I think he's proven that he's unreliable. Whether I believe him or not, he's given me the ammunition I need to make sure that the jury doesn't believe a word he says."

He was right. Hell, I was waffling all over the place on Randall's guilt. If you took away the box of souvenirs, I'd be certain of his innocence. He was a square peg that didn't fit into my profile, and Scott Harden was officially untrustworthy. All Robert needed was one juror to have reasonable doubt. He'd get that, and Randall Thompson would be free.

I let out a breath and considered the sobering thought that the Bloody Heart Killer was still out there. Watching us. I glanced at the view, the dark drop-off before the scenery of faraway lights, and suddenly didn't feel so cozy and protected.

"I've been rereading your BH profile."

"And?" I brushed a lock of hair away from my mouth.

"It has holes."

An accurate statement. One that a DID or PS diagnosis would help to fill. I took a sip of wine and didn't respond.

"How certain are you that the BH Killer is gay?"

He was referring to the section of the profile where I dissected the anal rapes and penile amputation of the boys. The highly personal and sexual nature of the abuse, paired with the victim selection, lent itself to that likelihood.

"I'm not certain that he's gay. I believe he has violently strong emotions about homosexuality and would repress those inclinations if he experienced them in his everyday life."

"Well, Randall Thompson is not gay. One hundred thousand percent not gay." He rose as if the discussion was final. I watched as he walked over to a bronze can and dropped the bottle inside.

"How do you know?" I challenged. "Have you spoken to his prior students?"

"No, but I emailed you his discovery file an hour ago. You can review it yourself. Every accusation made against him was made by a female student, not a male. Is Randall a little creepy?" He paused. "Yes. Would I trust him to babysit my fourteen-year-old niece? Hell no. But he's not gay, and he's in horrific shape, so he's not moving bodies in and out of trunks unless he has an inhaler handy and some help."

It was a valid point and underlined the fact that Randall was too old for my psychological profile. He was pushing retirement, and the BH Killer was much more likely to be in his early forties, physically fit, and not in an environment where he was surrounded by students every day.

"Look," I yielded, "I didn't come here to convince you that he matches the profile. But there's something off with him."

"Sure, he's a sexual predator." He shrugged as if the information was unimportant. "Three students have filed complaints about him in the last twenty years."

"Wait, what?" I paused. "Why didn't you mention that before? When I asked you, what . . . ?" I tried to think about how long it had been. "A week ago? I asked you if any students had complained about him."

He pulled a fresh bottle from the ice bucket and twisted off the cap. "I didn't want your initial impression of him to be tainted. You're the one who preached the need for a clean mental slate when creating your profile."

Fair point. Still . . . "If he's a sexual predator, that only puts more validity—"

"They were all females. Thirteen- and fourteen-year-old girls. It's a completely different MO."

I fell silent and processed the information. He was right, it was a different MO. Was that the vibe I had gotten from Randall? Molester versus killer?

Maybe I had been wrong.

He studied me, then turned toward the house. "Enough talk about death. Let's head inside. I want to show you something."

~

"What do you think?"

I stared at the wall of items, letting my eyes drift over each of them. There were too many to absorb, and I drifted closer, then moved slowly down the line. Each was housed in a clear box and lit with a spotlight that protruded from the wall. "What is this?"

"It's my collection of oddities. Each birthday and Christmas, I buy something unique to add to it."

I appraised the collection. At least thirty items, ranging from figurines to photos. "How long have you been doing this?"

"My wife began the tradition. She always selected items of significance, ones that carried a personal story from our life. After she died, Gabe and I continued it on our own."

The importance of what I was looking at sank in. Not just a wall of expensive knickknacks. This was an intimate look behind his veil. While the kitchen was devoid of life, this room was heavy with it. It could have felt dark and mournful, but there was a peace in the reverence. Robert seemed more relaxed in here, more at home. Stopping before a pair of short swords, I bent to read the gold plaque. "'Splitting the eyebrows.' What does that mean?"

"Those are samurai swords from the 1800s. They tested the sharpness of them by cutting a human skull in half. After they passed the test, the owner engraved the saying on the underside of them."

He ran a finger over the glistening surface of the blade. "Gabe picked these out. *The Last Samurai* was his favorite movie. This summer, we had plans to spend two weeks in Japan and visit the Kakunodate district and Hagi castle town." He swallowed, his eyes wet, and pulled his hand back.

The reality of his life hit me. Past the expensive suits, the confidence, the courtroom record, was a man living alone with ghosts. Everyone he loved had been taken from him. Was it any wonder he had shown up at my home with flowers and stayed long enough to put together a puzzle?

Pushed for dinner, then almost begged me for this evening of drinks? Approached a stranger in a bar and gone home with her?

I may have only had my cat and a DVR playlist of romantic comedies, but my life was absent of grief, and that additional force took loneliness and drenched it in agony.

I cleared my throat and moved down the wall, examining a baseball that looked like it had been put through a garbage disposal. He followed, his arm brushing mine, and I struggled not to reach out and touch him, to comfort him.

"Now, that ring"—he pointed to an antique emerald solitaire, one in a gold setting and surrounded by diamonds—"has an interesting story."

I waited, afraid to ask if it had belonged to his wife.

He lifted the open ring box off its stand, removing it from the spotlight. "It's over four hundred years old and has been lost to the sea twice. The first time was in 1622, when a Spanish treasure ship sank off the coast of Florida in a hurricane."

"The *Atocha*," I remarked, familiar with the history.

He raised an eyebrow, impressed. "That's right. When hunters found the treasure in 1985, this ring was recovered, polished up, and gifted to the wife of a prominent investor, Debbie Stickelber, who wore it on her finger every day for ten years. Every single day, except for one." He paused and I grinned up at him, enjoying the theatrics of the story. It was no wonder he was good in the courtroom. As a juror, I'd listen to him all day.

"The morning of October 4, 1995, Debbie was woken up by her husband, who screamed at her to get dressed and grab anything of value. A hurricane was coming. The umbrellas and patio furniture on the porch of their beachfront home had already smashed against the railings. Storm surge was beginning to creep up their sand." His voice took on the dark tones of a ghost story. "She grabbed the small safe from his office and a Van Gogh that hung just outside their bedroom and ran for their car, leaving behind her wedding ring, watch, and this ring, still lying on the bedside table, where she took them off each night."

"Why hadn't they gotten out earlier? Don't you know days in advance about a hurricane?"

"The Stickelbers were known for their parties and had decided to ride out the storm with a few dozen bottles of liquor and champagne. It wasn't until that morning, when the husband woke up and realized the size of the storm, that he decided they needed to leave—and it was a good thing they did. Hurricane Opal destroyed their house, wiping it completely off the sand. When they returned one week later, the only thing left was the concrete pilings that their home had been tethered to. Along with their belongings, the hurricane took over five hundred *Atocha* coins, six silver bars, and her jewelry. A search party, complete with backhoes and divers, searched the shore and ocean for weeks, looking for the re-lost treasure."

I looked down at the ring. "And they found this?"

"Yep. Four houses down, a hundred yards out, under two feet of sand. They eventually found two of the bars, and around half the coins. The rest was never recovered, or"—he gave me a wry grin—"I suspect some was pocketed by members of the search crew."

"How did you end up with it?"

He chuckled. "Debbie Stickelber ended up leaving her vast estate— including the ring—to her dogs, a decision that infuriated her children and led to quite a legal battle."

"I wasn't aware you did estate litigation."

His grin widened. "I don't. But when one son tried to kill his sister over ownership of the teacup poodle with the net worth of some countries . . . that's when I was hired. The assets were frozen by the court, but the sister slipped me this ring, and we called it a day."

"I love that story." I held the ring box out to him.

"You should keep it. Consider it my payment for the profile."

I choked out a laugh. "Wha—what? No." I pushed it toward him. The stone was two carats, if not three. The value of it . . . with the history . . . I couldn't even fathom. "Don't be absurd."

"I don't have anyone to give things to, Gwen." His voice dropped. "Just take it. Please. I don't want to be that guy who leaves everything to his goldfish."

I met his eyes, and another protective layer was gone, his emotions exposed, the haunted look in his eyes almost unbearable. Impulsively, I reached forward and hugged him. His back was stiff, his body language tense, but I still wrapped my arms around him and squeezed. After a moment, he responded, softening into the embrace. "Thank you," I said quietly. "It's the nicest thing I'll ever own. And there is no way that goldfish lives past the month."

He laughed and kissed my forehead, a surprisingly sweet gesture that affected me more than it should. When he stepped away, my body ached to follow. "Just promise me you won't lose it in a storm."

"I won't." I closed the lid and glanced back at the empty space. "I'm going to get you something to replace it. It won't be a priceless emerald, but I'll find something. Something cool."

"Cool," he repeated, walking down the row, his attention already off the vacant spot. "I think I'm too old for cool."

"Which is your favorite?" I shivered as I passed in front of the air vent, my thin dress not enough for the chilly room.

"It's too hard to choose." He glanced at me and moved closer, reaching out to rub his palms along my upper arms. "Do you want to go outside where it's warmer?"

I couldn't think of a response, because his attention had fallen to my mouth, his hands tightening on my arms, and when he tugged me forward, I sank into his chest, like one of those mindless heroines in a romance novel. Right into the arms of the vulnerable and lonely beast.

CHAPTER 35

I woke up naked in his bed, tucked underneath layers of silky sheets and down feathers. It felt like a cocoon, one that I never wanted to move out of. I closed my eyes and savored the moment before my brain would fully engage and I'd overthink this entire situation.

The mattress shifted, and I turned my head and found Robert seated at the edge of the bed, dressed in slacks and a button-up, his hair already in place, tie already knotted.

He was facing straight ahead, his eyes on the windows. "Tell me what John told you. How much you know about what he did."

I worked myself up and onto my elbows, holding the covers to my chest. "Excuse me?"

"John Abbott." He turned his head and stared into my eyes. "Tell me what you know."

I swallowed, my brain trying desperately to wake up and perform. "I don't really know anything. I mean, other than what he told me. But I—"

"You've been lying to me since the day I met you." He swore, then ran his hands over his face. "Shit, Gwen."

"Not lying," I countered. "I haven't lied to you." I scooted farther back on the bed, so I was fully upright.

"You did. You knew all about John." He measured and weighed his words carefully, as if he were grinding them through a stone. "The monster he was. You could have stopped him."

I dropped my gaze, avoiding the judgment in his face but still hearing it in his words. Weeks together, and he'd known the truth of Brooke's death the entire time. Had he been waiting for me to bring it up? Watching to see what I told police? "Yes," I said softly. "I should have done more. I should have called the police."

The mattress shifted as he rose, and I searched for something to say, an explanation to give. When I finally found the courage to lift my gaze, he was moving through the bedroom door, his steps sounding down the hall. I waited, listening, but I could feel the emptiness of the house when it took over.

~

I found my dress and underwear by the foot of the bed, my sandals at different corners of the room. The curtains were drawn, and I parted them enough to see that it was late morning. My phone was probably still in the kitchen, tucked into my purse. The battery was likely dead, and I tried to remember what my day looked like. Luke Attens had finally called the office and was on the books at eleven. Hopefully I had time to swing by the house and shower first.

I stepped into the bathroom long enough to use the toilet and wash my hands. Glancing in the mirror, I paused, taking a moment to smooth my wild, dark hair into place. Looking into my eyes, I took a deep breath.

It will be okay. I repeated the phrase twice, inhaling and exhaling deeply. Maybe Robert was going to the police now. Maybe he wasn't. After all, he had asked me what I'd known. He hadn't known my guilt for sure. What he had known was John's guilt. And now, from my own admission, he knew mine.

Despite what Meredith said, despite all the excuses my mind liked to throw up, Brooke's death was my fault. If I had answered John's call that morning. If I had listened more closely during his sessions. If I had reached out to Brooke and warned her, or gone to the police or flat out done a better damn job with my client.

Should I destroy John's file? Burn or bury the evidence? How much should I do to protect myself? I inhaled sharply as my stomach heaved and I bent over the sink, waiting for last night's dinner to come up.

It didn't. The moment passed, my stomach settled, and I straightened. I needed to get out of here. I passed through the arched doorway, back into the bedroom, and hesitated, seeing the black-velvet box on the stained-teak bedside table. The ring. I considered putting it back in its place on the wall but decided to leave it there, my urge to leave outweighing my need to return things to where they belonged.

I'd need to get a client-termination letter prepared as soon as possible. I had a template I'd used before and could have Jacob complete it and send it over to Robert. My outstanding invoice, which I hadn't yet submitted to Cluster & Kavin, I could void. Have Jacob include an attachment of the canceled bill, just to make it clear that I wouldn't be asking for any payment.

It all felt too little, too late. I should have ended this the moment it had begun. In the bar, with the peanuts and beer. Instead, I was neck-deep, and everything in my life was in danger of drowning.

Hurrying down the hall, I found my purse where I'd left it. I threw the thick strap over one shoulder, grabbed my keys, and fled.

~

"You look like shit." Luke, who was meticulously put together in a powder-blue suit, coiffed hair, and Versace sunglasses, eyed my worn jeans and loose blouse with a critical scowl.

I didn't bother with a smile. I had barely made it to the office in time for this appointment. "Good morning to you, too, Luke." I stirred a sugar packet into my coffee and gestured to the conference table. "Please, sit."

"Seriously, what's wrong with you?" He dropped into the closest chair and eyed me with concern. "Blow-dryer on the fritz?"

"Nothing's wrong." I glanced through the glass wall and found Jacob and Bart in the lobby, watching. "Can we talk about Randall Thompson without you screaming in my face?"

His concern flipped to annoyance. "I wasn't screaming. You over-reacted and were a huge baby over the entire thing." He drummed his manicured nails on the arm of the chair. "And why are we still not in your office? I know what's in there, you know."

"Yes," I said calmly, taking a seat that was a safe distance away. "Thank you, by the way, for the broken lamp." Too late, I corrected myself. I knew better than this. Inflammatory statements weren't the right way to handle Luke, and if I wasn't so tied up in knots over Brooke and Robert, I'd be aware of that. I softened my tone. "Luke, in our last meeting, you were trying to tell me something about Randall. What was it?"

"You lied to me, Doc." He pointed toward my face, and it was a little too aggressive for my liking. "You told me you weren't working with him."

"I wasn't working with him. I was hired to do a psychological profile of the BH Killer."

"Hired by his attorney." He lifted his foot and rested the ankle of it on his other knee. It was a good sign, a change in body language, and I relaxed slightly at the new pose. "I saw you on the news, Doc."

"Yes, I was hired by his defense," I admitted. "But I quit."

He looked at me with skepticism. "When?"

"This morning." Jacob's email had gone out at 10:15 a.m., and so far there'd been no response from Robert. I thought of the anger that had been in his voice. So raw. So emotional. Why did he care so much about John Abbott? Yes, I had been negligent. Yes, a woman had died. But they had barely known Robert. Service provider and client. If there had been more of a relationship there, Robert had never mentioned it.

Through the glass walls of the conference room, I saw movement by the elevators and tensed. Meredith walked past, and I forced my hand to relax its iron grip around my coffee cup. Would they come for me today? Would it be Detective Saxe or someone else? Or would Robert sit on my confession and continue whatever cat-and-mouse game he was engaged in?

Meredith paused by Jacob's desk.

"If you aren't working for Randall anymore, why do you want to know about him?"

"Honestly?" I returned my attention to Luke. "Personal curiosity. I haven't made up my mind if he's innocent or not. It would help me if I understood what he did to you. But Luke"—I set down my coffee cup—"you and I are protected by doctor-patient confidentiality. Regardless of whether or not I'm working on that case, I can't share anything you tell me with anyone. And obviously, if you'd prefer not to tell me things, you don't."

"Randall never touched me." He twisted the diamond bezel on his watch.

I frowned. "I thought—"

"It wasn't me. He put his hands on my first girlfriend. Kept her after class and pinned her against the wall and fingered her." His fury was gone, the words delivered in a cold and clinical way that was nowhere near the Luke of before. Where was his rage? Had that outburst been about Randall, or had Luke just been on the bad end of an emotional dip?

I sat back, slightly deflated. "Did she tell anyone?"

"No. Another girl . . . a freshman, had told the guidance counselor that he raped her in the science lab—and she'd been ignored. And remember, this was twenty years ago." He shrugged. "Back then, the guy wasn't old and fat. Some of the girls liked him, and the girl in question was already a slut. No one believed her. Kristen didn't want to be a repeat act. And she didn't tell me about it until years later, when we were in college."

I dropped my head back against the chair and tried to push the silenced girls in question out of my head. While the story was tragic, I needed to focus on how this information fit into my profile. The problem was, it was another puzzle piece that didn't. It matched what Robert had said—Randall was a sexual predator, but toward women, not men.

Maybe Robert was right and Randall wasn't responsible for the BH deaths. At the moment, I couldn't find a clear thought in any of this.

I looked back at Luke. "Do you have my wallet and keys?"

"Nope."

A lie if I'd ever heard one. I gritted my teeth and wondered if I could fire him as a client, too.

I met his gaze, his obnoxious smirk twisting one side of his face, and mentally lifted a middle finger to everything he stood for. Why not fire him? If I was going down in flames, I might as well go out swinging.

CHAPTER 36

Marta Blevins was in the running for Realtor of the month. One more signed contract and it would be her name on the plaque, her Tahoe in the premier parking spot. She needed a sale, and this showing could be it.

Unlocking the home, she stepped inside, crinkling her nose at the dingy green wallpaper and cheap assortment of furniture. She moved deeper into the shallow living room and pulled open the blinds, flooding the room with light. At least it was neat. Last week she'd shown a Culver City home that had piles of rancid clothes everywhere you looked.

On the street, her clients' blue sedan pulled up to the curb. The newlyweds from Texas had been dismayed at the prices of the last two properties she'd shown them. Hopefully their budget would help them overlook the stigma brought on by this home's history. Not that she had told them. California law was lenient with what had to be disclosed, and deaths were specifically off that list.

She watched them through the window. The husband was on the phone, which would give her a few minutes to walk through the place. You never knew how other agents would leave the house, and there had been a fair number of showings since the last time she'd been here.

The master bedroom was in order, and she took a moment to turn on the bedside lamp and open the blinds. The second bedroom had been converted into a flex office, and she toed a dead roach underneath an abandoned treadmill that was parked against one wall. Glancing in the laundry room, she was grateful to see the pull-down entry to the attic easily accessible. The husband was a home inspector, a fact he mentioned ad nauseam, and he had wanted to see the crawl space and attic of every home they'd viewed. In preparation, she pulled at the cord, pleased to see the folding stairs smoothly extend out, the construction well done and reinforced in multiple places. Normally, these attic access stairs were barely functional death traps. This looked like something that was built to last.

Hearing a tentative knock, she hurried back down the slim hall to let the couple inside.

~

As expected, the husband beelined for the access, enthusiastically gripping the handrails and clipping up the stairs and into the ceiling.

"I don't know . . . ," the wife said doubtfully, looking around the space. "Do you think they'd consider a lease purchase?" She adjusted the skinny red belt that cut across the middle of her white sundress. "My company is paying for four months of relocation rent. And I asked if we could use it on a mortgage, but they said—"

From the top rung of the stairs, her husband cleared his throat. "Um . . . Marta?"

"Yes?" she called out sweetly, sneaking a glance at her watch. Appetizers were half-price until six thirty, which meant—

"You need to see this."

His tone was odd, steeped in trepidation, and she peered up the ladder at him. "What is it?" Mold? Asbestos? She mentally crossed her fingers. Please, not raccoons.

He climbed the final rungs and disappeared in the hole. She waited expectantly, but he moved deeper into the attic without responding.

Marta gripped the handrails of the stairs and gave them an experimental shake, testing their stability. It was really amazing. The owners had obviously swapped out the traditional steps for a commercial-quality set. She took the first step dubiously, then gained confidence on the second, then the third. By the time her head cleared the attic opening, she felt a small burst of accomplishment. And her ex said that she never got her hands dirty. What did he know?

She twisted toward the husband. What was his name? Wyatt? Wayne? Wilbur?

He was standing still, his attention on a mattress pushed against one of the attic walls. And wow, this was an actual room up here! Livable square footage, if you didn't mind roughing it a bit. She pulled herself to her feet and spotted a work light, like the sort you see at construction sites, clamped to a nearby beam. She fumbled along the back of it and switched it on. The dark space illuminated in brilliant white light, and she turned back to the husband, pleased with herself. Wes. That was his name.

He was still just standing there. Staring at the bed. No, not actually at the bed. At something between him and the bed. A worktable of some sort.

"This is pretty nice," she chirped, brushing off her hands and moving closer, curious to see what he found so intriguing. "I—"

Her words, her sentence, her thoughts all ceased. Everything in her subconscious halted as she stared down at the neat row of amputated fingers.

She stumbled back as her attention swept across the room. The mattress, its tan sheet stained with dried streaks of blood. The towel rings affixed above the mattress, ropes hanging from them. The camera set up by the bed. A bucket with flies buzzing above it. She inhaled and was suddenly aware of the smell. Iron and shit. Sweat. Fear. Was that sound coming from her? That low moan, that horrible, horrible moan?

She swayed to one side and looked for the stairs, zeroed in on the open hole in the floor. The wife was calling her name, was now climbing the stairs, but she couldn't come up here. No one should be up here. She lunged for the exit and slipped, her hands scrambling across the unfinished plywood surface. Splinters peppered her palms, and she gagged at a tuft of hair that was stuck in between two boards.

Making it to the opening, she shoved her feet through, narrowly missing the face of the wife. "Go!" she yelled. "Move! Move out of the way!"

"Is it rats?" the woman screeched, hurriedly retreating down the stairs. "Cockroaches?"

Marta launched off the access and ran down the hall as fast as her heels would allow her. Snagging her purse from the couch, she burst out the front door and gulped in the fresh air. Digging through her purse, she cursed, then dropped to her knees in the grass and dumped it upside down, shaking the canvas tote until it was empty, her phone finally visible among the makeup, pens, business cards, and tissues. Unlocking it with a shaky hand, she took a deep breath and dialed 9-1-1.

CHAPTER 37

"I can't believe you fired Luke Attens midsession." Meredith pulled out a chair from the break-room table and dropped into it. "That took some serious balls."

"It was stupid," I countered, glancing into the hall and pulling the door shut to give us some privacy. "Between the time I wasted on Robert and ditching Luke, my billable hours this month are going to be pitiful. Oh . . . plus, one of my clients died, so I'm down to Lela Grant and a handful of randoms."

"This town is full of crazy people," Meredith said cheerfully. "And you were on TV. You're a D-list celebrity now. That'll bring in the nutjobs."

"Oh, great." I opened the fridge and bent over, seeing what was available. "Just what I want." Other than the coffee during Luke's appointment, I hadn't had anything to eat, and my stomach growled in protest at the almost empty shelves. Jacob's job was to restock the break room, and I made a mental note to nudge him with a reminder.

"Hey, if money gets tight, I can always send over a few of my sexual sadists," Meredith offered. "Technically, they could be classified as violent."

"You know, I think I'm good." I squatted and looked through the collection of plastic containers. "How old is this spaghetti?"

"It's still good," Meredith assured me, fishing the remote out of the basket in the middle of the table. "Two days old, max. There should be a date on it somewhere." She turned on the ancient TV that sat on the counter and flipped to the grainy news channel. "Any word from your sexy attorney?"

"Complete silence." I pried the lid off the leftover pasta and placed it in the microwave. "If cops get off the elevator, flash them your boobs so I can slip out the back."

"I hate to break it to you, drama queen, but they can't arrest you for not reporting someone's emotional deliberations."

I squinted at her. "Uh, yeah, they can. Emotional deliberations are called premeditation."

"If only we had an attorney to ask," she intoned, pushing to her feet. She cracked her back, then sighed. "Honestly, I can't decide if he was a gentleman or an asshole to unload the accusations postpenetration."

I considered the options. "Both." Definitely both. The one thing I hadn't needed was that reminder of what good sex and intimacy felt like. Curled against Robert's side last night, there had been a solid period of time when I had thought that maybe he and I were something. Something with a future.

Stupid of me. I hadn't been so stupid since tenth grade, when I believed Mick Gentry when he told me that having sex proved we were in love.

"What do you think he's going to do?"

"I have no idea," I admitted. "I'm so confused by the entire thing. Why hire me at all? Why not just confront me, right then, when he read John's file?"

"Maybe he liked you," Meredith mused, flipping on the faucet and washing her hands. "Like, *liked you*, liked you."

I made a face. "Remind me again, how old are you?"

Meredith turned off the faucet and ripped a piece of paper towel off the roll. "Okay, I know you're trying not to think about the case, but I haven't spoken to you since the news broke about the fake escape story. So can I just say how weird it is that the killer just let this kid go?" She dried her hands, then balled up the towel. "Why?"

"I don't know," I admitted. "Scott was the only victim from Beverly High. If the killer was Randall Thompson and he was going to let someone go, it doesn't make sense for him to release a victim who could ID him. Randall's not a genius, but he also isn't stupid. The more I'm finding out, the more convinced I am that he's not the BH Killer. And there's a chance Scott Harden isn't a BH victim at all."

"Are you writing this stuff down?" Meredith asked. "This could be your book-deal moment. How awesome would it be if Scott Harden isn't a BH victim? Seriously." She leaned against the counter and crossed her arms over her chest.

"Totally awesome," I deadpanned, pulling open the microwave door and testing the temperature of the food with my finger.

I needed a vacation, I decided. Somewhere far away from the LA traffic, the smog, and clients who might cut my throat if I missed an appointment. Somewhere I could take an entire week and not think about the Bloody Heart Killer or Robert Kavin or dead wives of horrible clients. Maybe Hawaii. Or Costa Rica. Actually, screw the heat. Alaska. I'd always wanted to see a whale.

I turned to Meredith to ask if she'd been to Alaska and paused; her attention was glued to the TV above the bar.

"Are you watching this?" she hissed, reaching over and jabbing her finger on the volume-control button.

I left the microwave open and moved beside her, concentrating on the wobbly news headline.

SEX PRISON FOUND IN ATTIC—IS IT THE BLOODY HEART KILLER?

An aerial shot zoomed in, past a partitioned-off street and a dozen uniformed officers who filed in and out of a white brick home. The newscaster spoke, and I had to grip Meredith's arm to stay upright.

". . . six pinkie fingers have been found, and our sources are confirming that this is, in fact, the lair of Los Angeles's most notorious killers of this decade . . ."

So much for not thinking about death. Randall Thompson was, in fact, innocent, and the names now displayed below the newscaster's face were heartbreakingly familiar.

John and Brooke Abbott.

CHAPTER 38

I drove home, speeding down La Cienega and cutting through the back of my neighborhood. I parked in the carport and missed the key slot twice, my hands shaking as I finally got the key in the side door lock and turned. Clem mewed at me from the windowsill, and I ignored her, dropping my purse and keys on the counter and practically jogging to my office. Flipping on the light switch on the wall, I sat at my desk and pulled John Abbott's file to the center of the desk. It had only been a week since I'd opened it, a week since I combed the section that Robert had seen, fearful of what he'd read.

Now, I had an entirely different reason for opening the file. I reached forward, my fingers trembling over the top of the manila cover, then stopped. Pulling open my drawer, I flipped through the tabs and found the second item I needed. I pulled it out and placed it beside John's file.

THE BLOODY HEART KILLER: A PSYCHOLOGICAL PROFILE AND ANALYSIS

DR. GWEN MOORE, MD

I didn't know where to start. John's file would take me a full day to properly review, but it would give me a deeper look. The psychological profile could be wrong. After all, I'd written it, and if the last twelve hours had proved anything, it was that Dr. Gwen Moore was a horrific judge of character. Still, right now, I needed to organize my thoughts and really explore this possibility. I took a deep breath and opened the psychological profile. Selecting a gold Cross pen and fresh notepad from the drawer, I wrote along the top of the page:

Is John Abbott the Bloody Heart Killer?

I stared at the line, unwilling to believe it could be true. All this time, as I watched the news reports and worked up possible scenarios and motivations—could he have been right there? Sitting across from me. Sharing.

I flipped past the introductory pages of the report, past the bullshit disclosures and history of the crimes, and slowed when I got to the first real meat.

The killer will research and stalk his victims prior to taking them. He will know their schedules and social life. He will be ultra-cautious in his selection of when to take the victims, and plan it down to every detail.

Detective Saxe had shared the Peeping Tom citations. John had been caught several times. All wealthy women. At the time, I hadn't believed the news, certain that John Abbott wasn't sexually interested in any women other than his wife, and maybe I'd been right. The police had assumed the most likely scenario, but John hadn't been interested in the rich middle-aged women. Even without knowing the women's information, I'd be willing to bet that they were mothers. *He'd been spying on their teenage sons.*

I read farther down the page, to my section on BH's personality traits.

Fastidious in his appearance and grooming. Neat and analytical in nature. Has a job that requires attention to detail. Precise in his lifestyle. Conscious of what other people think.

It was John to a T, as if I'd written the analysis just for him. I cupped my forehead in my hands and inhaled, feeling my palms tremble against my forehead. "Oh God," I whispered. "This is bad."

Where had the signs been? Had I missed them? Had he mentioned the victims in our sessions? Had he wanted treatment for those inclinations and used Brooke as an excuse?

No. While I might have missed some references to the boys, I refused to accept that he hadn't truly struggled with violent inclinations toward his wife. The emotion he had shown in our sessions, the heated anger that had come into his face, the crack of his voice . . . he had been vulnerable and honest in those moments. I know he had.

I closed my eyes and thought of my last session with him. He'd started screaming, spittle flying out of his mouth as he had ranted about Brooke and their neighbor.

"I can see it in the way she looks at him." John had sprung to his feet, pacing the area in between our chairs with short, stiff strides. "The way she talks about him. She's thinking about him during sex, I can feel it. She's glowing like a damn high school girl," he'd sneered. "And she's home alone all day? They're screwing—I know they are." He kicked at the small wastebasket next to my desk, and it flew across the room and banged against the wall.

That had been just two weeks before Scott Harden's release and Brooke's and John's deaths. John had told me that the guy was a new neighbor, but looking at the timeline . . . what if it had been Scott Harden?

I inhaled deeply, trying to slow down my thought process. If John's jealousy had been about Brooke's interactions with Scott Harden—and, prior to that, Gabe Kavin—then that meant that Brooke was interacting with the victims. That she was aware of what John had been doing.

I had thought John was paranoid, but maybe he hadn't been. Maybe Brooke had been sleeping with the men. The rapes . . . Had she been involved?

The salve. The kind gestures. I had assumed it was a dissociative identity, but what if it hadn't been a second personality? What if it had been a second person?

Brooke.

An awful foreboding hit in the center of my soul like a knife as the possible implications sank in.

A woman might explain why Scott Harden had lied. An inexperienced teenager, sleeping with a grown woman—it was a much easier leap to Stockholm syndrome, especially if she was a good cop to John's bad. Had she developed true feelings for Scott Harden? Was she the one who had let him go? And was that why John had killed her?

The dates lined up. I had never put two and two together, but Brooke and John died the same morning that Scott Harden reappeared. My hand trembled, and I squeezed my pen to stop the motion.

I thought of John's repeated insistence that she was developing feelings for the neighbor. What had he said the morning of their deaths? That he thought she was going to leave John and run away with him. Maybe he'd been right.

Dread suddenly settled as a half dozen pieces clicked into place.

I told him to get rid of the landscaper.

I practically tore the front of John's file open and flipped furiously through the pages, skimming my finger down my notes from our first month of sessions. Background info . . . his history with his wife . . . there. The landscaper.

John had been concerned they were getting too close. Had heard them laughing together. Holding eye contact with each other. Had found dirty dishes in the sink and speculated that she had fixed him lunch.

My neat script recorded my solution to his agonizing insecurities.

I suggested he solve the problem by firing the landscaper.

Those initial meetings with John had been dominated by his concerns over her and this landscaper. John had wanted to *kill* Brooke over the fear of her alleged affair and feelings for the man. So I had pushed him down the path of least resistance. It was easy. Remove the landscaper from the equation and focus on rebuilding and strengthening his relationship with his wife.

But if the neighbor in our most recent sessions had actually been Scott Harden, then the landscaper was . . . I let out a pained sob and fisted my hands in my hair. Gabe Kavin. *I told him to get rid of Gabe Kavin.*

The dry drowning. The death that was different from the others. Had his furious jealousy been the trigger for the violent manner of death? Ohhhh, and I had handed him the solution, my voice soothing, the opinion delivered with confidence.

I pinched my eyes shut, trying to block out the autopsy photos. His glassy stare. The blood caked around the heart. He was so young. So innocent.

"Hello, Gwen."

I flinched, my hands jerking away from my head as I looked up to see Robert in the doorway of my office. Loose at his side, the blade catching in the light, was a knife.

CHAPTER 39

Scott Harden stood in the shower and tilted his head up toward the large rain head. Steam rose off his skin as the hot water peppered across his cheeks and shoulders. Pinning his lips together, he closed his eyes and let the tension ease out of him.

For those seven weeks in the attic, he had dreamed about this shower. And now, in the middle of the giant space, his bare feet against the flat pebbles of the floor, he only wanted to be back. Back in the attic. Back in the bed. Back on that metal folding chair where she would run a giant sponge across his naked body. Over his cuts. Along his back. In between his thighs. Thinking about it now, he hardened, but when he reached down and stroked himself, the same thing as before—an instant softening. Like she was the only one with the power to bring him pleasure.

Maybe it was because she was his first. The girls at school had always talked about that—like the guy who took their virginity had some sort of power over them. He'd always laughed at the thought, but maybe they were right. Maybe that was why he had fallen so quickly and so hard. Was that why she wouldn't leave his mind?

He picked up the shampoo and squirted a glob of the pale-purple liquid into his hand. There hadn't been an easy way to wash his hair in the attic. And she hadn't trusted him enough to let him downstairs.

He raked his soapy fingers through his hair and remembered her long nails, how they would scratch and massage his scalp. The soft brush of her lips against his forehead.

It was different, being with an older woman. The girls at school all seemed so pointless and immature compared to her. Her confident look as she had straddled his naked body. The seductive purr of her voice in his ear. She had loved him. That's what she had whispered in his ear as that asshole had watched. She had *understood* Scott.

And each day, after her husband left for work, she showed him. She kissed and treated the wounds from the previous night. She put on her lace outfit and lay beside him and talked all about the life they would share. Without Jay. Without school. She hadn't seen him as a kid; she had seen him as a man. She had wanted him.

And he wanted her. Even now, a month later. Especially now.

"Scott?"

He swore at the sound of his mom. She wouldn't leave him alone. Always hovering. Always watching, a sharp line down the middle of her forehead as if she was trying to figure him out. He wished she would just stop. Go AWAY. Monitoring his phone calls? Didn't he have privacy anymore?

He put his head under the water, washing away the shampoo, and ignored the second call of his name, this one louder. Closer. Good thing he'd locked the door. She probably had her mouth to the crack, those giant fake boobs pushed against the wood.

Why had she gotten those anyway? Dad hadn't cared. Dad had barely even noticed.

Brooke's breasts had been perfect. She had let him spend all day touching them, had let him ask whatever questions he wanted about them. They'd been natural, she'd told him that.

There was a loud crack, and a crash of something right outside the shower door. Scott wiped the condensation off the glass and saw the bathroom door open, both of his parents standing there. *What the hell?* He reached over and turned off the water.

"Scott?"

Why did his mom keep saying his name? He pulled the towel off the heat rack.

"Scott, the news is showing some sort of room they found. An attic." His father spoke in a stern tone that Scott hadn't heard in a long time.

He paused, the towel pressed against his face. An attic. He dabbed the water from his eyes and slowly wrapped it around himself. He opened the shower door and stepped out.

His parents stood side by side, their shoulders touching. His mother in a red blouse and white shorts. His dad, his hair almost fully gray, with hands propped on his hips.

"Can I have some privacy?"

"Did you hear us?" his mother repeated. "They found an attic filled with things, and they are saying it's where you were kept."

"And it's not at Randall Thompson's house," his father added grimly.

Of course it wasn't. Randall Thompson was a pawn, one who deserved to rot away in a jail cell for the rest of his life for what he did to Brooke. Scott tucked the towel around his hips and walked past them and to his walk-in closet.

"Were you kept in an attic?" his mother asked.

He pulled a white T-shirt from the stack and wondered what the police knew. How had they found the attic? If the house was listed for sale, and Brooke and Jay were gone—wouldn't they have emptied out the attic in their move?

"This is the house it was found in." His mother held her cell phone up to his face. He tried to turn away, and she moved it closer. "Look, Scott. Recognize this house?"

Of course he did. And of course he couldn't admit that. Because, according to what he'd told the police, he'd been let go a few miles from his house and hadn't seen wherever he'd been kept.

"I don't know. No." He knocked her arm out of the way.

"They found two dead bodies in this house the day you showed up here." His mother's voice was steel, her feet firmly planted.

Two dead bodies? His hand, which had been reaching for a pair of shorts, paused in midair. "Who?"

"John and Brooke Abbott." She swiped the screen on her phone, then held a new image up for him to see.

John and Brooke Abbott
John and Brooke Abbott
John and Brooke Abbott
John and Brooke Abbott
John and Brooke Abbott

Everything in his mind came to a stop at the image of the couple. Brooke was wearing a red sundress, her long hair in wavy curls on her shoulders, a grin across her face. Jay was in a collared shirt and khakis, his dyed black hair swept over his balding forehead. It was them, right under a bold black headline that said, THE BLOODY HEART KILLERS REVEALED.

Jay. Was John his name? No wonder Scott hadn't found anything about them on the internet, though that had been impossible anyway without knowing their last names. Now, he took the phone from his mom and stared down at the photo of them. The man who had destroyed his life, and the woman who had saved it. Three months, she had said. *Wait three months and then call me.* She'd tucked a note with her number inside his pocket. *Three months.* She'd kissed him on the lips. *Then we can be together.*

But he hadn't been able to wait three months. He'd gone crazy without her, felt lost in his old life, and had so many questions. What to tell the police, whether she had seen him on television, and if he could see her. Just from afar, at least. If he could just talk to her, then maybe the dull sensation that was sweeping through him would stop.

So, he had called her. Early, he knew. But he had still expected her to answer or at least return his calls. When she hadn't, he had started texting her. And then her voice mail was full, and he had broken all their rules and traced the path he had run back to their house. He hadn't had a plan. He was just going to drive by. Maybe park a few houses down and walk by. Maybe wait until she left the house and then follow her.

The day he drove there, it had only been three weeks since his escape, and yet they were gone. Window blinds pulled shut. Car gone. The grass was freshly cut, and there was a **FOR SALE** sign in the yard. When he called the number on the sign, a lady said no one lived in the house.

Brooke had left him. Abandoned their plans of a happy ever after and *left*. That's what he had thought, his heart breaking as he had driven back to his empty life, ignored his parents' questions, and crawled into bed.

But maybe she hadn't left. Maybe she had . . .

"Scott, is this who took you?" It was his father's turn holding up a phone, and his display was now on a photo of Jay's face, that ugly smirk exposing the crooked top row of his bleached white teeth. He'd had that same smirk when he'd stopped Scott in the school parking lot. Kept that smirk on as he had pinned Scott down to the mattress and spread his legs. Later, Brooke said it was a domination thing. That Jay had been abused as a child, and that something about taking pain and innocence from someone else gave him peace.

Jay had needed a lot of peace. The more Scott had screamed and begged through his gag, the wider that stupid smirk had become. And Brooke had sat there quietly and watched it all happen. Let it happen because if she hadn't, he would have turned it all on her. She had been a prisoner, just like him. And she had healed him each day while Jay had been at work, and he had healed her, too.

His father shook him so hard that his neck snapped back from the force. "Scott!"

"Who's dead?" Brooke wasn't dead. That wasn't right. That wasn't why she hadn't answered.

"John and Brooke Abbott." His mom moved closer, and he felt trapped in the small space, both of them getting closer and closer, glaring at him as if he'd done something wrong. "Scott, the police are going to be here soon, and they are going to arrest you."

He looked from her face to his father's, but he still didn't understand.

She had been alive. She had pushed him out the door with a kiss, the feel of her lingering on his mouth, and they'd had a future together. Three months. Three months, then forever.

CHAPTER 40

I weighed my options very carefully. Robert stood at the only exit to the room. My phone was on the desk beside me, in arm's reach if I lunged for it. He stepped forward, and I stiffened, watching as he dragged the short tip of the blade along the top of my desk. It cut cleanly through the leather topper, dissected the phone cord, and suddenly that lifeline was gone.

I met his eyes, and this was a new Robert, one I hadn't seen before. One who was holding on to sanity and reason with a very tired grip. He regarded me with a mix of pity and disgust. "You let my son die, Gwen."

He was both right and wrong. While my intentions had been true, my awareness had been flawed. A better psychologist might have asked different questions and unveiled the true depravity of John's thoughts. With that knowledge in hand, a better psychologist might have called the police, saved Gabe, and locked away John long before whatever hell Scott Harden went through.

But would I have known about Brooke? Would I have found that piece? Probably not. And John had been smart. He had been calculating. He had known exactly what to tell me and what line to toe without alarming me to the point of calling the authorities.

I may have made mistakes, but nothing that I had done, or not done, had been intentional. My deception, my evasion . . . all that had happened after Brooke's and John's deaths and wouldn't have changed any of these horrific events.

Robert lifted the knife, but I kept my attention on his face, searching for a hint of compassion in his eyes. There was none, just tired and unfiltered hate. He wasn't a killer. I knew that he wasn't a killer. He was hurt. He was angry. But he would not harm me, not if he knew everything.

I believed it. I had to believe it.

"Robert," I whispered, "I didn't know John was the killer."

"Bullshit," he spat. "You *told* me you knew. John Abbott was seeing you while he had my son tied up in his attic. He was seeing you when he killed my child. He was seeing you when he stole Scott Harden away from his family." He gritted out the words and repositioned the knife in his hand, getting a better grip. I thought of Detective Saxe's somber tone when he had delivered the news of John's death.

The man was stabbed in the stomach. The angle and situation lead us to believe it was self-inflicted.

"No!" I shook my head, searching my desk wildly for something to prove my innocence. "When you asked if I knew what John had done, I thought you were asking about Brooke. He killed Brooke. That's what I was hiding from you. That's what I should have told the police." I pressed my palms together, pleading with him. "And I was treating John because he was behaving violently toward her."

He paused, and at least he was listening. Human nature would dictate that he wanted to believe me. I just had to give him the pieces to justify it in his mind. I tried not to look at the knife. Now was not the time to give him a reminder of it.

"No," he said tightly. "No. You said clients confessed things to you. You said you could have stopped him from killing, and you didn't."

"I was talking about Brooke. All we ever talked about was Brooke," I said firmly, then placed my hand on John's file. "This is his file. It has every session I've ever had with him. Read it. All my notes are there.

Brooke was cheating on him, and he was furious over it. He was worried he would hurt her, and we were working on it."

"Working on keeping him from killing his wife? What about my son?" He clenched his free hand into a fist.

"I didn't know about Gabe," I said softly. "I had no idea." I gestured to the profile and my notepad, still mostly blank. "I just saw the news, about the attic, and came right home. I needed to go through everything and see . . ." I faltered, emotion coming over me, and I pinched my lips together and attempted to swallow the emotion. "I needed to see—" I tried again. "How I had missed something so horrible. Had he given me clues and I hadn't caught them?" My voice caught. "I'm sorry, Robert." I gasped out the apology. "I'm so sorry."

He swallowed, and I saw the raw crumble of his features, the loss of control from a man who was so tightly wound that he was going to break. He slowly sank into the chair, his gaze tight on mine. His eyes intense and searching. "Don't lie to me, Gwen."

"I'm not." I held the eye contact and took a deep breath, needing to collect myself, to control my emotions and stay levelheaded. His anger was receding, but he was still very dangerous and emotionally volatile.

I thought of the time we'd been in this room. When he had been standing over my desk, the slow turn of his head toward me when I'd entered the room. The continual questions about John Abbott that had fed my fear that he'd known about Brooke. But he hadn't. His anger was over the Bloody Heart Killer, not Brooke's death. So if . . .

My mind whirred through all the suspicious moments, the constant feeling that he was two steps ahead of the game, his steadfast insistence that Randall Thompson was innocent and Scott Harden was lying. "You knew," I said quietly. "You knew that John was the BH Killer."

His face didn't change. He didn't nod. He didn't acknowledge it. He didn't deny it. But I knew I was right. The clues were all there—I had just been missing a few cards.

"What did you think?" I asked slowly. "You thought I knew John Abbott was the killer and I still put together this ridiculous profile?"

"It was pretty spot-on for him," he said quietly. "And I asked you if it fit any of your clients."

"Well, I wasn't thinking about my dead clients," I said, frustrated. "And my interview with Randall Thompson was what—a test? Every conversation I had with you, where I argued about Randall's innocence . . . you thought that was what? Me *pretending* to be an idiot?" My voice rose, and getting into an argument with an emotional, armed man was the number one way to get killed, but I couldn't stop myself.

"I needed to know what John had told you." Some fire was coming back into his eyes, and this switch in topic was either the smartest or the stupidest idea I'd ever had. "And you were cagey about it, so I finally just came out and asked you."

I resisted the urge to check and see if the knife was still in his hand. "You didn't come out and ask me if John was the BH Killer. You asked me something . . ." I blew out a frustrated breath. "Something like . . . did I know what he did, or something that was general as hell that I took as a reference to Brooke. Do you think if I was hiding the BH Killer's identity that I would have let you get within a hundred feet of me? Hire me? Sleep naked in my bed?" I lifted my hands in frustration. "I think we can all agree that my powers of intuition and deduction as far as John Abbott was concerned were . . ."

"Horrendous," he provided unhelpfully.

"Flawed," I allowed. "But I'm not an idiot. I'm not stupid. Tell me you believe that."

In response, he slowly placed the knife in between us, on my desk. He paused, then released his grip on it. An olive branch with a four-inch blade.

I stared at it and felt every muscle in my body give way to relief. It wasn't safety, but he believed me.

"Robert," I said carefully, "when did you find out that John was the one?"

His face tightened, and there was more there. I had confessed my crimes, and he needed to confess his. "October second."

I looked down at my desk, clicking through the timeline in my mind.

"It was the day before he died." His voice was flat and matter-of-fact. When I studied his face, it was grim but without remorse. "The day before I killed him."

And there it was. The confession.

"I—uh—I came in the kitchen and found him kneeling over his wife. He was crying. Shaking her. Performing mouth-to-mouth, but she was dead."

I wasn't surprised to hear that John had regretted the action. I told him, so many times, in so many sessions, that killing her wouldn't solve anything. That it was a brief moment that would ruin his entire life. He had loved her fiercely, unnaturally so, in the sort of rare attachment that the selfish reserve for their toys.

"He didn't hear me. I had a gun, but I set it on the counter and pulled a knife from the block."

His words were dusty, as if they had waited a long time to come out. He examined his palm, rubbing his fingers against the surface of it. He dropped his hands and met my eyes.

"I knew Scott was gone. I'd been watching the house. And it—it sounds so wrong, but I was mad when I saw Scott leave. I didn't understand why he could be let go, but Gabe hadn't. I . . ." He paused and took a deep breath. "I had gloves on. I crouched behind him and reached around and stabbed him as hard as I could, in the gut." He frowned. "The knife was long. And sharp. He fell back and couldn't move. He tried. He tried to sit up, to roll over, but he couldn't."

I stayed silent, and I could picture it. Everything he was saying. The look that would have come over John's face. The pain that wound would have caused. But had he appreciated it? Had he looked at Brooke, dead beside him, and felt that he deserved that fate?

Robert gave a sad smile. "He recognized me. He knew why I was there. And he couldn't move, but he could talk. I sat at the table, and for fifteen minutes, I watched him die."

Three loud raps sounded on the window of the front door and caused us both to flinch. Robert stood and stepped into the hall. I watched as he looked down the length of it, toward the front door. I knew what he was looking at. My front door was modern, three tall rectangles of glass that eliminated the need for a peephole.

"Whoever it is can see you," I said. "It's dark outside, light in here." The knife was in front of me. If I stretched forward, I could pluck it off the edge of the desk. I kept my hands in my lap.

He glanced back at me. "It's the police."

CHAPTER 41

I didn't have a chance to process the announcement before Robert strode down the hall and out of sight. I stood to follow and heard the front door swing open.

"Detective Saxe," Robert said warmly, and the man deserved an acting award.

I stepped into the hall and moved slowly toward the front door, wondering why the detective was here. Earlier, I'd been concerned about being arrested for my failure to report John's premeditations toward Brooke. Now, with his BH Killer label in place, did any of that really matter?

Another possibility entered the fray. Detective Saxe could have the same opinion that Robert had held—that I'd known the BH Killer's identity this entire time. My stomach turned.

"Good evening, Mr. Kavin." The detective stood on the front porch and eyed me as I came to a stop beside Robert. "Dr. Moore."

I cleared my throat. "Hi. Come on in."

Robert moved to the side and the detective entered, his badge glinting from his hip. I gestured them into the study and flipped on a lamp beside the chair.

"So, you're both here." The detective looked at each of us. "Again. Is this a thing, or do you guys just really love talking about dead people?"

I rubbed my forehead and wished I had eaten the spaghetti back at the office. I felt light-headed from lack of food, and I needed every bit of my limited brainpower right now. "We saw the news. I'm surprised you aren't at the scene."

"I was, but only because it was originally *my* scene. The task force and feds have taken it over now. Detectives are headed to Scott Harden's house, but I thought I'd swing by here first. I tried to call, but you didn't answer."

I looked in the direction of the kitchen, my purse still on the counter where I'd left it. "Sorry, my phone's in the kitchen."

"Well, we're trying to figure out what happened. We've got two dead serial killers and a kid who escaped the morning they died. Before I start looking at Scott for that murder, I wanted to know if you had any insights, especially since John Abbott called you that morning."

I met Robert's eyes for a heartbeat, then looked away. How many people, other than him and me, knew that he'd killed John?

And how had he known John was the BH Killer? The latter was a question I still needed the answer to.

"Right? Isn't that what you told me initially? That John left you a short voice mail, asking you to call him back?" Detective Saxe looked up from a small tablet. "Care to change any part of that story?"

"Two dead serial killers?" I frowned. "You have definitive proof that Brooke Abbott was involved?"

"There's no way she couldn't have known. Not with him keeping the boys in the house. Now . . ." He let out a frustrated sigh. "Anything else I need to know? Because I got to tell you, Doc, given what your patient was up to, there's about to be a lot more attention on your pretty little head."

He was right. And if this was the moment that I lost my medical license, so be it. "John killed his wife. I don't know that for certain, but I know that his desire to kill her was what I was treating him for, and I spent a year listening to him talk about it. You probably did a tox screen on her for poisons, but I would check for vitamins that can be deadly in combination with whatever her heart medication was." I made it the short distance to the closest seat and sat, immediately relieved by the confession.

Detective Saxe peered down at me as if I were crazy. "John Abbott wanted to kill his wife? You expect me to believe that's what you were treating him for?"

"Yes. His client file's in my office. Take it with you, if you need to."

"Wow. Suddenly singing and ready to unveil client confidences." He looked at me with thinly veiled disgust. "You could have just told me this from the beginning. Saved the department and myself a lot of time."

"They were both dead," I said simply. "I didn't know about the teenagers. I thought he was just a jealous husband, one who was trying not to hurt his wife."

"I don't think Dr. Moore should say anything else." Robert stepped in, and it was sweet how a man who came here to kill me was now protecting my legal rights.

Saxe paused, and I waved him forward. "Keep going."

"And John Abbott never said anything about the boys tied to a mattress in his attic?"

I forced myself not to go down the psychiatrist rabbit hole, but the details were fascinating. Brooke's awareness of the acts. Her potential romantic involvement with the victims. Keeping them in their house.

In the expectant silence, I shook my head. "No. He never mentioned that. Never even hinted at it. I came right home as soon as I heard the news, to go through his file and see if there was something I missed, but . . ." I looked between the two men. "I don't think I did. They were two separate silos. Morally, he was fine with being the BH Killer. Enjoyed it, if I had to guess. But his dark thoughts turning to Brooke . . . that scared him. That's why he came to me. I just didn't realize what I was dealing with." I swallowed.

It was clear from Detective Saxe's expression what he thought of my competency. Well, screw him. I had tried my best with the information I had been given. Yes, I'd kept things secret, in order to protect my career. But so had Robert. And probably, at some point, so had Detective Saxe. It was human nature to protect ourselves.

"So, John killed Brooke?" Saxe asked.

"I'm pretty damn sure. Like I said, I'd run the tox screen."

"And who killed John?"

Robert's eyebrow twitched, and now was the moment. I could just tell Saxe, right now. He was armed, he could protect me. Arrest Robert and take him away. That was my civic duty, right? Instead, I pinched my facial features in a confused look. "I thought you told me that he killed himself. Stabbed himself in the gut."

"I did . . . ," he said slowly. "But now we know more. There's a lot more reasons for someone to want him dead." He regarded Robert. "Take Mr. Kavin, for instance. Your son was his sixth victim. I'm sure, if we put a knife in any of the parents' hands, they would have done the deed. Would you agree?"

If I was sweating, Robert was as cool as ice. "I'd have gutted him like a fish," he said without hesitation.

Detective Saxe chuckled. *Chuckled.* I guess I wasn't the only one unable to tell a killer when he was standing right in front of me. The cop returned his attention to me. "So, you think suicide is still consistent with his mentality?"

"He was hopelessly in love with his wife. If he broke and actually hurt her—killed her? Yes. Absolutely. Killing himself would have been very plausible, if not expected." Since no one else was seated, I gripped the arms of the chair and stood.

"Okay." The detective nodded. "I'll be back in touch with any more questions. Kavin, looks like you caught a break with your client."

"I wouldn't call it a break," Robert said. "Thompson's life has been ruined."

"Well, sue Scott Harden, not the police department." He tucked his tablet into his breast pocket. "Stay in town, Dr. Moore. We'll probably be back for that file."

"Sure," I said tartly, and I didn't even feel a little guilty at letting him believe that John had killed himself.

As the detective left, Robert stayed in the foyer. He turned to face me, and there was a moment of silence as we stood just a few feet apart.

"Don't feel guilty about Brooke's death," he said gruffly. "She was as much a monster as him. While he was dying, he told me everything." He closed his eyes and sucked in a pained breath. "It was bad, Gwen. He was physical with the boys, but she was emotionally cruel. It was a sexual and emotional game between them, with the boys as pawns. She deserved to die, and in a lot worse way than she went."

I hugged my arms over my chest. "I'll try not to, but the guilt is still there. Now in about a hundred new ways."

From the street, the detective's car rumbled to life. Robert twisted the knob and pulled open the front door. "Goodbye, Gwen."

I stepped forward. "Wait. Robert."

He ignored me, moving onto the porch and pulling the door shut, quick enough that it almost hit me. I jerked back and watched him through the thin panes of glass. He stepped into the dark yard and didn't look back. A few seconds later, car lights illuminated at the curb, then pulled away.

I flipped the dead bolt, then moved to the kitchen and repeated the action at the side door, irritated with myself for leaving it unlocked. Returning to my office, I took my chair and picked up the knife that he'd left behind. It was one of the ones from his collection, one he hadn't shared a story on. I turned it over in my hands, then placed it in my desk drawer and let out a sigh, looking over the papers spread out before me.

An hour ago, I was frantic to look at John's file and find the clues I might have missed. Now, it was the last thing I wanted to do. And did it really matter? At some point, the file would be confiscated by the cops or the courts. My work would be a news story, a Wikipedia entry, and a cocktail-party conversation piece. I would become famous as the most inept psychiatrist of all time. Randall Thompson would be released. Scott Harden . . . I frowned, unsure what would become of him. Obstruction of justice, surely. Was that in my future, too?

I didn't care. I had spent the last month paralyzed with guilt over a woman's murder, and she had turned out to be a monster. I now had the blood of two teenagers on my conscience and would spend the next couple of decades microanalyzing every conversation I'd ever had with John Abbott.

Just a week ago, I'd been bristling with excitement over the chance to speak to Randall Thompson. I'd considered it a once-in-a-lifetime opportunity, to sit across from the Bloody Heart Killer. Now, I knew that I'd had a year of interactions. I'd doodled in the margins of my notebook while Los Angeles's reigning killer had spoken.

I had failed, and I wasn't sure I'd ever forgive myself for it.

CHAPTER 42

ONE MONTH LATER

Scott Harden stood in the tall grass and watched Randall Thompson through the window. He sat at a table, his chair pulled close, his belly snug to the edge, and scooped forkfuls of pasta toward his face. His gaze was fixed and unmoving on the screen in his hand. The faint sounds of voices came through the window, a sitcom playing on the device.

In Scott's hand was the knife. The same knife Brooke had given him that morning, when she had snuck him outside, their plan in motion the moment John's car pulled out of the drive. "Just in case," she had said, then pressed a kiss on his forehead. They hadn't discussed what *just in case* covered, but killing Randall Thompson was as good a reason as any, one that would have made Brooke proud. One that, if John Abbott had really loved his wife, he would have taken care of himself.

But he hadn't, and now this asshole was suing Scott, and his parents, and the police department, and was going to collect ten million dollars, according to their attorneys.

That wasn't how this was supposed to happen. That wasn't what Brooke had wanted. She was the one who'd risked everything and snuck into her rapist's house, putting the box of souvenirs under his bed. She was the one who had planned out everything so that this sack of shit would finally get what he deserved. She was the one who had trusted her teacher and had her innocence stripped in return.

The science teacher had raped Brooke. Raped her without a condom, and when she'd missed her period, she'd had to tell her mother, who had still refused to believe it was him, but marched her down to the clinic and berated her during the entire termination process.

Brooke had told Scott how no one had believed her. The girls at school had called her a slut. Everyone had dismissed her claims, even her parents. She'd had to stay in Randall's class, in a front-row seat, and feel the heat of his gaze on her for the entire semester.

He had done that to her, and to others, and *never* been forced to pay for his actions—not until now. Scott eased around the edge of the house and toward the back door. From inside, Randall laughed. Beside Scott, an air conditioner clattered to life.

Scott thought of Brooke, her soft hair falling in his face as her lips brushed his. He moved down the skinny side porch and reached for the doorknob.

"Scott."

He jumped and turned, raising his fists in self-defense. Pausing, he peered into the dark yard. A small figure in a blue velour jumpsuit stepped closer, and his hands dropped. "Mom. What are you doing here?" he hissed.

"Give me that knife." She climbed the steps onto the saggy wooden porch and jerked forward, snatching the knife from his hand before he had the chance to hold on to it. "We're going home."

"No." He reached for it, and she stepped back, her expression stern and brokering no room for arguments. "You don't know what he—"

"Tell me about it on the car ride home, and then we'll find a solution—together. But going into a man's home with a knife is only going to end badly, and I am NOT LOSING YOU AGAIN." Her soft voice shook with emotion, and he couldn't do this, couldn't handle the tears that were welling in her eyes.

Tinny laughter came faintly through the windows, and he glanced back inside, where Randall continued to eat, oblivious of the conversation happening on his porch.

"Come on," she ordered, gripping his forearm and pulling it with the strength of a woman twice her size. "Let's get in the car and you can tell me all about it."

He didn't want to tell her all about it. He wanted Brooke, and he wanted the life they had planned, and he couldn't take another minute of the horrible things his mom was constantly saying about her. She hated Brooke, and she didn't even know her. Didn't understand that Brooke had been protecting him, caring for him. That Brooke loved him.

Whenever he tried to explain it, his mom just looked at him as if he were crazy.

She pulled on his arm and he resisted, glancing back at the window, where Randall Thompson was twisting the cap off a fresh beer. For one final moment, he considered ripping away and kicking down the door. Wrapping his hands around that thick old neck. Squeezing until his face turned purple and spit bubbled between his lips.

He considered it, savored it, then he followed his mother toward their vehicles.

CHAPTER 43

TWO MONTHS LATER

A text message alert pinged in the middle of Lela Grant's long and uninteresting recap of last night's Netflix session. I glanced at my cell, didn't recognize the number on the display, and returned my attention to her.

"So, the kicker is, the guy is actually her stepfather, but you don't realize that until the very last scene, when he pulls out his gun and shoots her in the face!" Her eyes widened enough for me to see her shimmery purple eyeliner.

"Interesting," I mused. "So, you'd recommend the movie?" I drew a decorative border around the film's title on my notepad.

"Well, no. Now that you know everything that happens." She looked crestfallen, then perked back up. "I saw that the LAPD is finally investigating Randall Thompson for molesting his students."

"Yes, I heard that."

"I think it's pretty cool, how all the moms of the Bloody Heart victims got together and created a victims' advocacy foundation. And they're, like, investigating old crimes?" She fixed her eyes on me.

Unsure of the correct answer, I nodded. "Yes. It's very nice."

And it was. I had watched the press coverage closely and could see the powerful and positive impact the nonprofit group was already having—not just with victims, but among themselves. They had felt helpless during their sons' abductions, then grieving and alone after their children's bodies had been found. But now they were united in a common goal—helping those without a voice find justice. They were formidable, well funded, and had embraced the ignored accusers of Randall Thompson as their first pro bono clients.

"You know, Sarah went to Beverly High."

Ah yes, Sarah. The horrible sister-in-law, worthy of killing.

"We've been watching the updates of the case together on social media."

I waited for a comment about Lela torturing Sarah for information, or plotting to wrap a laptop's extension cord around her neck, but she stayed silent.

"That's nice," I managed. "Together? Or—"

"Oh no." She shook her head. "I mean, she lives way out in Pasadena. But we've been texting about it. She wants to come to the first hearing with me. She didn't have him for a teacher, but she was a student there and saw him in the halls, like, every day. Plus, she knew Jamie Horace—who was one of his victims—like, personally. They were cheerleaders together, practically best friends." She beamed. "I requested to be Jamie's friend on Facebook, and because I was a mutual friend with Sarah, and not some random stalker, she *accepted* me." She twisted a lock of her hair with one finger. "So it's cool, because she has that connection, and I have my whole connection with you . . . so we're both, like, *really* invested in the case."

I digested that sugarcoated pile of garbage and managed not to react. "So, you're getting along with Sarah?"

"Yeah. I think I'm over the 'killing her' thing." She frowned. "I mean, not that I want to stop sessions or anything. I have other problems if that's—"

I held up my hand. "I'm happy to be here for you, without the need for violence. We can talk about anything you want to talk about in your sessions."

"Oh, good." She bounced a little in her seat, and I fought the urge to smile. She was, however ridiculous, a pleasant burst of innocence in days now full of darkness. My professional reputation, which I had considered doomed, had actually grown in the months following the Bloody Heart unveiling. I had appeared on a dozen interview spots, turned down two book deals, and had a waiting list of clients, all anxious to speak about their inner aggressions. It was refreshing to sit here with Lela and talk about movies and celebrity gossip and her daughter's improvements. Maggie was now in regular sessions with a therapist and progressing nicely.

A few minutes later, I walked Lela to the door and waved goodbye, passing her off to Jacob, who deserved a gold medal in ass-kissing. Returning to my desk, I picked up my phone and checked my messages. The text from the unknown number was short.

It's been a while. Hope you're well. —Robert

I stared at the message, unsure how to respond. After he'd left my house that fateful afternoon, he'd disappeared. No texts, no phone calls, and—when I checked the internet—his profile was off the firm's site. When my curiosity got the best of me, I drove over to his office in Beverly Hills and rode the elevator up to his floor. Stepping off, I was surprised to see that his name had been removed from the sleek glass doors, a woman now visible through the open door to his old office.

I hadn't driven by his house. I had gone too far already by snooping around his office. I had accepted that if Robert Kavin wanted to talk to me, he could call me. And now he had. Sort of.

I placed my cell on the desk and nudged it away from me. I didn't know how to respond to the text, and the swarm of butterflies stealing through my chest was definitely not a good thing. The man had come to my house to kill me. Granted, he hadn't—but what if I hadn't convinced him of my innocence?

Sane individuals didn't turn to murder. Then again, the death of a child could cause anyone to lose their mind. I didn't blame him for killing John Abbott, and I didn't blame him for turning his anger and hatred on me when he thought I had willingly let his son die.

In the last three months, an investigation had thoroughly dissected every moment in John and Brooke's gruesome history. I'd turned over my files, as useless as I believed them to be, and sat through hours of questioning. Thankfully, the state believed my story and didn't pursue any charges for obstruction of justice, their focus quickly shifting back to the growing horrors of John and Brooke Abbott.

The Bloody Heart killings weren't their first crimes. The first had been a high school classmate of John's who—if I had to guess—had sexually abused John Abbott. An audit into John's pharmacy unveiled a massive number of misfiled and appropriated prescriptions, along with a connection among the victims. At least four of the six teenagers had had ongoing prescriptions filled at Breyer's Pharmacy.

Picking up my cell, I considered responding. What harm was one simple text?

I'm good.

There. No one could call that flirtatious. I dropped my cell in my purse and rolled closer to my desk, vowing to return all my outstanding emails before I looked at my phone again. A slight buzz came from inside my purse.

Okay, four new emails. I clicked on one, read the first paragraph of it twice, then gave up and retrieved my phone. Settling back in my chair, I opened the new text.

We should have a drink and catch up.

A drink. It sounded so simple, so innocent. I typed a response before I could second-guess myself.

Sure. When?

CHAPTER 44

We met two days later in a candlelit bar off South Beverly Drive that had a Bugatti parked out front and a hostess with more diamonds and plastic surgery than sense. He was already there, seated at a gold stool at the bar, and I paused before approaching, not certain that it was him.

In three months, Robert Kavin had become a different man. His short-cropped beard was now thick and paired nicely with a rough brush of salt-and-pepper hair. He was tan, and his eyes held a new glow of life that they hadn't had before. He wore a collared golf shirt and dark-blue shorts with small whales embroidered on them.

"Wow." I paused next to his stool. "You look . . . beachy." I glanced down at my outfit. I was still in the navy suit and nude heels I'd worn at the office. "I probably should have suggested a more casual place. And changed."

He stood and leaned in, brushing my cheek with a kiss. His beard felt foreign against my skin, and he smelled like coconuts and soap. "I like you like this. Though . . ." He gestured to the open stool beside him. "I'd love to see you let down your hair. Literally and figuratively." He tugged on my low bun, and I batted his hand away, annoyed to see that he'd stolen a bobby pin.

"I'd like to see you with less hair." I scowled at him. "What's with the caveman look?"

He smiled. "I threw away my razor when I got rid of my suits." He tugged on the side of his short beard. "You don't like it?"

"It's okay," I said grudgingly and picked up the bar menu. In truth, he looked good. Really good. Melt-your-panties-off good. "How do the clients like it?"

"I wouldn't know. I left the office and moved to Venice Beach. I found a fixer-upper on the water and am renovating." He reached for my hand, and I pulled it away. "You were wrong, you know."

"There's a shocker," I deadpanned. "In what way?"

"My goldfish is still alive."

I laughed. "You brought him home?"

"Yep. Gave him the guest bedroom. He's helping me with design choices. He seems to like living at the beach."

"You seem like you do, too." He seemed lighter, the cloak of intensity gone.

"Oh, I love Venice. I always told myself I'd retire on an island in the Caribbean, but . . ." He shrugged.

"No extradition?" I asked dryly.

He laughed. "Well, no, but my reluctance to leave was a little more noble than that."

I caught the eye of the bartender and ordered a vodka tonic. "Yeah?"

"Well, you're here."

I paused, confused. "And?"

"And we have unfinished business." He eyed me. "Think you can squeeze in one more client?"

I set down the menu. "You know, grief counseling really isn't my specialty. My clients are normally a little darker than that."

"I have a few skeletons in my closet," he admitted.

"And they shave."

He winced. "I can shave."

I scraped my fingers across his jaw and tugged at the wild, thick tufts. "Nah. Keep it."

He pulled the edge of my stool, bringing me closer to him. "I also wanted to give you this. You left it at my house."

He pressed something into my palm, and I looked down to see the emerald ring. "Robert . . . ," I protested.

"Stop," he ordered. "We went through the argument about it already. It's yours. Take it. Consider it a peace offering for me wanting to kill you." He winced. "Now, can you forgive me?"

"I don't know." I slid the ring onto the ring finger of my right hand. "Can you forgive me for not realizing what a monster John Abbott was?"

He studied me, his pupils moving minutely as he read, judged, and processed what he saw in my eyes. "I think I already have."

He hadn't. The chances were high that he would never forgive me.

"How did you know that he was guilty?" I asked. The question was the one thing left unanswered, and it had followed me for three months.

He sighed, and I knew he didn't want to walk back down that path, but I had to know what he'd seen that I had missed. "The autopsy report on Gabe. The blood labs." He turned back to the bar and picked up his drink. "His insulin levels were perfect, as if he'd worn his pump the entire time. But in order to do that, he'd need infusion sets."

"So why wouldn't you suspect another diabetic?"

"There are dozens of variations of infusion sets, but more importantly, I hadn't gotten the call to pick up his prescription. Which I didn't notice or think about at the time. I mean, my son was missing. I barely knew what my middle name was, much less if I hadn't gotten a call from the pharmacy. And if I had noticed, I would have chalked it up to them knowing that he was missing. But months later, almost seven months after he was gone, I was at the pharmacy, picking something up, and I thought about it." He looked at me. "So I checked with the insurance company, and someone else had picked up his prescriptions. The insulin and also his inhaler."

"And then you figured out it was him?"

"No." He sighed and took a sip of his beer. "And then I ran background checks and wasted a shitload of time looking at all the wrong employees of the pharmacy before I figured out it was John."

"Oh." It was a cruel irony that the one thing that had probably put Gabe Kavin on John's radar was the same thing that led to his killer.

"I had a dozen talks with John about Gabe, before, during, and after his disappearance, and I never suspected a thing." He met my eyes. "I was a prick to assume it was any different for you."

I shrugged. "I'm a professional. It was my job to have seen something." And we had both been, at multiple points in this journey, pricks and liars.

"Here." He raised his bottle. "To cradling sorrows to sleep."

I clinked my glass against his. "I'll drink to that."

I smiled at the familiar toast, remembering when I had given it in the run-down country bar. It seemed like a lifetime ago. We had been strangers, our history linked without us knowing, our focus on distraction from our grief and problems.

William S. Burroughs once said that no one owns life, but anyone who can lift a frying pan can create death. He was right. Killing is the easy part. The act of living—of finding happiness in life—that's the hard part. Moving past grief and guilt, and learning to love and to trust . . . I wanted to take that path, but I rather liked cradling my sorrows. I enjoyed the well of emotion, the proof that an empathic soul still existed in my aching chest.

One day, I'd move on and forgive myself. I'd live a proper life. But for today, I just needed to survive. To survive and make room on my calendar for one new client. A scruffy, bearded killer who smelled of sunscreen and had a goldfish as a pet.

Robert reached for my hand, and this time, I didn't pull away.

ACKNOWLEDGMENTS

It's interesting, because first drafts are such solitary journeys. Late nights, your back cramping in protest, a pile of empty soda cans beside you, your dog wheezing out a loud snore as you try to manage just a few hundred more words before bed. There isn't anyone to turn to, anyone to pass off the keyboard to and say, "Hey—mind finishing up this chapter?" We're stuck, in a hypothetical canoe, in the middle of the lake, with no one to row but ourselves.

But then . . . we make it to the other side, and there's a group there, waiting to pick up that heavy manuscript and help. The group I had for this book was fantastic, and I could fill another two hundred pages singing their praises. For now, I'll try to be concise.

Maura Kye-Casella, thank you for being such a source of support and wisdom for the last eight years. You continually believe in me and my stories, and I am so grateful to you for all that you have done for my writing—and my career.

Megha Parekh, this book is all thanks to you! Thank you for your insight and ideas, for brainstorming plot points and for sifting through the half dozen concepts until we found the right one. I'm so happy with how this book came together, and so blessed to be a part of the Thomas & Mercer family. Thank you for your vision and support.

Charlotte Herscher, your edits and feedback made this story so much stronger. Thank you for pushing hard where I needed it and for giving me room where I was stubborn. And for all the late-night emails and the phone calls—I appreciate your willingness and dedication more than you know. We've now got two book babies under our belt—I hope there are many more in our future.

To Laura Barrett, copyeditor Sara Brady, proofreader Jill Kramer, and the formatting, cover design, and Thomas & Mercer team: thank you for your attention to detail, your creative talents, and your support of this novel. I sincerely appreciate your efforts.

And finally, the readers. You have no idea how important you are. Thank you for picking up this book. Thank you for stepping into Gwen and Robert's world. I hope you enjoyed reading their story as much as I enjoyed writing it.

Until the next book . . .

Alessandra

ABOUT THE AUTHOR

Photo © 2013 Eric Dean Photography

A. R. Torre is a pseudonym for *New York Times* bestselling author Alessandra Torre. Torre is an award-winning bestselling author of more than twenty novels. She has been featured in such publications as *ELLE* and *ELLE UK* and has guest blogged for the *Huffington Post*. In addition to her writing, Torre is the creator of Alessandra Torre Ink, a website, community, and online school for aspiring and published authors. Learn more and sign up for her monthly updates at www.alessandratorre.com.